WINDSWEPT

A SEA GLASS INN NOVEL

JULIE CAROBINI

DOLPHIN GATE BOOKS

JULIE CAROBINI writes inspirational beach romances and cozy mysteries … with a twist. *RT Book Reviews* says, "Carobini has a talent for creating characters that come alive." Julie lives in California with her family and loves all things coastal (except sharks). Pick up a free ebook here: www.juliecarobini.com/free-book/

CHAPTER 1

"She's an imposter."

Sophia jerked up, her hands poised around her cheeks like parentheses. Water dripped down her fingers and into the dingy airport bathroom sink as two women burst into the space behind her, deep in conversation. A droplet fell from Sophia's chin and slithered past blotches of darkness and into the drain.

She peeked into the mirror again. Each woman slipped into a stall, pulling a suitcase behind them, their conversation never slowing.

"I don't know why I agreed to come here anyway and watch this sham of a wedding take place," the first woman continued.

"Well, that's exactly why I decided to come," the other woman answered from behind her stall door. "You know me— I love the drama!"

The first woman cackled. Sophia could hear her saying, "That's for sure," above the sound of flushing water.

The women were strangers to Sophia, but the pettiness in

their tones was all too familiar. She reached for a paper towel and mopped the water from her face. She froze, the paper in her hands bringing forth a memory she'd just as soon forget, one written in the hand of someone she loved. Despite the angry missive on paper with ink, she hadn't so much as burned or tossed it away. Instead, though she longed to forget the angry words, she kept them. Perhaps as a reminder.

Sophia sucked in a breath and gazed into the unclean mirror above the sink. She took in the taupe half circles beneath her own eyes. The green of those eyes, once vibrant, now looked more like a plate of overcooked broccoli. Pitiful. She hoped her brother, Jackson, had come alone to pick her up. Not that she was particularly vain. Sophia had conquered that mountain long ago, before she'd started her fledgling company ... and long before she'd ever even met her brother.

Fledgling. A peculiar word that meant new, underdeveloped, and yet she had spent her whole life, it seemed, creating her company's underpinnings. And for the past year she had watched that carefully built foundation begin to crumble, the weight of revelations and timidity causing it to buckle.

The women emerged from their stalls simultaneously and approached the wall of sinks, surrounding her. She swallowed, not looking anywhere in particular. They continued their conversation, speaking over her as if she were invisible, and as if doing so was the norm. Maybe she really was invisible to them.

As always.

"I heard she's gained all sorts of weight," one said.

The other snorted. "Perfect for the wedding photo album. Most people look back on the good ol' days before baby weight —not this time, ha!"

Sophia heaved a sigh and turned abruptly, startlingly sure

that her bathroom companions had not noticed. She couldn't stay in that unremarkable, gray restroom a minute longer, listening to cruel chatter. Her makeup-less face would have to do. Soon enough, she would be in her brother's car, making the hour-long trek to a new life.

She couldn't wait.

At baggage claim, she glanced around at the throng—strangers, every one of them. Her temples constricted, her head dizzy. Though she had lived in some of the busiest cities in the world, she had always preferred the solitude of her own nest. She longed for that now, but pushed herself to move forward, to tear her gaze away from the masses and search for her suitcase. She spotted the brightly colored scarf she had tied around its handle, thankful for a friendly sight. Just as she bent to reach for the handle, a tap landed on her shoulder. She pivoted and smiled, expecting to see Jackson.

But a stranger standing tall and powerfully built watched her, his eyes laser focused on Sophia's face. "Care for a ride, m'lady?"

She shrank back. "I-I, no. I ..." She'd heard of this sort of thing, men targeting women alone in airports and other public places when their guard was down. He looked normal, though. Kind eyes. Nice wave of wheat-colored hair above his brow. The scar that emerged from the edge of his beard, traversing to his temple, made her wonder. Had he been the victim of an accident? Or had he earned that particularly jagged mark from a stint in prison?

Her bag!

She spun back toward the baggage carousel and bit her lip. *Stupid, girl.* Had the stranger purposely delayed her? Had she fallen prey to a perilous kind of distraction? Did he know that she had left her latest design inside? After all, someone once stole her identity. How much easier might it be to steal her designs too?

She sucked in a breath, wishing away her frantic thoughts. She was not this person, or at least, she hadn't been until recently.

Sophia searched the carousel again and exhaled. Her bag, jet black except for a glint of the cobalt blue scarf she had tied around its handle, had passed her by. But it was safe. Still in view. She glanced around. Unless she cared to scramble aboard the conveyor belt wearing spiked heels, or jostle her way to the front of the crowd that stood three-people deep to await their own luggage, she would have to wait for it to return to her. This also meant she would be unable to gracefully extricate herself from the cab driver—or whomever he was—who seemed overly concerned about her need for a ride.

She turned at another tap on her shoulder. "Sophia?"

She frowned. The man knew her name? She took a closer look at him and spotted the cardboard in his hands. Had he been holding that sign all along? The one with her name hastily written across it in red ink?

"Did my brother send you? I apologize that I seem to have mistaken you for a ... " *For a what? A stranger who somehow knew her name?* She pulled herself together. "Are you ... are you one of my brother's valets?"

The corners of his eyes crinkled when he smiled, as if the folds of a curtain holding back laughter. "I am if it means you'll come home with me."

Her bag nearly passed her by again. He was either teasing her or a con man, and Jackson, she was convinced, would not have sent either type to pick her up at this large and lonely airport. Sophia forced her way between two teens wearing backward Dodger baseball caps standing elbow-to-elbow in front of the carousel. She lunged between them and grasped the scarf of her suitcase, tugging until she could reach the bag's handle. "Excuse me." She gave the handle a yank, hauled the bag off the conveyer until it landed on the scarred linoleum with a clatter, and strode from the baggage area as fast as safely possible. She would have to rethink wearing heels in an airport again.

"Sophia. Wait!"

With one hand on her phone, she zeroed in on a security guard at his post, a round, graying man who she hoped could rustle up some strength if she were to ask for his assistance. She picked up the pace while also texting her brother: *Did you send a weirdo to pick me up?*

She stepped up to the guard and opened her mouth to speak, but the man behind her spoke again.

"Seriously, Sophia," he said. "Your brother sent me. Jackson's waiting in his car nearby."

Sophia stopped. Was that laughter in his voice? She faced him. "You really are here to retrieve me?"

He smiled at her now, the tip of his scar more pronounced. "Jackson's circling the airport as we speak. LA traffic delayed us. He was worried you'd feel stranded if one of us wasn't here to greet you."

She exhaled. Her gaze lingered on him and he seemed to jolt.

"I'm Christian ... Capra. It's good to finally meet the famous Sophia Riley."

Sophia ... Riley. Would she ever get used to hearing the name she'd always known paired with the one she'd only recently learned about? She continued to eye him until her phone dinged with an incoming text: *Yeah. Sorry. Christian's harmless.*

Christian extended his hand to her.

With a sigh, she took it. "Hello."

He dipped his chin and glanced at her bag, reaching for it. "Is this it?"

"For now."

"Well, then. It's enough."

~

THE LULL of the engine made the fight to keep her eyes open that much more difficult.

"Meg's got your suite all set up for you. I think you'll really love it," Jackson said.

"I'm sure I will."

"You could have stayed with us, you know. Our home is yours."

"Thank you, but I think newlyweds should be left alone."

Christian piped up from the back seat. "Until they fill their mansion with babies, you mean."

Sophia perked up. "Is this true? Are you ..."

Jackson chuckled. "Not yet, no. Right now we're just ... practicing."

Sophia turned her chin toward her brother, a moniker she was still becoming used to. "This is why the suite in your hotel will be just fine for me."

"Correction. In *our* hotel." He paused. "Meg calls the place 'magical.'"

She smiled.

"You'll find the staff very happy to see you. All friendly people. Although Meg and Liddy already have been talking about dragging you out for wine with some of their friends." He gave her a sideways glance. "My bride is worried you'll be lonely."

Christian cleared his throat. "I'll keep you company, if you'd like."

She turned enough to see him in the shadows of the back seat. Was this his attempt at flirting? Or was he showing genuine concern?

"Unless you still think I'm an ax murderer."

Jackson nearly choked on a laugh. "A what?"

She shook her head, her mouth grim. "I did not think that."

Christian chuckled. "C'mon, sis, you did. Or at least a deranged guy trying to pick you up in the airport. Sorry I scared you, by the way."

Her brother turned to her. "Wait. Sophia, does this have something to do with your text about a weirdo picking you up?"

Christian scoffed. "Made an impression, I see."

"What did you do?" Jackson glared at Christian in the rearview mirror. "And only one of us is calling her sis, got that, old man?"

"Got it. And I'm a mere two years older than you." He chuckled. "You want to tell him, Sophia?"

Sophia laughed this time. "It's not important. But I will say that I did not immediately see the sign he'd created—my eyes were tired." She paused. "Plus, I have not been called m'lady ever in my life."

Jackson groaned. "Oh, brother. I should've warned you that my college roommate would be meeting you at baggage and that he's got a strange sense of humor."

"Hey. I resemble that remark."

Jackson glanced at her and rolled his eyes. "And that he'd be moving into the Sea Glass Inn to finish his next book."

"You're a writer?"

The smile on his face faded and he glanced out into the

night, the glow from street lights occasionally illuminating him. "I am but I've been on a sort of ... sabbatical."

Jackson broke in. "Sabbatical, huh?" He paused. "Whatever we're calling it, my friend here has always been a wanderer. I gave up trying to keep tabs on his whereabouts a long time ago. Even his forwarding orders don't work."

"Sad but true," Christian said.

"Well, I can understand the need for an artist to take a small break," Sophia said. "It's good for the soul—and for the art, too."

Christian turned his chin enough that their eyes locked in the passing light.

Jackson cleared his throat. "I know you're tired, Sophia. After you've had a good night's sleep, though, I need to speak with you. Actually ... our financial advisor will be in tomorrow morning. I'd hoped you would meet with us." He paused. "Can you do it?"

She nodded, aware that though a part of her had looked upon this move as an extended vacation, the truth was, she had years to make up for where Jackson and the Sea Glass Inn were concerned.

"Of course. Whatever you need from me, I will be there."

"Thank you. Wade and I plan to have breakfast in the dining room at 8:30. You join us when you're ready, and then afterward we'll huddle in my office. Sound good?"

"Yes. I will be there."

Somehow she would need to make time to work on a few dress designs if she was ever going to revive her company. She pressed her lips together and took a deep breath through her nose. She did not care to think about anything other than stepping into the calm and quiet of her new home, densely populated as the inn may be.

THE NEXT MORNING, Sophia stared at the ceiling trying to decipher the unfamiliar sound. A wave. The first one crashed onto shore, then another. She'd heard about the red-flag alerts on this stretch of the coast, how the waves could be positively monstrous, but she had not considered the impact that water could make when it landed. The experience had already provided her a vastly different wake-up call than that of car horns honking and sirens blaring. Not that the sounds of Manhattan bothered her. On the contrary, she had become so accustomed to the cacophony that on those occasions she had traveled elsewhere, such as to her beloved Italy, she found herself unable to sleep in with the lack of background noise.

On her feet, Sophia cinched a hotel robe around her and stepped out onto the balcony, inhaling the odd, somewhat-addicting scent of water and air and salt.

"Never gets old, does it."

Her eyes widened. She hadn't seen him standing out on his deck jutting from the room so close to hers. "Hello, Christian."

"Good morning."

"Are you usually such an early riser?"

He seemed to stare at her for a beat before answering, one of his eyebrows gently cocked upward. "All depends on the view I'm waking up to."

Heat rose in her cheeks. She smoothed her hair with one hand, letting her fingers drift to her collarbone.

He quirked that smile and glanced out to sea again. "Besides, how could I stay asleep with all that racket going on out there?"

"Yes. I know. It'll take some getting used to."

He swiveled a look back at her, frowning. "You're not serious."

"Is that a question?"

9

He gave his beard a scratch. "Does the sound of waves bother you? I think there are medications for that."

She shrugged. "I meant that I'm used to something a little bit—how shall I say it?—a little more hustle and bustle outside my window. Something less magnificent, more frenetic."

He winced. "The City."

"You don't care for New York?"

"It's not that I don't care for it, it's just that, well—" He screwed up his mouth before looking her straight in the eyes. "All right. No. I really don't care for it. At all."

"I see. And the reason for that is?"

"Pretty near impossible to choose just one, but, okay. Let me see." He shifted. "For one thing, it smells."

"I see. Example?"

"Like sewage mixed with stale coffee grounds."

She scoffed. "I cannot imagine why you'd say that."

"Really? Have you ever strolled over a manhole in Manhattan? Or traversed that stench-filled maze lovingly known as the subway? When I think of New York, I think of dirt and grime and the shower that I always had to take at the end of the day to wash off the soot." He paused. "No offense."

"I think maybe that you have not experienced the same New York that I have."

"And what New York is that?"

"Standing shoulder-to-shoulder with people from all over the world for more than fifteen minutes just to buy a bagel—"

"Not too convincing."

"Okay, how about pulling on my wool coat and favorite boots to walk after dark, when the city's lights blaze. There is so much magic to the nights there."

"That's actually criminal activity." He crossed his arms and took a sip from a mug.

She sighed. "I give up. Maybe you are just not a fan of coffee."

He set the mug down. "Not hotel coffee."

"Ah."

"What?"

"A coffee snob."

It was his turn to scoff.

She tilted her head. "I admit that I agree with you—it's difficult to find a good cup of coffee outside of Italy."

He groaned. "Not you too. Meg has poor Jackson grinding coffee beans flown in from a roaster near Florence."

She eyed him. Their first encounter aside, she'd enjoyed the way he and Jackson had bantered on the way home, like old friends saturated with memories and shared jokes. Today he was a grouch.

Pity.

She pushed away from the railing. "I retract my question."

"What question was that?"

"I asked if you were an early riser, but I see that you are not."

He spat out a coarse laugh and crossed his thick arms across his chest, his skin swathed in golden hair, that coffee mug of his dangling precariously from two fingers. His eyes narrowed, the line of his mouth still dancing. That shaggy-boy mop of chestnut hair tried to charm her, but she'd already seen his mood and doubted its ability to win her over.

"Au contraire. I've been up since dawn."

She startled. "Truly? How can that be? We arrived home so late last night. The only reason I'm able to carry on a conversation without so much as a sip of coffee is that I am still on New York time. But you ... you must not have slept all night."

He shrugged, watching her.

Sophia became suddenly cognizant of the fact that she'd

11

neither brushed her teeth nor combed her hair. What in the world had she been thinking when she'd slid open the door to this deck?

Of course. She thought she'd be alone. Like usual ... before ... before she suddenly wasn't. Unlike some people, the quiet had never bothered her. When her mother died and she extricated herself from her half-sister's mean-spirited ways, Sophia found herself going deeper into her art of design. The caress of fabric between her fingers, the whir of the machine, her mind entranced by simple transformations.

Ironically, those designs created in solace had sent her barreling into the spotlight. Well. Not exactly a supernova-type spotlight, but her name—and her face—had quite suddenly become the talk of fashion bloggers here and there and she had quickly learned how their word-of-mouth admiration could carry more weight and more propulsion than a million-dollar ad campaign.

And how that propulsion could slow to a drip as quickly as it had appeared.

She took a step back.

He cleared his throat. "Writer's block."

"Sabbatical over?"

He gave her a sharp, shuddering shake of his head, never taking his eyes off hers.

She frowned until a proverbial light switched on inside her mind and she nodded. "Ah, so this is the reason you were up most of the night."

He closed his eyes now, giving her one succinct nod.

"And the reason you are such a grouch today."

He coughed a laugh and put a fist to his chest. "I'm hurt."

"You are not."

He laughed now. "Yeah, you're right. I'm not."

"I understand."

"You mean about the writer's block?"

"Designers get stuck sometimes, too." She did not tell him that her "sometimes" was now.

His kind eyes returned, recognition in them. "Thanks. I appreciate you saying that."

She smiled at him, knowing her pearly whites would have to make up for her otherwise lack of daytime readiness. "I'd better get inside."

"Right. The breakfast meeting. Nice of your brother to give you time to settle in."

"I don't mind. Although ... I hear the coffee's not very good here."

He laughed harder this time and wagged his head. Warm red rose in his cheeks. "My apologies to the chef."

She held her finger to her lips. "Sshh... I won't tell."

CHRISTIAN STOOD out on the deck, his fingers curled around his mug of now-cold coffee. In the rolling waves, he saw a goddess. Or was it a mermaid? No matter. She glided closer to shore and rolled onto her back, floating, her skin luminescent, her eyes lolling gently. He leaned across the railing now, hearing snippets of her voice, like a song. It carried on the wind, but he couldn't catch it completely. Still, the soothing sound of it calmed the tremor that had pounded in his veins all night, the one that had grown in intensity the more he thought about the voicemail he'd found on his phone.

He should have ignored it. He'd come back to his cozy suite at Sea Glass Inn, content after spending the evening with Jackson—and his sister. What a schmuck he'd been. He had missed Jackson and Meg's wedding. Had been too caught up in

13

a drama of his own making to come out of hiding and be found—even by good friends.

If he hadn't been so myopic, so seething with both self-doubt and indignation, he very well might have been at their wedding. No doubt he would have become hypnotized by the woman who stood in stark contrast to the shrew who had successfully—for a while—stolen Sophia's identity.

He blew into the wind, his cheeks deflating. He'd allowed the presence of a voicemail to disrupt the flow of his newfound motivation. He'd turned a corner, or so he thought, newly inspired by a chance at starting over. At reaching deep inside himself.

At writing, once again, a book of his heart.

Then that blasted voicemail turned his thoughts to a darker place. He'd have to listen to it completely next time and avoid the urge to delete it altogether. All he really wanted to do was forget. Forget everything.

He stood there a moment longer, fighting to keep calm. One thing he couldn't seem to forget was the sight of Sophia drifting out onto the deck next to his, her hair in disarray, those crystal eyes of hers attempting to adjust to the morning light.

She was lovely.

And then he offended her. Made snide comments about her beloved New York and watched her countenance fall. Such an idiot! And what did she do in retort? She offered him an olive branch in the form of laughter.

He shook his head.

What was it about Sophia Agli Riley that caused him to both be on his toes and push the envelope. He'd certainly pushed it at the airport. And then again, this morning. And still she spoke to him without a haughty look or condemning word.

It was humbling. Christian had done his share of eating crow over the past year. He'd had to after bringing shame upon himself and disappointing those who had believed in him. Had believed he had changed. People like Jackson.

He swallowed a gulp of that cold coffee, the taste of it bitter, as if he deserved to take his caffeine with a little punishment on the side.

Christian looked out upon the horizon again. Sophia's diamond-shaped face framed by bedhead popped into his memory and he laughed out loud. On the heels of that memory he was reminded of the way she shrank back when he'd sidled up to her with a handmade sign and spoke to her in a weird accent. Had she really been planning to turn him in to one of the guards?

He laughed out loud again.

"Man, you're sure in a good mood for so early in the morning."

His yanked his neck, causing it to spasm. "Sor—"

The woman continued, "If only my ex had worn a smile like that in the morning, we'd still be married."

Unlike Sophia, the woman on the opposite balcony had obviously run all kinds of styling tools through her mountainous blonde hair. Her face had an airbrushed quality, and he forced himself not to shade his eyes from the brightness of her lips.

"It's a beautiful day." He looked out toward the sea. "And the beach is outside my window. All kinds of reasons to be in a good mood, I suppose."

She licked her lips, eyeing him. "Sure is. Join me for a mimosa on the restaurant patio?"

He held back his knee-jerk reaction, the one shouting "no." He tilted his head and conjured up a regretful smile. "Sorry. On a deadline."

She pushed away from the railing. "Another time then."

"Perhaps."

Inside his room, he lowered himself to the desk chair next to his bed, the one that squeaked and groaned as if he were an unwelcome visitor. He'd have to mention that to Jackson. He was thankful for quick thinking and looming deadlines. He swallowed a chuckle, then opened the page that had pushed him outside in the first place.

It said: Chapter One.

CHAPTER 2

*S*ophia made her way through the dining room, chin up, eyes and mouth smiling. She had determined to help her brother after the horrendous year he had suffered thanks to her half-sister. Gia had stolen her identity, cheated Riley Holdings, and nearly chased off one of the company's most loyal employees—Meg. Would Jackson and Meg even be married today if her sister's crimes had not been exposed?

She shuddered. Though Sophia would have preferred to curl up in bed with her sketchpad and forget about all that had transpired, she soldiered on. Her father, God rest his beautiful soul, would have wanted it that way.

"Sophia." Her brother stood, took her right hand, and kissed her on the cheek. Another man had stood as well. "I'd like you to meet Wade Prince. Wade, my sister, Sophia."

Solidly built with salt-and-pepper waves of untamed hair, Wade took her hand and enveloped it in his. He smiled, tan and ageless, revealing a deep dimple, and shining brown eyes. Like a younger Antonio Banderas. She'd always heard that California cultivated celebrities, and Wade Prince, with his crisp, white shirt opened at the collar, appeared to have sprung from the state's verdant garden.

"It's a pleasure." Sophia took her seat.

Jackson shifted. She'd sensed a slight bit of tension in her brother's demeanor last evening, but now he gave her more than a glimpse. He smiled, but the stiffness of his posture—his back hardly grazed the seat back of his chair—alerted her.

Wade appeared not to notice. "I see you practice what you preach."

She leaned her head slightly. "Sorry?"

"I understand you are a fashion designer. That dress is beautifully made. Did you design it?" He gazed at her, but not in a way that put her on guard. On the contrary, the warmth of his voice glided through her consciousness.

"Yes. Thank you."

"It looked like one of yours." He paused, then smiled in that sheepish way, as if being caught. "Meg has shared some photos of your designs with me."

She laughed lightly. "Well, I don't make all of my own clothing."

"But you once did?"

She nodded. "It was my hobby for many years." She could have said more, but her past still held many moments that she preferred to keep private.

Jackson cut in. "It was more than your hobby—it was your passion. And I for one am anxious to see how you will be inspired by a change of landscape." He paused. "I hope and pray it suits you."

A light went on in Wade's eyes. "Yes, of course. A city girl has moved to the coast. Will tropical prints and Hawaiian shirts be in your future?"

Gratitude for laughter after a long flight and a short night of sleep filled her. "Well, I wouldn't plan on too large of a shift just yet. Besides, I'm here for more than the scenery." She gave her brother a sad smile. "To make up for lost time, mostly."

Wade's smile turned almost grim. He took a sip of coffee but did not remove his gaze from her. "I understand. Your brother has filled me in. I'm terribly sorry for all the pain that you've gone through."

"Well," she said, "I'm here now."

Wade lifted his coffee mug. "That you are. Welcome to your new life, Sophia."

She tipped her head to the side. "Thank you very much."

Jackson signaled for the waiter, though Sophia had not so much as glanced at the menu. The waiter appeared. "What can I bring you this morning?"

Sophia ordered her usual poached eggs and potatoes. A macchiato. And no bread. Wade and Jackson both ordered omelets and black coffee.

Jackson's posture stiffened again. "Wade has been a friend for several years, and after I became aware of how much debt we had acquired—"

"Because of my sister."

"Right. Because of Gia's involvement in the inn ... anyway, Wade's skills as a business consultant have been helping me dig us out ever since."

"Are you an accountant, Wade?"

He shook his head. "I worked as an accountant for a few years before discovering that my strengths lie more heavily in marketing and management. So, I made a switch." He paused. "The inn's remodel—coupled with the financial strains of late that have affected the other properties as well—have been an enormous undertaking for Jackson. He has handled it all in stride, at least that's what I see from my chair."

"But you believe the inns need a better presence online. Simple enough."

"That will help, though there is no quick fix." He spoke slowly. "Ultimately, I believe word of mouth is the best advertising a business can have. I have seen this proven time and time again."

She studied him. A certainty of concern showed in his eyes, and yet, did he not believe he could help? Were the inns in more trouble than she had first believed? Was he concerned that not enough progress had been made?

She spoke directly to him. "But you have much more to say."

Jackson touched her hand and gave Wade a look that she could only describe as cautionary. "Before I knew you, I was forced to sell the other inns—all except this one and Sea Castle in Florida. Now Wade has advised me to sell that one too."

"I see."

A server appeared with their breakfasts, quietly delivering the correct dish to each person. The presence of other patrons in the restaurant dimmed, as if they had gone quiet. Though that well may have been Sophia's imagination. Another dagger to her heart had been inserted with this latest news—news that likely would not have had to be delivered if it weren't for ...

"Is there something wrong with your order?"

Jackson's voice woke her to the present. She shook her head and lifted a fork. "It looks lovely." She hadn't the heart to tell him she had suddenly lost all interest in food.

Her brother sighed. "Let's eat before getting into more specifics. It's been a long night. For all of us."

Wade nodded and dove into his breakfast. She supposed it would be easier for the messenger to eat than it could possibly be for those who had the task of dismantling what a father had built. As she considered this, he glanced up. Their eyes met and lingered, his full of that concern she'd seen moments ago.

She glanced away, aware of the heat in her cheeks. She'd

been caught mistrusting him. She didn't know the man, so why would she assume he cared less than he did?

SOPHIA RETURNED TO HER ROOM, her mind filled with numbers and proposals. When Jackson and Meg had suggested she move to the inn, she'd jumped at their proposal. The deeper she had moved into the business of design, the more she had grown unsure of the direction of her life. Her existence, it seemed, had cut a swath toward its own path, regardless of where or how she may have tried to direct it herself.

A housekeeper had plumped her pillows and tidied the room, so she kicked off her heels and sank into the bedding, eyelids heavy. Plenty of travelers took noontime naps, did they not? Still, the thought of not pressing on, of not *doing* something during the daylight hours, felt akin to slothfulness.

She woke to pounding on the door. With a start, Sophia hopped out of bed and hurried across the room.

"So good to see you, my beautiful sister!" Meg flung her arms around Sophia's neck and hugged her close. "I had to arm wrestle your brother over who got to see you first today."

Her sister-in-law's best friend Liddy strolled in behind her. "Yeah, and Meg won," she said. "She let Jackson have you first only so he could save face."

Meg laughed and glanced back at her friend. "Don't let him hear you say that."

"He's just mad that I've been making you work out with me." Liddy turned to Sophia. "Look how toned she is—I kind of hate her."

Meg tsked. "Please."

"Seriously, I've been running for years and you lift one weight and look at you—you're more cut than a freshly mowed

21

lawn." Liddy put an arm around Sophia's shoulder. "Hey, gorgeous."

Sophia blinked.

Meg gasped. "Were you asleep? Oh no!"

Sophia stroked the air with her fingers. "Not to worry. It was just a catnap. I need to be up now anyway so my body doesn't get confused."

Liddy clucked. "My body hasn't had its head on straight since my son was born. Not sure if it'll ever be the same."

Sophia smiled. "You have a beautiful body and a sweet baby. I would be proud to dress you both."

Liddy leaned her head to one side and gave Meg a frown-smile. "That is the sweetest thing I've heard in a long time. I would love that!"

Meg plunked down on the king-sized bed and kicked off her flats. "We were hoping to steal you away before you get too settled in." She glanced at Sophia's bags near the couch, one still open. "Is this all you brought?"

Sophia shook her head and walked over to the couch with the open suitcase. "I apologize for how I've left things. This is all I have for now." Idly, she pulled a cotton blouse from her bag and draped it over her arm.

"I love that fabric," Liddy said. "Gorgeous."

"Thank you." Sophia continued to unpack. "The rest of my things were shipped or put into storage. I don't need everything right away. Thank you for the suite, by the way. Once my things arrive, I will be utilizing every corner. Oh, and the large wooden table is perfect."

"Don't thank me—it's your home now. This inn is magical … I'm sure you'll find that out soon enough." She winked. "By the way, the table was Jackson's idea. He's so cute. He actually called a couple of designers and asked what you might need."

Sophia's heart squeezed.

"Anyway," Meg continued, "we knew you'd need much more than a room to live in. I'm sure you'll realize that once all your boxes arrive."

"I'm sure you are correct." Sophia didn't add that she'd left far more behind than she had shipped. The sense that this move might be temporary continued to shimmy its way through her heart. "As for now, I'm more than ready to see more of this city."

"Hold on," Liddy said, approaching her. "What is that?"

Her sample. Not the design she was working on for a possible new line, but a dress sample she'd made for herself on a whim long ago. She'd forgotten about it until she had found it tucked into a bottom drawer when she was packing to come here. She had already shipped the rest of her things, so she'd had no choice but to bury it in her suitcase. Or burn it.

"May I?" Liddy asked, reaching toward the dress.

Sophia hesitated before shrugging. "Be my guest."

Liddy lifted the raspberry-and-white garment from the suitcase and held it out in front of herself. "I love this so much —I could eat it up. If only I weren't nursing, then I'd steal it from you and wear it myself."

"That looks so cool and comfortable, Sophia," Meg said, joining them. "I can tell by the cut that it's one of yours, but that color! So different."

Sophia reached for the dress and gently folded it over the other garments hanging on her arm. "Yes, I suppose it is."

Meg reached for it again and held it by its armholes. "Oh, please wear it today. I want to see it on you."

Liddy nodded. "Me too. Let me live vicariously through your svelte-ness. I beg you."

Meg danced the dress in front of her, turning it left to right like the steering wheel of a car, her smile imploring. "Put this on and then we'll do some sightseeing before Liddy has to get back to the baby. So much we need to get caught up on."

"He's still nursing, so I can't leave him for too long," Liddy added. "I hope you two don't mind me butting in, but" —she shook her head—"the story of how you came to be here, in this family, is still so surreal to me. I'm so glad you're here, Sophia. Truly."

"And I am glad you're here as well. You two are like sisters —I can see that."

Meg tilted her head to one side, still holding the dress in front of Sophia with that pretty-please smile on her face.

Sophia relented, headed to the bathroom, and slipped into the dress, mindful of the way the fabric embraced her skin and gratified her curves. She stared at herself in the mirror for three long beats. The dress was dated, but still fit her well. She had bedhead, though, from her nap, so she took a hair tie from the drawer, twisted her hair at the crown, and rolled the excess into a messy bun.

"Hey, beautiful," Meg called out. "You ready?"

She emerged from the bathroom to Liddy's reaction. "Gorgeous! What a pretty color on you. And you have the perfect chin line for that hairdo—my profile is the pits."

Meg clucked her tongue. "Really, Liddy, I don't know how you come up with things like that. There's nothing particularly hideous about your profile."

Liddy tilted her head to the side. "Hear that, Sophia? One of us used the word hideous in a mention of my profile, but it wasn't me."

Meg cracked up. "I can't win with you. Let's get out of here."

Meg drove, Sophia sat shotgun, and Liddy took the backseat driver position. Sophia took in the green-blues of the sea that abutted their drive. They made a quick stop at the harbor museum, jogged up the stairs, then lingered at the telescopes that opened a view to the Channel Islands in the distance.

Sea air filled her lungs and refreshed her soul. When was the last time she'd thought of anything other than her designs? Her business? Her ... problems?

Meg interrupted her musings. "I know it's not Italy, but isn't that ocean gorgeous? And those islands?"

"They are so lovely. In a small way, though, those islands floating out in the sea remind me of Italy's coast." She turned to Meg. "I often traveled by train by myself for the day—for inspiration."

Meg hugged her neck. "Oh, you are a girl after my own heart."

Liddy tilted her head to the side. "Meg ran away to the coast one day. Didn't you?"

Meg's eyes widened. "I absolutely did. I was mad at your brother." She laughed. "So I took a train to some cute little hilltop villages—there are five of them."

"Cinque Terre?"

"Yes! Well, only one of them. I went to Vernazza."

Sophia's heart lifted. "One of my favorite places to go. Did you have a meal? Their fish is the freshest I've ever tasted."

Liddy rolled her eyes. "Did she! She tells the story every chance she gets."

Meg put a hand on her hip. "You're sick of me? Is that what you're saying?"

Liddy sighed and hugged her friend. "I could never get sick of you. Go ahead and tell your story for the *thousandth* time."

Meg's eyes shined. "I ran off to Vernazza and made a friend there. A woman who was traveling alone. We had lunch together and—you're not kidding about that fresh fish—it still had its head intact."

Sophia smiled. "Of course it did. You didn't think they would serve you frozen fish, I hope?"

"What was that woman's name again? Your friend?" Liddy said.

"Priscilla."

Liddy's voice sounded wistful. "There's something charming about running off to a foreign country and making a friend who can wander those cobblestone streets with you and share your angst, isn't there?"

Sophia smiled, unsure if Liddy was joking or dead serious. It did sound rather charming, but given the circumstances of what was happening in Meg and Jackson's life at the time, Sophia doubted the excursion to Cinque Terre was as awe-inspiring as all that. She bit the inside of her cheek. Then again, it wasn't her story to tell. Who was she to judge Meg's memory of a day in Cinque Terre?

"Penny for your thoughts," Meg said.

Sophia shook her head and mustered a smile. "Sorry. I was, uh, thinking about how nice it may have been to have run into you in Vernazza. Those happy little houses on the hill can do wonders for a person's countenance. Wouldn't you agree?"

Meg watched her, pensive. She nodded. "You do understand."

"It's no wonder you made a friend there," Sophia added. "Sometimes a physical change of place makes it easier to let go of the ideas that plague us. It sounds as if you and Priscilla were good for each other."

"Yes, yes, we were. Sometimes I wonder how she's doing, whether she's been able to conquer the mountain she faced as I have."

"Perhaps someday you will find out."

Meg smiled. "I hope you're right."

Liddy lifted her phone and motioned for Meg and Sophia

to scooch closer to each other. "Let me get a pic of you with those islands in the background."

The breeze lifted tendrils from Sophia's face, and as she tucked the wayward hair alongside her shoulder, her gaze caught sight of the raspberry blush of her dress. The glimpse startled her. She had temporarily forgotten that she'd forgone her usual black, white, or gray aesthetic.

Then it hit her. Sophia's mind churned. Why hadn't she tossed away this dress when she'd found it? Too much time had passed for it to be considered fashionable, but more than that, it reminded her of thoughts and feelings she'd prefer to leave behind. One's clothing—like art and books and other items people hold dear—were like that. Maybe her hesitation to part with it felt akin to letting go of history. Like throwing away a child's first baby shoes.

History. Some things were written about to be remembered, while others should never be thought of again. Such as the contents of her stepfather's note, the one he'd written after one too many shots of grappa.

Hadn't she already conquered this mountain? She'd taken his words into consideration, made adjustments, and found a modicum of success. She supposed that the dress she wore now had played a part in that success. And perhaps for that she could manage to be glad.

Meg cinched her closer. "Say cheese."

Sophia made herself smile.

Liddy lowered the camera phone and plunked it into the designer diaper bag she carried in place of a purse. She patted her stomach, which looked as if it no longer contained even a smidge of baby fat. "Are you ladies ready for lunch yet? I'm starved."

Sophia had hardly touched her eggs at breakfast this morning, and though time had melted away, her appetite had yet to return.

~

HE'D WRITTEN ALL DAY. Not that he had been aware of time, but the darkness that descended upon his room was a sure indication that he'd managed to pour more words onto a page than he had in months. The mermaid who swam into his consciousness early in the morning had lingered. She'd splashed him with her shimmering tail and he'd held on, praying his hands would not slip from her silky scales as he tirelessly put her story on paper.

The ride had, at times, made him breathless.

Christian hit "save" again, then popped his knuckles in one loud rumble. His stomach reacted by grumbling back, so he stood and searched for something to fill it. A half pack of saltines ... two sections of a peeled tangerine ... and one slippery slice of processed ham stuffed into a baggie in the mini fridge.

He'd have to do better than that.

Before he'd had the chance to lace up his running shoes, the click of the slider door of the suite next to his reminded him that he was not alone. He threw open his own slider and stepped out.

"Evening, Christian," Sophia greeted him, her face awash in moonlight.

He stroked his beard, burying a yawn. "Evening yourself. Been busy today?"

"If you count sea gazing and wine tasting busy, then yes. Yes, I have been."

"Ah. I see you've been out with Meg."

"What happens at the beach ... stays at the beach." She

laughed. "Meg and her friend Liddy told me to say that, but nothing really happened."

"You won't find me judging."

Her smile reminded him of a little girl's, gentle and shy, but those eyes. From this spot across the divide, her unwavering gaze seemed full of questions. If he did not break away soon, they'd cast a spell on him and he'd soon find himself lying beneath a hammer, as if he were the shell of a coconut awaiting its fate.

"If you don't mind me saying, you look ... quite exhausted."

He pressed his lips together, the light dawning. "Was it the slippers that gave it away?"

She stood on her tiptoes and braced herself to look over the railing and onto his deck. "They have seen better times, haven't they?"

"Hey!" He gave her a mock glare then shrugged.

She only laughed quietly.

He leaned his tired body against the railing, allowing the night air to bring him a second wind. "I'd be insulted if you weren't a fashion designer, you know. But hey, maybe you could design something more to your liking."

Now it was she who shrugged. "I don't do feet."

He lowered his voice. "But you haven't seen mine."

She gasped a little. Had he crossed the line? Would not be the first time he had opened his mouth and stuck in a foot— pun intended. Though when had this ever bothered him?

A way to a woman's heart was through her gut, in a sense. If he could make her laugh—really belly laugh—she'd be his. His father had always told him that and he'd found it to be true. But Sophia ... she was different. Jackson's sister. Ethereal. A porcelain figurine in the next suite over ...

And he didn't care to cause her to break.

"I suppose I could make you a pair of socks." Her melodic voice interrupted his internal struggle.

"Excuse me."

"Shoe design is not part of my repertoire, ah, but socks. Socks I can do, though I would need to remind myself how." She lifted two palms and gave him a little shrug. "It would not be a problem."

"You're serious."

"Well, I would hate for you to get sick."

He scrutinized her expression in the moonlight.

"From all those holes in your slippers," she deadpanned.

He crossed his arms in front of him. "Well, now you're just pulling my leg."

She squealed as softly as a whisper and covered her face in her hands, her shoulders shuddering from deep and abiding laughter.

He'd won. And he kind of liked that.

CHAPTER 3

"You look bereft. How can I help?" Wade stood near the empty chair at Sophia's table in the hotel restaurant. One hand beneath his elbow, the other holding his chin, his expression imploring. She gestured for him to sit.

"I am right, aren't I, Sophia?" he said once he'd slid into a chair. "You need help with something."

Sophia swallowed, thinking. Slowly, she said, "I think I may. The problem is, I'm not exactly sure what kind of assistance I need. I can't bother Jackson with my problems right now ... not with all he has on his schedule."

Wade wore a perfectly tailored heather-gray suit that contrasted beautifully with his dark hair. She surmised that he must be on his way to a business meeting. Perhaps with Jackson. Or a vendor. Still, he sat across from her, one elbow on the table, his chin leaned into it, concern knitting his brow. "What is it?"

"My sales rep called. She is preparing to represent my dresses at a show in New York in September, but she says interest is low and she's not sure there will be enough orders to sustain my business. I'm afraid I'm going to lose her too. Plus, the small manufacturer I've been using is asking for guarantees."

"And this has taken you by surprise, I take it?"

"In all honesty, no."

He gave her a succinct nod. "So you have had indications? To what do you attribute the drop in sales?"

She answered him with a shrug and a small shake of her head. Could she finally admit that this news of a downturn only served to highlight her lack of confidence? No matter what success she had found, even for a short while, she could not shake the opposite sense of herself. Unsure. Critical. Wary of her artistic imperfections. Sophia preferred to stay inside her head with only music and her thoughts to occupy her.

"But you would like to recapture your sales, right?"

She exhaled a breath. "Yes, but I admit that I have been very distracted with personal upheaval in the past year. I've not given my designs the attention they need—and my creativity is rather flat right now."

Wade's expression turned pensive, his lips pursed. He rubbed his fingers together while in a fist, almost as if squeezing a baseball. As he did, he watched her, the effect like the brush of fresh pine needles up and down her arms.

Finally, he said, "First, I think you need to find a new manufacturer."

She coughed a laugh. "I hardly think I can do that now, not with Fashion Week only a couple of months away. No." She shook her head. "I've only just arrived and now it appears that I need to book a flight back to New York to meet with them. They are lovely people. Truly."

Wade wrinkled that space between his eyes again, his mouth curved as a smile burgeoned on his face. "Can I talk you into holding off? As I'm sure you know, Los Angeles is a hub for apparel manufacturing. There are many full-package manufacturers in your own backyard, so to speak."

He was right. She knew this, but Los Angeles had never appealed to her. Not like New York and Milan. For some reason, every time she pictured LA she saw gray. Not silvers of shimmering fabric that paired well with white and black, but the drab kind of gray that started out white, only to fade to a colorless swatch.

"Or perhaps it's time that I let it go."

"Your design business?"

Maybe her purpose in it had already been fulfilled. "Yes."

"Sophia, one thing I've learned over the years is that the time to think big—really big—is when you're at the bottom."

She laughed at this. "With all due respect, Wade. I can't imagine that right now."

"Well, you're in luck. And as it happens, I will be driving to LA in about"—he pulled his phone from his pocket, checked the screen, then re-engaged her with his gaze—"in about an hour. I have a meeting with a client in Santa Monica. Should be brief, and if you don't mind waiting, I would be glad to take you downtown to visit some of those manufacturers by the middle of the afternoon. If nothing else, you will be inspired by the garment district."

She thought a moment. One of the benefits of working with companies in New York—other than the fact that they were in a city that she adored—was their willingness to take on a boutique designer like Sophia. Hers, a small family-owned manufacturer in a small walk-up where rents had grown tenfold in a short amount of time. Still, they prevailed. She had wandered in one day with a suitcase of her garments and myriad questions.

"Can you help me produce my dresses in multiple sizes?"

"Do you handle distribution?"

"How do I create a tech pack?"

Lost in the memory, she smiled at her own ignorance.

Wade leaned his head to the side, appraising her. "What's on your mind?"

She startled. "Pardon?"

"You were smiling."

"Oh, that." She laughed gently. "I was thinking back to when my design hobby turned into a business. I had no idea what I was doing, so I packed up my dresses and walked into a small sewing studio and asked for help."

"Remarkable. So you had no plans to start a business?"

Her smile dimmed. An unkind memory circled her mind, unwilling to land. She gave it a mental swat, reminding herself to stay in the present. "I suppose I had thought about it, but never very seriously. I was young. Sewing and designing had been my passions for as long as I could remember, so it came as a surprise to me when I received a message about a dress I had worn in a photograph."

"I'm sorry—I don't understand. Who was it that saw your photo?"

"My friend Carla had taken it and framed it. We had been traveling through Positano and the weather had turned unbearable, so I decided to try the sample I had brought with me. Its fabric was breathable and light, a crinkled cotton, perfect for the Italian coast in summer."

"Are you telling me that your business was started with a photograph?"

"You could say that, yes. A friend of hers saw the photo on her mantle and asked if she could sell the dresses in her boutique. I suppose you are right. That first boutique spread to more than a dozen—enough to run a small design company."

"Old fashioned word of mouth. Social media is powerful

and an integral part of my business, but I'm sure you know that."

Sophia shrugged. "I am an anomaly. I don't care much for social media. All those angry voices in one place cause me to struggle."

"Struggle?"

"With humankind, in general."

"I see. That's understandable, but I hope that I can prove you wrong."

She leaned to one side, considering him. His eyes sparkled, as if he hid a secret. "Is that a challenge?" she asked.

He laughed. "One that I think I will win."

"Okay. Let's see if you can change my mind—and prove me wrong."

Wade sat back, a triumphant smile on his face. He looked as if he believed he had already convinced her of the power of social media. "I can't believe your brother never mentioned to me that your business was started by a simple photograph." He leaned toward her. "He does know how your business came to be, correct?"

Sophia thought for a moment. "Actually, I'm not sure that he does. The subject never came up."

Wade smacked the table, his mouth open in surprise. Though she believed him to be as much as twenty years her senior, give or take, he reminded her of a little boy who had just discovered the joys of Fortnite—or the video game du jour.

Her waiter appeared, his voice shaky. "May I get you something, sir?"

"Yes, as a matter of fact, I'd like a large iced coffee to go," Wade said. "And that slap on the table was not meant for you."

"Yes, sir."

"I think he meant it for me," Sophia said, teasing.

Wade wagged his pointer finger at her. "Not really. I just love a good challenge."

The waiter wavered, rocking on the balls of his feet, as if wondering if he should stay or bolt. "Ma'am?"

"Nothing more for me. And please, call me Sophia. I'm Jackson's sister and I'll be living at the inn for a time."

"Yes, ma—I mean, Sophia. My name is Ryan. If there is anything else that you need, please let me know." He turned to Wade. "I will return in a moment with your coffee."

After he'd gone, Sophia quirked her head in Wade's direction. "I think you scared him."

"Really?" He leaned across the table, catching Sophia's gaze with his. "And what do you think of me, Sophia? Do you think I am ... frightening?"

She swallowed back against the flush in her cheeks. "I hardly think you're frightening, Wade. Though, perhaps, a little intimidating. That poor waiter was trembling."

His smile grew broader. He leaned back and surveyed the room before landing his gaze back on her. "I can accept intimidating," he said. "Besides, if I'm going to help you negotiate a manufacturing contract, I'll need to have intimidation in my back pocket."

She scoffed. "I don't think that will be necessary, Mr. Prince."

Ryan returned with iced coffee in a to-go cup, then scurried off.

Wade's eyes held a question. "Jackson asked me to stop by his office. Why don't I ring you when I'm ready to leave, say, in a half hour or so? Will that give you enough time?"

She stood. "I look forward to it." On her way back up to the room, Sophia asked herself over and over again: *What have I agreed to?*

~

CHRISTIAN PACED the green-blue pattern of the carpet in his suite. Why had he waited this long to play back that voicemail? How long had it been? Weeks? A knife twisted at the base of his neck, metaphorically speaking maybe, but it might as well have been real as far as he could tell. The sharp pain shot through his neck and up into his head, and there did not appear to be a thing he could do about it.

He glanced at his open computer screen, his curser blinking, coaxing him back to write the scene he'd left splayed open. He'd been writing the hero's point of view, something that usually came quite easy for him. But today he'd become stumped. Not that he didn't understand what Nickolas thought about the graceful being from the sea who dazzled him. No, he had a quite good idea of what the man was thinking ... but how to convey those emotions with mere words?

Instead, he had allowed himself to stop the flow, to interrupt the world of avengers and hawks that had been writhing and swelling within his mind since early morning. He'd taken a swig of water and visited the bathroom, and on his way back, his eyes caught sight of his cellphone, that voicemail waiting.

What did that windbag want from him now? Hadn't they already said all that needed saying?

He'd listened to the message only long enough to recognize the grating rasp of his ex-agent's voice. Burns Golden called only when he wanted something, even if that something was nothing more than to badger Christian to perform better. Write faster. Produce content in rapid succession, each story better than the first.

He frowned. He was no longer beholden to Burns's schedule. Burns had taken care of that with one well-placed punch that had both made headlines and caused his agent to lop him off from his roster like a chicken's head at dinnertime.

So he'd listened to the full message, this time his sense of curiosity stronger than his desire to fully eliminate Burns from his life. Now, as he stood hovering over his computer, he wished he could simply forget the voicemail's contents and dive back into the story that had been causing him to lose sleep the past few days.

Instead, Christian sat in front of his computer, opened a browser, and logged into his Facebook account. He rarely checked Facebook anymore, deeming it a soon-to-be relic. However, not everyone felt the same disconnect with the social media site and it appeared that someone he knew well had inadvertently let his secret slip.

Even if he were to ask her to delete the post—something he planned to do—the damage had already been done.

His fingers flew across the keyboard and then he scrolled. And scrolled. And scrolled more. There. His cover designer's name beside a post with heart and happy face emojis embedded in it.

So excited to show off my latest cover design for a very important author! I can't disclose his name here (which is why there's a black mark across the top), but isn't the cover divine??

And there was his cover. The painting he'd commissioned, the embellishments he'd asked for, and the title. Everything but his name.

Christian groaned. *Marci* ... He'd plucked her from a stack of recommended cover designers because he'd seen her work and it had impressed him. Until recently, she'd been employed by a publishing house that, by all accounts, had managed to stay afloat.

But that had been marketing. Or, he'd guessed, a straight-out lie. As Heidi Klum said on *Project Runway*, "One day you're in, and the next? You're out." Unfortunately for Marci and others on the editorial and design teams, they were all out. Without even a day's notice.

The publishing house's loss had been his gain—at least until she'd made an error in judgment to "out" his new book on Facebook before he'd had a chance to announce it to his readers himself. He had hopes for this book to relaunch his career, but had yet to plan how that would all happen. Marci's post had complicated that process and he wasn't sure what to do about it. A knock on the door interrupted Christian's plans to take a midnight flight out of the country ...

A second knock, more like a pounding, hurried him along. "Just a minute!" Christian opened the door to find Thomas, a valet, standing next to a cart full of boxes. "Yes?"

THOMAS STOOD THERE LIKE A REED, his chin lifted, making Christian think he either had a question or wanted to clock him with an uppercut. Weird vibe from that guy, for sure.

"Can I help you?" Christian's gaze slid to the cart full of shipping boxes.

Thomas frowned and looked down at the call slip in his hands. "Wait."

Christian shifted and crossed his arms.

Patches of red enflamed Thomas's cheeks. "Looks like I have the wrong door. These are for Ms. Riley." He paused and finally looked up. "Sorry."

"No problem." He should have shut the door and gone back to the task at hand—dealing with the angry voicemail and the cover that had stirred his former agent's ire—but curiosity piqued him. Besides, Christian convinced himself, Sophia might need help moving those heavy-looking boxes around her room. He certainly didn't want to see her stuck paying the valet to stick around when he could do it.

When Thomas's knocks on Sophia's door went unheeded, Christian called to him, "You can bring them to me after all. I'll take Sophia's boxes to her when she returns." When Thomas hesitated, Christian unfolded his arms and dropped them to his sides with a growl. "For heaven's sake, I'm living here too. Jackson and I have been friends since college. I'm not going to steal her sewing machine."

Thomas grunted. "Suit yourself."

With Sophia's items securely in his room, Christian questioned himself. How was he going to explain this if she asked? And what if she was gone for the day and he was left to step around the maze of boxes he'd collected without much thought?

He swiped a palm down the gristle of his beard, the sound of it rustling in his ears. Nearly missed the sound of a nearby door clicking open and shutting with finality. Christian glanced at the door then back at the packages.

Already?

He padded down the hall, regretting that he'd neglected to put on his shoes. He didn't normally wear them when writing. Why bother, right?

Sophia's smile greeted him, then faltered. "Christian."

"I see that you're thrilled."

She shook her head and tsked, shaming him. "I was just expecting ... oh, never mind. Come in!"

Her brilliant smile had returned, but he held up a hand. "I forgive you for not being more excited to see me. Just came by to let you know that my suite is filled with boxes that are addressed to you ... m'lady."

The way she stomped one petite foot and rolled her eyes

nearly made his knees buckle. He soldiered on. "Now that you're back, I'll bring them to you."

She hesitated and her eyes darted to the hall. "Oh, but I hate to bother you with them—there are so many."

Secretly, he was grateful to have anything but Burns's voicemail to deal with right now. "It's no problem. Put one of those pointy heels in the door and I'll be right back."

He lugged two boxes stacked on top of each other down the hall wondering why he hadn't slipped Thomas a twenty to leave the cart. No matter. He was young. Virile. Sitting at a desk writing all day was not akin to being a couch potato—no matter how many times he'd been punched in the shoulder by a buddy to prove otherwise. So what if he wasn't cut with ridges? What woman wanted to be sliced open with those when he went in for a kiss?

Sophia cleared her throat, and he realized he'd been standing in the parlor of her suite holding those two boxes for he didn't know how long. He flashed her a smile as if to say, *I've been waiting for you.*

"Please, Christian. Just put them anywhere. I don't have time right now to open them anyway."

"You got it." He pushed the boxes into the corner, went back to his suite to gather more, and returned a few minutes later.

Sophia walked into the parlor wearing a different outfit—a sleek skirt paired with a sleeveless ruffled blouse. She held a necklace in her hand. "Would you?"

"Of course." Christian took the delicate gold chain from her hands and stepped behind her. She had scooped up her shiny brunette hair and twisted it high above her nape, allowing him access to the back of her long and slender neck. A sweet scent of floral reached his senses and the clasp of her necklace taunted him, but he wouldn't be riled. Both his mother and sister had asked this of him, and he would not allow himself to be vexed by a flimsy piece of metal!

"Are you able to do it?" she asked.

"Not to worry. I'm an expert at necklace clasping."

"Oh, are you now?"

A bead of perspiration bubbled along his temple, and he nearly gave up, when at last—success. "There! See?" He turned her around by the shoulders. "And you doubted me."

Her smile dazzled, the upward tip of her chin drawing him like a magnet, her mouth curved into a crescent. "I would nev—"

A rap on the open door. A male voice. "Am I interrupting?"

Sophia spun around. "Wade. You're here."

Christian took a step back and put his hands into his pockets. The guy's suit was atypical for this beach town. He'd seen plenty of tailored suits like it in New York. Shoot, he'd owned a few and probably still had one. Somewhere.

Sophia stepped quickly to the door and touched the guy—Wade—on his forearm. "Wade, this is Christian, one of Jackson's oldest friends."

"Hey, I'm not that old," Christian cracked. He shook Wade's hand. Firm. Confident. Would make a great antagonist in his next book ...

"A pleasure," Wade said. He turned to Sophia. "I was planning to call but had to dash up to my room so I thought I'd pick you up on the way down. Ready to go?"

Sophia's gaze met Christian's, her apology shining through.

"I was on my way out anyway." Christian tapped a naked toe on one of the boxes he delivered. "That's the last of them. You two kids have fun now."

"Thank you for delivering my boxes, Christian," he heard her say as he exited Sophia's suite. "I owe you!"

In front of his own door, Christian paused. His heart hammered in his chest. Unease slithered around his insides.

He'd been off his game for weeks. Months, really. Had only finally found momentum yesterday, all of a sudden, in fact, when he'd knocked out nearly four thousand words in one morning. Exhilarating. Therapeutic.

Terrifying.

He swallowed. He should walk right inside and do it all over again. But then again, lightning rarely struck twice. Or so he'd been told.

He glanced down the hall. Sophia and what's-his-face had yet to emerge. Not that it was any of his business. He had a book to write. Remember? And a fire to put out where his agent was concerned. He exhaled roughly, then fished his key card out of his pocket, allowing it to hover in front of the key reader.

Click. Laughter. He slid a glance down the hall just as the door to Sophia's suite opened wide. Christian shoved the key card back into his pocket, turned away from his room, and darted through the fire escape doors. He took the stairs two at a time, wondering all the while where he'd go when he finally hit the first floor.

CHAPTER 4

The Pacific Ocean crested and surged, drenching Sophia with possibilities. They'd taken the coast—Pacific Coast Highway—into Santa Monica after Wade checked his GPS and learned about a wreck to avoid on the 101 freeway south. The water, blue and endless, kept her from vomiting.

Because, unfortunately, Wade drove like a maniac while talking on the phone to clients and weaving in and out of traffic on the winding highway. By the time the ride was over, Sophia was drenched all right, but from sweat.

"We're here." Wade unclicked his seat belt. "Why don't you come up and wait inside the air-conditioned building while I have my meeting?"

Sophia uncurled her hands, which she'd kept clenched in her lap, stretching her fingers to allow the blood to reflow through them. They exited the parking garage and entered the stream of pedestrians traversing the sidewalks near Third Street Promenade.

She stopped. "If you don't mind, I think I'd like to walk."

He frowned. Everything about him screamed cover of *GQ* . The wavy hair, cut of his suit, sunglasses. Two blondes in shorts, tanks, and flip flops passed him on the sidewalk, turning their chins at the same time, like synchronized swimmers.

"Tell you what," he said, oblivious. "I'll text you the moment I'm done, and we'll meet back at this spot. A word to the wise— this place is bigger than it looks." He pointed at her heels. "Your feet could get pretty tired in those."

"Wade, you don't have to worry about me. I've been walking everywhere my entire life. Italy, New York, everywhere."

He crinkled his brow. "You do drive, Sophia, right?"

"Actually, no, I do not."

"You have a driver's license, but you prefer not to drive. That's what you meant, correct?"

"Not correct."

His mouth hung open.

"I do have an ID card, of course."

He crossed his arms and leaned back slightly, his gaze sweeping over her. "My grandmother didn't drive. She's the only adult I've ever known who didn't have a driver's license."

"She sounds like a lovely woman."

He grinned now. "Indeed."

He left her there to wander, the sun on her shoulders, warming her. High-end retail stores mingled with mom-and-pop shops, the vibe bustling and touristy. She stepped inside one store and breathed in the scent of hand-poured candles. In another store, she admired the glimmer of polished silver.

Back in the throng, Sophia meandered past street singers busking, grateful for the chance to forget about all she'd been thrust into over the past months. She ducked into a wine bar, longing to sit at a patio table and people watch with a glass of prosecco. *If she were in Italy* ... She let the thought linger as the waiter hovered, but ultimately, with plans to visit potential vendors later that afternoon, she ordered an iced coffee instead.

Just beyond the low railing between her and the promenade, a man in black-and-white striped pants and a wife beater stepped into the center of the crowd and unrolled a thin mat. He flipped over onto his arms for a handstand. After a second or two, he put one arm behind his back and continued to balance on the remaining arm. Not one teeter or totter. She pulled a sketchpad from her oversized bag and began to draw.

The waiter brought her coffee, but she barely noticed. She drew the length of the performer's arm, the thick cords of his muscles, the jut of his chin, the strength of his hand, his fingers spread wide, unyielding. Though no music played on the street, she heard notes in her head. Pachelbel. Tchaikovsky. Cherubini.

"Where did you learn to draw like that?"

"Scusami?" The question had broken her concentration and she'd been so absorbed, she'd lapsed into Italian. In this sidewalk café with its streets teeming with visitors, she could have easily been back in Florence.

"You drew that so quickly." He was an older man, short-cropped hair, gray—almost shorn—his entire ensemble black: black button-down collared shirt, black slacks, black shoes. In the middle of summer. Perhaps he was on staff.

"I've been drawing my whole life." She glanced at her sketch, then back to the man. "It's not that good."

He reached for it. "May I?"

Sophia hesitated, a familiar tension creeping up her neck. As he examined her drawing more closely, she looked away, fighting off a sudden and desperate need to pull a cloak around her body, covering herself.

"You are quite talented. Thank you for sharing your art."

47

She nodded a thank you, though a smile was less forthcoming. Her dalliance with paper and pencil had been less than successful. A poor-quality replication of real life.

"May I call you sometime?"

She met his eyes. Her throat closed, her mouth dry. Discomfort rippled through her.

"Give me your number." He delivered his request as a quiet but steady command, his brows, she noted, like arrows.

"No," she whispered. She stood, dropped several bills on the table, and fled. As Sophia made her way out of the restaurant and onto the promenade, she spied a trash can. She ripped the page with the cursory drawing from her sketchbook, wadded it in one hand, and pitched it into the can.

Her chin set, Sophia marched down the sidewalk, past street musicians and families—moms, dads, children—licking ice cream. She'd lost track of where she was, of how far she'd walked from the spot where she had promised to meet Wade. Had much time passed? Had she even sipped her coffee?

A lump formed in her throat. Sunshine shone all around, but somehow, a rain-bloated, metaphorical cloud had blown in. She slowed. Taunts from her past mushroomed in her mind no matter how hard she worked to tamp them down. Words flung at her from her spoiled little sister. Why now? Had she not put Gia's behavior behind her? Or had she ever really dealt with it at all?

A tear of her own dripped off her chin and landed on her hand. She sniffled, suddenly awakened. When the song ended, she reached into her purse and pulled a wad of cash from her wallet. Without a glance at the amount, she stepped forward and spilled it into the violinist's case.

She spun around and right into Wade's chest.

"Whoa." His voice was low, gentle. "That looked like a lot of money. Be careful about who you give to here."

Sophia looked up, comfortable in the safety of his arms. She swallowed. "She's not a beggar. I appreciate her art ... and her service."

His smile held a hint of surprise. "I understand." He breathed in, as if thinking. "Let's go now, shall we? Those tours await."

He let her go then, and they walked side by side, past the restaurant where she'd left her coffee untouched and the myriad tourists, until they reached his car, climbed inside, and headed east.

CHRISTIAN SAT beneath the beating sun long enough to shake the cobwebs of writer's block that had knit their way into his mind once again. While lounging on the beach near the inn, he'd seen her. She'd emerged from the sea, a goddess, her tail curved, seductive. He laughed aloud, certain mothers would steer their young away from him.

But he couldn't help himself. He'd seen and written her in his mind, and now, as he dusted the sand from his lap and followed the path back to the inn, he kept her memory alive.

Back in his room, he darted for his computer, which had waited patiently for inspiration to strike. He pulled up a chair, scratched his bristling beard, and began to type. He glanced out to sea more than once, especially when memories of Sophia's delicate neck attempted to edge out the novel that needed writing. Or when the angry voice of his agent—his *ex*-agent—attempted to overshadow his muse.

Sweat soaked through his pores. The story, like a song, poured from his fingers and onto the page, a shower of blood. *His* blood, *his* sweat, and on occasion, *his* tears. There was no holding back.

Hours later, he sat back, breathless. The words on the screen blurred, but a sense of adrenaline told him that what lived on those digital pages, even in their rawest form, were noteworthy. In some ways, after many months of wandering in the desert, he'd found a way to connect again with his readers —through the power of story.

He whispered a silent prayer of hope ... may he never lose his way again.

The shrill of his phone startled every nerve in his body. He stuffed back a swear word and glanced at the screen. *Burns Golden.* He had nothing to hide. He'd paid his dues, and though he would have preferred to keep his plans quiet, his overzealous cover designer had made that impossible.

She'd been thrilled to work with him (and he with her). Could he truly fault her for that? He pressed the green answer button.

"Burns."

"So this is how you treat the person most responsible for your long success."

His back stiffened. "Quite a surprise to hear from you. You know, after what you said in court on my ... *behalf.*"

"Whatever I did or didn't say, you and I have a valid contract and you are violating it. You don't think I'm gonna let you get away with that, I hope."

"Last I heard, any contract we had was null and void. You did say that yourself, Burns. Wait. Let me pull up the exact quote." Christian's fingers flew across his keyboard. He scrolled until Burns's words, as reported in *Monthly Words*, the publishing industry's top magazine, popped onto the screen. "Yes, yes. Here it is: 'CJ Capra is out. Gone the way of mood rings and pet rocks. I assure you that you will never see my agency represent him—or his drivel—again.'"

Burns hauled phlegm up his throat and spat it out. Christian could not see this, of course, but he knew from the scraping, hacking sound of it—and from the branded memory in his head, something he'd never been able to erase—that a wad of his curse-filled spit had landed somewhere next to the agent's own two shoes.

Christian stood and began to pace. He crossed an arm under the one that held his phone. "You oughta get that checked, Burns."

"I'll be the one to decide what gets checked!"

Christian pulled his phone away from his ear.

"I've got eyes everywhere, you miserable hack. Even if that stupid girl hadn't posted that cover I would've found you out. I can smell a skunk for miles and your stink has outed you. You think I'd let you get away with this?"

He didn't want to bite. He knew he shouldn't. But this had to end now. He was determined to put a stop to whatever claim Burns Golden thought he had on Christian's work.

"Whatever contractual agreement we had in the past is over now, Burns. Let it go."

"There's where you're wrong. I shopped that book you're writing and I'll tell you when it's over. Now. If you want to go around and write about broads in bikinis, you can. But mermaids are mine—do you hear me?"

Christian broke down, coarse laughter spilling out. "Do you hear *yourself*? I hardly think—"

"That's right. You hardly think. Why else would you throw a sucker punch at the one guy who could have hurled your sorry self into the stratosphere?"

Christian looked down at his bare feet. He swallowed back a retort. His mind had been primed and pumped by a day of writing and a million responses rose to the top, ready to spill out. Instead, he controlled his tongue.

Burns continued. "Let me tell you how this is going to

work. You're going to connect me with your publisher. And he's going to be informed that I have a fifteen percent claim on all future books relative to the one that I spent my time and dollars on."

Christian cleared his throat.

"Understood?"

"That's impossible."

"Don't screw with me, Capra."

"It's impossible because that publisher you're talking about? He's me."

"What the—"

"I am publishing my own book." Christian shifted and drew in oxygen, grateful for the second wind that had recently come his way. "And as publisher, I reject your claim."

Silence. Then a roar that curdled Christian's already upside-down stomach.

"You are *self*-publishing your masterpiece?"

"It's called indie publishing, and yes. That is correct. Now, if you'll excuse me, I have a book to finish."

More churlish laughter filled the line, followed by another gag-inducing spume of phlegm. "Nice try."

"I'm serious."

"No doubt, but it won't work. Anyone else and I'd laugh this off. Self-publishing is for losers—the whole industry knows it —but it's part of your master plan and I won't let you get away with it. You think you can hide your royalties from me? I'll have the court make you cough them up."

He'd given Burns enough of his time—too much, really. He couldn't fathom why. The man had been his undoing, had pulled the threadbare rug from underneath him when he desperately needed steady ground.

Not that Christian didn't have it coming. He raked a hand through his hair as he paced. No. He'd let someone get to him, someone who had needled him for years, but he should've known better. He should have stayed on higher ground that night at the bar, but he'd let his emotions do the talking. Emotions plus a few too many beers.

Still, he had expected his long-time agent, gruff and ornery as he was, to support him. When he didn't, Christian paid an even larger price than that punch he threw had extracted.

"That's some twisted math you're doing, Burns. Not sure what you think gives you the right to stake a claim to a book that, until now, hasn't been written—"

"You know very well that you and I talked out this masterpiece of yours together. I counseled you. I gave you pointers from my vast experience. And how do you repay me? By taking what I've given from my own generous nature and keeping it all for yourself."

Voices in the hallway caught Christian's attention. He padded across the room and peered through the peephole just as Sophia and what's-his-name passed by. He glanced at the time—7 p.m. *Made a day of it, apparently.*

"You'd better give me your word about this, Capra, or you'll be hearing from my lawyer."

Yeah, yeah, lawyer, yada, yada, yada.

"Well?"

Christian looked out at the sea through his open window just in time to see the tip of a tail before it plunged beneath the surface. He frowned.

"I'm giving you three seconds to assure me that you're onboard with our partnership."

"One."

The tail had vanished. Had its appearance been a signal of some type?

"Two."

Christian exhaled. *Am I losing my mind?* The harsh scrape of

Burns's breathing assaulted his ear, awakening him to the real threat posed by his former agent. "Don't bother counting any higher," he finally said.

"Ah, I see you've come to your senses, Capra."

"That I have. And what I need you to know is—you won't be getting a dime from this book, or any others that I write in the future. Don't bother calling again."

Christian tossed the phone onto the rumpled sheets of his bed and sank into his desk chair, his mind now void of any kind of creative thought.

CHAPTER 5

*M*eg held a top in front of her. "But does it really say 'resort'?"

Sophia tilted her head to one side, thinking. Her legs were crossed, her feet shod with sneakers. She hated to admit it—but Wade had been right. She woke up this morning with throbbing feet, not to mention a sunburn. Hence, the comfortable footwear today—and a generous slathering of Aloe vera gel.

"My honest opinion ...."

"Please," Meg said. "Be honest."

Sophia sighed. "Well, the fabric ... it's too heavy. If I were making it, I'd want it to be breathable in some way. Also ..."

"Yes?"

"The body is too hidden with this design. It is cut into a box shape. Perhaps it would be better as a grocery bag."

Meg collapsed onto the couch in her office, an errant tendril of dark brown hair landing in her eyes. She blew a breath upwards to dislodge it. "See?" she said, focusing again on Sophia. "This is why we NEED you!"

Sophia laughed. "Please stop. Your wardrobe is impeccable. I have every confidence that if I had not come here, you would have chosen the perfect pieces to add to the inn's resort wear line."

Meg sat up, still holding the thick felt. "Do you?" She held the sample in front of her. "Seriously, do you? I don't believe that for one second. Not for one second!" Tears shone in her eyes.

Sophia frowned. "It's just a hoodie."

Meg dropped her chin. "I don't know what's wrong with me. I'm so emotional these days. I've never been like this—not ever in my entire life." She looked Sophia square in the eyes. "Do you know how happy your brother is to have you here?"

"I think I do. I am happy too."

"Did I hear you went to LA with Wade? What the heck?" Meg pointed at her. "What was that all about? Not thinking of opening a hotel in LA or anything, I hope."

Sophia cringed. "Meghan."

Meg spiked the air with both palms. "Sorry. No, of course not. Maybe you and he are ... you know. A thing? Older men are the bomb, or so I've heard."

"Please, stop. No." Sophia sighed. "He invited me to accompany him to downtown LA to tour possible manufacturers for my dresses."

"Yeah? And did you find someone? Wait." She shrank back. "What does Wade know about that anyway?"

Heat rose in Sophia's cheeks. She'd wondered the same thing. He'd told her he was a consultant for many businesses, so she'd just assumed ...

Meg batted the air with her hand, shrugging off her own comment. "Never mind. How'd it go?"

"Pretty well. We toured two facilities and I believe I've found one to take over production and fulfillment of my designs should I decide that a change is necessary." She relaxed into the couch. "I'm relieved, Meg. I left so much up in the air when I left New York. I even toyed with leaving design behind."

"Oh! But you can't do that!"

"It was just something I considered. But now that I have found a manufacturer so close"—Sophia turned her palms over and over, as if weighing an invisible package—"I am encouraged."

"I'm glad! So ... you'll help me then with this resort wear?"

Sophia laughed, feeling it to her toes. "Of course, I will. But can we go to lunch now? I haven't eaten and I'm afraid that if I were to design on an empty stomach, the gift shop would be filled with T-shirts with images of steaks on them."

"Let's go!"

They took a table near the outer edge of the inn's restaurant where the views of the water could be seen in 180 degrees —from the harbor to the sea.

"I want to talk to you about the sale of Sea Castle," Sophia broached.

"Did he tell you about the bite we got?"

Sophia's eyes widened. "Already?"

"Just happened." Meg's eyes flashed, then softened. "You know that Jackson will share every bit of the company's details, right? He is very driven. Can be quite headstrong— you've probably noticed this already."

Sophia laughed lightly. "It's true. I have."

"He doesn't mean to shut you out ... if that's what you're thinking."

"I didn't think that at all. I am just so sad about all my sister has caused."

Meg reached a hand forward, laying it on Sophia's. "We've been over this, but it is worth saying again. You are not at fault, my sweet Sophia. You were a victim. You are not to blame. I can tell you, wholeheartedly, that Jackson does not blame you."

"But he blames himself. Yes?"

Meg continued to stare at her, sadness permeating her smile. "Unfortunately, he does. He still does. There is nothing that I've been able to say to help him through that."

"Except 'I do.'"

Meg's smile relaxed. Her eyes sparkled, tears unshed. "Well, I guess that helped. A little." She caught eyes with Sophia. "Marrying your brother has been the smartest thing I've ever done. Your father—dear William—he would have been so proud. I wish he were here."

Sophia's voice dropped to a whisper. "I do, too."

Meg pulled her hand back slowly and mustered a smile. "I think we both better eat something soon."

Sophia nodded and shut her menu. "I don't know about you, but I'm having the largest burger the chef can create."

Meg gasped.

"Don't judge."

An hour later, Sophia strode along the path that curved its way around the inn. The chef had taken her up on her request for a burger—calling it the William's Special—and now she regretted it. Well, *half* regretted it. Every bite of that burger was delicious, but now all she could think about was working it off so that she could fit into the clothes she had brought with her.

"Whoa, there. Why so fast?"

She hadn't noticed Christian parked on the bench alongside the path, and she could not imagine why. From the moment she'd met her brother's friend, he'd alternately rattled her nerves or soothed them. She slowed. "Hi there."

"Still got some of the New Yorker in you, I see." He squinted up at her, one arm lolling carelessly on the back of the bench.

With a flicker of his gaze, he took in the tennies beneath her skirt. "From what I recall, athletic shoes are high fashion in the City."

"And you don't approve."

He assessed her with a tilt of his bearded chin. "They suit you."

"Hmm."

"I bet you could design a line of them with sequins or something equally as sparkly."

"Did you say 'sparkly'?"

"If that's what you heard."

She smiled, glanced out to the horizon, then back at him. "My non-sparkly sneakers and I are going on a walk, if you would care to join us."

His smile dimmed and Sophia's heart dropped. Had she put him on the spot with her invitation? Did he think she wanted more from him than mere companionship on an afternoon walk? Surely he knew that she understood his time at the inn would be only a blip until another adventure called out to him.

"Sorry," she said, adding a nod toward his iPad. "I see that you're busy. I'll—"

"You aren't getting rid of me that easily." He stood and tucked the iPad under his arm. "I'm goin'."

"Okay, but you need to keep up with me."

He raised both brows. "Is that right?"

"Mm-hm." A soft breeze alighted on her skin as they walked, goose bumps rising on her arms. She picked up the pace, searching for something to fill the silence. "How's the writing coming?"

"I've had a productive couple of days."

"So that's good, then."

"My characters have been behaving themselves, so yes, I'd say so."

"And today? Are you taking a break?"

He paused. "Just allowing some things to percolate. If that makes any sense."

"I think so. I find it fascinating, what you do."

"Which part? The agonizing over writer's block or the gnashing of teeth when I realize that what I've written isn't fit for wrapping fish?"

"Hmm. The second part."

He laughed. "You're honest."

"I truly am fascinated by your process. I think it's because I have never felt as comfortable with words as I do with needle and thread. They were my constant companions when I was growing up." Her chest tightened. Why had she told him that? "So," she asked, "what made you start writing?"

"Women."

"Pardon?"

He walked along, one hand in the pocket of his shorts, the other gripping the iPad. "Girls, actually. I was in fourth grade when I wrote my first love letter."

"Were you really?"

"Uh-huh. She had curly red hair and sat two desks in front of mine. I honed my joke-telling skills that year." Christian turned his chin to her as they walked. "I wanted to make her laugh. Used to like to watch her freckles dance when she giggled."

"It never occurred to me that boys could be romantic." She wrinkled her nose and glanced at him. "Aren't they usually more interested in using sticks as guns and rolling in dirt?"

He feigned offense, clutching at his heart and gasping. "Nine-year-old me is pained."

She clucked her tongue. "I doubt that very much."

"Okay. To be straight with you—my Romeo days were over

by fifth grade. If I recall correctly, I had no use for women that year."

"How very sad."

He shrugged. "No need to weep. I was back in the saddle by sixth grade—with a vengeance. By then, my buddies and I had formed a posse to identify eligible ladies and to let them know of our most ardent affections."

"Well, Jane Austen would have been so pleased."

"Man. Don't get me started about her Mr. Darcy. That guy made it tough on the male species around the globe. We were lucky to land a peck on the cheek after that guy raised the bar to such heights."

"Don't be dramatic." She slid a glance at him, taking in the tiny smile. The scar that trailed up his cheekbone turned scarlet and she looked away.

"Speaking of dramatic," he said. "I sensed the other night that the breakfast meeting Jackson had set up for the both of you was a serious one."

She bit her bottom lip and kept her eyes focused on the winding path in front of them.

"I've known Jackson for years," he continued, "and though he doesn't often spill his guts, I can tell when he's got something heavy on his mind."

"It has been rough for him, recovering from all that my sister stole from ... us." She heaved a sigh. "I will do everything in my strength to help him restore what has been lost."

"Is that why you're really here?"

Her mind fiddled with that question. Why was she here? Was it simply to reconnect more fully with the brother she never knew? She had walked away from her apartment, her small circle of friends ... even put her fledgling business at arm's distance with this move.

And yet, she knew. Sophia knew the impetus that had

caused her to dislodge her roots and take Jackson and Meg up on their offer to move to this funky seaside town. She'd found a seemingly insignificant bump from her past buried inside a box of memories, something she probably should have burned or shredded. But for some reason, she hadn't, and when it fluttered to the ground while she was digging for evidence of her newfound family, it struck her once, then twice. A memory on which she had pivoted.

Those few lines revealed so much to her.

"Sophia?"

She startled. "Yes. Sorry. I was distracted by ... by all this beauty out here."

"Aha, so you admit that the City is not all it's cracked up to be."

"I will admit no such thing." She shook her head and pasted a flabbergasted smile on her face. "You don't give up, do you?"

He was quiet for a moment as they walked. "No, I'd have to say that, no, I don't give up easily."

They reached the door to the chapel. She tilted her head. "Would you like to go in for a moment?"

"Why not?"

Their steps echoed in the simple space. Goose bumps lit along her arm, like they had that first time she'd entered through those doors the year before. White walls, high ceilings covered in shiplap, rough-hewn beams stained to a warm tone —it was magical. "Jackson and Meg were married here."

Christian looked around, one hand in his pocket. He wore an expression of regret. "I wish I could've been here."

"Did it conflict with your schedule?"

He looked at her, then slowly shook his head. "I didn't know about it."

"Oh." She felt herself blush. Had he not been invited? "I'm sorry."

"Don't be. Jackson had sent me an invitation, but I had already moved. It didn't reach me in time."

So this must have been the reason behind Jackson's cryptic remark about Christian's forwarding orders. "That's too bad. It was a beautiful, inspirational ceremony."

He stared at her long enough to cause another round of blushing. She looked away, toward the steps at the front of the room, remembering Jackson and Meg saying their vows beneath a rough, wooden cross.

"Well, like I said, I would have liked to have been here."

She nodded. "And then I would not have tried to run away from you at the airport!"

He laughed. "I'll never forget that wide-eyed look you gave me. Your eyes were like ... well, they were like wild willow, only on fire."

She shrank back at this. "I don't believe I've ever heard my eyes described as anything other than *green*."

He stepped close to her, his voice husky. "Well, then, stick with me, beautiful."

Sophia froze a moment, but when a smile stretched across his face, she answered with one of her own. They stepped back out into the sunshine, continuing to banter. On their second loop of the hotel grounds, each of them lobbing a gentle serve of words to the other in a non-stop exchange, they noticed him. Jackson stood at the farthest point of the outlook over the sea, his body bent, his forearms resting on one rugged length of fencing.

They surrounded him like bookends.

"Hard day?" Christian asked.

The surf tumbled onto shore, the sound of it a soothing backdrop.

Jackson sighed like an old man. "Something like that." He

JULIE CAROBINI

turned to Sophia. "Hey, sis." The words seemed to bring a light to his face.

She rested her arm on his back and leaned the hollow of her cheek against his shoulder. The three of them stared at the horizon for several beats, a comfortable silence among them.

Christian broke that silence. "Legend has it that a mermaid wandered into the Netherlands through a fissure filled with sea water."

Jackson continued to stare out to sea, but his composure flickered.

"She was injured on the journey, of course."

Jackson kept still. "Of course."

"She was taken to a lake then," Christian said, "for rehabilitation."

Sophia had been peeking around Jackson as Christian spoke, watching for a sign that one of them would soon crack. But Christian went silent and she couldn't wait any longer. "Well? What happened then?"

Jackson swung a look her way that said *don't encourage him.* He rolled his eyes.

Christian's forefinger and thumb were cradling his chin now, his face pensive, calm. All that was missing was a smoking jacket. "The locals nursed her back to health and she became a productive member of society." He crossed his arms at his chest and peered back at her. "Was baptized and everything."

Jackson dropped his chin into his chest, laughter rumbling out of him. "You're an idiot."

"And that, my friend, is how you fall for fables—hook, line, and sinker."

Jackson groaned.

Sophia's face split into a grin that she could hardly hide. "Has he always been this way?"

Jackson groaned again, only this time the sound of it light-hearted. He put his back to the railing and leaned against it, eyeing her. "What're you doing out with this character anyway? You need me to call security?"

"Hey, I *am* her security. She begged me to join her on a walk."

"An invitation is not begging," Sophia said, though she noted Jackson studying her. "A simple walk. Nothing more."

Jackson pushed himself off the fence, the seriousness of his expression deepening. "Whatever it was, I'm glad I ran into you. Can we meet for coffee?"

"Of course. I'm supposed to meet back with Meg later this afternoon, but I'm all yours."

"Great. Let's head to my office."

Christian raised two hands and began to back away. "Hey, no, you two go on ahead. No need to join you."

Sophia laughed, but Jackson had already cupped her elbow and started walking. They moved swiftly toward the inn's front doors, leaving the breeze and salt air behind. *What was the rush?*

"Mail call, Christian," Trace, the inn's quirky concierge shouted across the lobby, holding up a stack of mail. There was something so comforting about knowing that the staff at Sea Glass Inn knew his whereabouts and were looking out for him.

And yet, not.

Truthfully, he was beginning to feel somewhat claustrophobic in the beautiful inn by the sea. He'd come here to start over, to live somewhat incognito away from the groanings of his former life in publishing. Not that it was possible to fully retreat from the living now that the internet had taken over the world.

But after he'd paid his dues and his lease was up, and after he'd wandered the country for a time, Jackson had come to his aid. "Stay at the inn and write another book. I insist!"

So he packed up and checked in. He'd insisted on paying rent—and now that he'd heard more about the inn's troubles, he'd upped it. Still wasn't up to the cost of a nightly rate, though. It wasn't money that he needed, but a change of environment for his muse to get lost in.

Maybe he should've settled for a cabin deep in the woods. A place like Cottage Grove, where he could hide among the pines and soaring redwoods.

"This one looks like a check." Trace doled his mail out one piece at a time, glancing at the sender of each piece before handing it over. She sighed each time and he thought he detected a slight shake of her head, as if quite put out for having to collect his mail.

He thanked her and turned while examining the envelope with a blue check showing through its window.

"Christian!" Meg gave him a squeeze as she bustled by wearing a sharp navy suit with stilettos. His buddy had married far above himself.

"What's got you on the run?"

"Group in-house is having audio problems!" She was hustling backwards now, moving quickly down the hall. "And they're out of coffee!"

Trace tsked. "We have people for that." She turned back toward her computer.

Christian waved his mail at Meg but kept the pace toward his own room. The envelope in his hand was from his publisher. Well, his former publisher. They still held the rights to his previous titles, though they'd buried them under threats from the jerk that he'd caught with an uppercut.

He expelled a breath in exasperation. *Move on already, Capra.* The one thing he could feel glad about was that the royalty check, tiny as it probably was, had come directly from the publisher—and not through the offices of his ex-agent. Some agents received the entire royalty, kept their fifteen percent, and sent the author the remaining eighty-five. But this publisher had agreed to Christian's request to send each of them their shares separately. He shuddered to think what might have become of his income otherwise.

Christian took the stairs two at a time, opting to forego the elevator. He'd had a standing desk in his apartment, but here he had found himself settling back into the BIC routine, i.e., "butt in chair."

Every writing book he'd ever read said that one way to break writer's block was to get the body moving. Climbing the stairs stirred up his brain cells. Already he began to feel his muse coming to life.

The other bit of advice he'd always heard about writer's block was to get outside. He'd been doing that—catching some of the sun's rays and fresh air—when Sophia's sudden presence about knocked the wind from his body.

He hadn't asked for it, or expected it, but Christian could not deny that he had, quite peculiarly, found Sophia to be ... disorienting. He had little time for that now.

The buzz of his phone broke into his thoughts and he answered without so much as a glance at the screen.

"Wasn't sure you had the guts to answer my calls," Burns said. "I'm impressed."

Immediate-onset heartburn took hold of Christian. "What is it?"

"Now, now, don't take that tone with me. I think we both

know that our last phone call ended, shall we say, too abruptly?"

He quit talking long enough to spit into something metal. Christian fought to keep bile from rising in his chest. Burns continued, "I think you'll be pleased with my reason for calling."

"Listen, Burns, don't give me any credit here. The reason I answered your call—the *only* reason—is because, quite frankly, I hadn't looked at the screen. I have to go."

"Shut up a minute. I have something to say that will please you."

Christian shoved open the stairwell door, marched down the hall, and entered his room. Burns continued to talk, all of it nonsense. Christian tossed the mail and his iPad onto the expertly made bed, slid the glass door open, and stepped out onto his deck.

He drew in a breath just as he realized Burns had said something about his book. He'd heard the words "contract" and "your publisher," but hadn't been listening closely enough to realize how those words had been strung together.

"Wait. Say that again?"

"See there? I knew you'd be pleased. As I said, I have decided to let bygones be bygones. To that end, I spoke with Lisa and she has decided to forgive your ... actions as well."

"Lisa?"

"Your publisher." Garbled laughter filled his ear. "Don't tell me you've forgotten the woman who gave you a writing career. Aside from me, that is."

Christian bit his lip. Lisa certainly had been his champion, especially with his first book. If he were going to credit anyone for giving him a start in publishing, it would be Lisa. She'd taken that first manuscript, and after going through it herself

—something he'd heard was unusual—she'd handed it to one of her finest editors.

But, he'd learned, that even one's closest allies can find reasons to withdraw their support.

"Listen, Burns, this will be our last phone call. Do you understand? I have to go."

"It's you who needs to understand. Now that word is out that you've decided to write the novel that I've already shopped, Lisa has decided to give it a look."

"She already said no."

"That was because of your dirty, no-good ... indiscretion. But I took the liberty of calling her to discuss the matter and she's agreed that enough time has passed and she is going to forgive you. She'll have a contract out to me within the week, but I'll need you to hustle and send over what you've got so far to Lisa. I take it the manuscript has not veered too far from the proposal." He paused. "And if it has—change it."

A slider door opened nearby. Christian glanced over to see Sophia standing on her balcony. She waved to him, but as he lifted his hand to return the gesture, what's-his-name appeared next to her, looking like he'd just stepped off a tennis court. White shorts. What self-respecting guy wore *white* shorts?

Christian turned his back on them and studied the balcony railing. A venomous heat threaded through him. He planted a fist on the railing, an unmovable decision in his head and heart.

"Burns, this conversation is over. I will not be sending you a manuscript so do not bother to send me a contract. Are we understood? There will be no more business between you, me, and/or Lisa. Got it?"

"I see."

"I'm glad that you do."

"Might want to take a good long look at our contract, though, slugger. Particularly the clause under future works. You may think you can take everything I gave you and keep all the proceeds for your greedy self, but my lawyer informs me that you are wrong." He paused, no doubt letting those words sink in. "The next call you'll be getting—is from legal representation."

With a click, Burns was gone.

Christian huffed, pulled up Burns's number on his phone, and hit "block." When he turned back toward Sophia's balcony, she—and that pretty boy—had vanished.

CHAPTER 6

$\mathscr{C}$hristian could no longer ignore the blather coming from his stomach. He'd tried filling his hunger with some of the contents of the mini-bar—chocolate-covered pretzels and trail mix—but found himself hungrier still. Not to mention nearly broke from the typical mini-bar cash grab. Had those prices been Wade's idea too?

Without thought to a comb or brush, he put on a pair of slippers and padded down the hall to the elevator, which he stepped inside without a passing glance at the other occupants.

The quiet of the inn's restaurant drew him in, and with no host at the front, he wandered inside and took a seat at the bar. The night bartender, Johnny, slid a menu over to him. "Calamari's fresh tonight."

"I'll wait to order it till it's day-old."

Johnny scrunched his eyes and stared. Christian sighed. He hated when people didn't get the joke.

"What'll you have?"

"Peroni. On tap. And a burger. No onions."

"You got it."

He glanced around while waiting, noting how few tables were occupied. An older couple sat near the window, neither talking. A few voices carried from a far corner. Not a great sign for his old friend. Then again, the place would be hopping by the weekend—and he'd be lucky to find even one empty seat at the bar.

His beer arrived first, followed by the burger. "Anything else?" Johnny asked.

"Got any miracles back there?"

Same scrunched-up face.

Christian waved him off. "Nah, I'm good. Thanks." His night might have ended there if he hadn't looked up during a particularly sudden and loud burst of laughter coming from the table across the restaurant.

He spotted her first. How had Christian not noticed them when he'd entered the place? Perhaps the self-absorption he'd dragged into the restaurant with him had something to do with that. She sat between Jackson and Meg, and across from her—probably looking deeply into her eyes—was Wade.

Christian took a larger bite, nearly choked, then grabbed his beer and threw it back so as not to require the Heimlich maneuver from a passing doctor. Or bartender.

Johnny grabbed the empty glass, his brows up. "Another?"

Before he had a chance to answer, Jackson's voice shot across the empty restaurant. "Hey, Christian. Join us."

With barely a nod in his old friend's direction, Christian folded his napkin in half, wiped his mouth, and slid off the barstool. He tossed the napkin onto his plate and approached the foursome, glad they hadn't had to watch him be revived on the dining room floor.

"Looks like a party," he said to no one in particular. Empty dessert plates littered the table, but the wine was still plentiful. "Hello everyone."

"My wife insisted I call you over. Said you looked sad and lonely over there."

"Jackson!" She looked directly at Christian. "I did not say that!"

"Oh, that's right. She didn't say lonely. I think it was pathetic."

Sophia's eyes widened and she covered her mouth.

Christian grimaced. "Sophia doesn't know you're kidding, Jackson."

Jackson smirked. "Who's kidding?"

Christian strolled over to her side of the table. He pulled a chair away from another table and pointed to the spot between Sophia and Meg. "May I?"

Sophia nodded. "Yes, of course." She scooted her chair over, and when he took a seat, she gave him a squeeze on his forearm. Wade sat across from him, silent.

"We were all discussing further renovations of the inn, you know, for when we're able to move forward."

"After the spa is finished," Jackson added.

Meg continued. "And Wade had this funny idea that we should rename all of the meeting rooms and give each one its own unique look."

"Like the Madonna Inn—without all the gold cherubs and pink wallpaper," Christian said, then added, "I hope." The Madonna Inn was a one-of-a-kind hotel on the coast that was beloved to some and less-than to others.

Meg laughed. Jackson looked annoyed.

"I know he was kidding," Meg said, "but I think it's really a fabulous idea. I travel all the time and haven't seen this!"

Wade shifted forward. "And to your point, Christian, instead of focusing on the guest rooms, I'm suggesting the smaller group meeting rooms be updated with one of Sophia's designs."

"Right," Jackson said. "And like I said, this is a way we could use Sophia's skills in the entire process and advertise it as such." He spread his palms wide as if outlining a name in lights. "Designed by Sophia Agli Riley. Who knows? It might help her —and us—if we put the word out that the hotel's meeting rooms had her designer's touch."

Christian swung a look at Sophia, who had remained quiet. "What do you think of all of this?"

"Me? Oh, I know they're kidding." She nodded to an empty wine bottle, a sly smile on her face. "This is just one of the many ideas they have pitched to each other tonight."

"But we're *serious* about this one!" Meg said.

Sophia had a way of masking her emotions. If he were a betting man, though, Christian felt confident that if he put his dollar on "she's having none of this," he would likely win. Sophia's face may have been lacking in strong emotional upheaval, but she had been toying with the napkin in her lap during the entire conversation.

Finally, Sophia said, "I am flattered that you all think I have the kinds of skills required to make the inn a ... a showplace. I'm not sure, though, if I have the expertise for this." She turned her chin toward Meg. "You do know I create dresses, right?"

Meg smiled. "Oh, but an interior design firm will be hired, of course. I know we were only brainstorming, and that we've been goofing around all evening, but to have a family connection apparent in the inn's design ..." Meg lifted her chin to the ceiling and her smile had turned giddy. "Well, I just think this idea has merit—a unique feature that will draw visitor interest. Does that make sense?"

Sophia's gaze grew pensive, intense but focusing somewhere in the distance. She licked her lips as if preparing a speech. "I have another thought. Perhaps we could design each room around a particular person in the family. We would of course create a room that epitomized Father, as well as your mother, Jackson. And you." She paused, her eyelashes fluttering.

Meg gasped and said, "Wow—another great idea! Would be an amazing way to honor William as the patriarch, as well as Jackson's mother, who I never had the good fortune to meet."

Christian nudged her gently. "And you."

Jackson spoke up. "Of course we'll have the 'Sophia' room."

She laughed. "My only concern is that it might look too ... self-serving?"

Wade's focus was on Sophia. "Not if it's done tastefully. I think this is a unique idea with the very real possibility of creating a bidding war for each of the room's use. It will stir up group interest, which, of course, is your bread and butter. No, no, I think you're onto something, Sophia. You'll want to hire an interior designer who is willing to work within the framework that you and the team creates."

Sophia turned to her sister-in-law. "And you won't feel awkward leading tours of the 'Jackson'?"

Christian chimed in, "Trying to picture that one. Hmm ... muscle cars on the walls?"

"Ha—you wish." Jackson paused for a moment. "I'm seeing a cigar lounge. Dark wood paneling, a wingback chair, polished brass."

"You're 007 now?"

Jackson laughed. "Sure. Works for me."

"You'll want to make sure to balance the colors," Wade was saying. "I'm no designer, but you don't want colors from one room to the other to clash."

Christian's attention had drifted to Sophia, whose mangled napkin now looked as if it had gone through both the washer and the dryer.

"Right," Meg said. "There should be a nice flow to the

rooms, especially since some groups will use more than one. Plus, we need to be careful to keep both a relaxed, coastal vibe that also looks upscale."

"Your interior designer can work with you on all that," Wade said.

Jackson agreed. "I don't think it'll be a huge problem, except that all of us appear to have a similar love of darker colors. The design firm will have to figure out a way to incorporate something lighter so Sea Glass Inn doesn't look like it belongs somewhere in the Rocky Mountains."

"All except for the 'Sophia,'" Christian said.

Jackson darted a confused look at Christian, his brows low to his eyes. "I don't know what you're talking about. I've never seen my sister in anything other than black or white or the combination of the two. Wait. Okay, maybe gray."

"So you're limiting the design of your rooms to the colors you wear?" Christian said. "I thought the rooms might be more of a reflection of the people they represent." He glanced at Sophia, who seemed to have retreated even more from the discussion.

"So what 'color' do you think my sister represents?" Jackson said.

Meg watched him with a tilt of her head, as if amused.

Wade's eyes, which had been stuck like glue to Sophia's face, had suddenly taken an interest in him.

Christian set his gaze on Sophia, whose cheeks had tinged pink. He ran his tongue over his teeth, thinking. "She's ... a watercolor painting."

The blush of pink on Sophia's face turned to plum and those eyelashes fluttered again. But then, slowly, her lips meandered into a smile.

A wadded-up napkin landed on Christian's cheek. "Hey!"

With his pitching arm still extended, Jackson said, "Man.

You didn't tell me you were writing cheesy romance novels now."

Meg laughed. Wade looked bewildered by the conversation. For her part, Sophia's smile deepened, so there was that.

As for Christian, the fire of his own face heating up made him grateful that his beard would likely mask the shock of red sure to be permeating his skin.

Sophia watched Wade through the lick of flames emanating from the outdoor fire pit. It was late, long past the time she usually stayed up—she was an early riser. But after Christian begged off to do some writing and Jackson and Meg left the restaurant, Wade mentioned he'd brought some paperwork with him from the two manufacturers they'd visited in LA. Given the sharp detour their dinnertime conversation had taken, he hadn't had a chance to show the sample agreements to her.

So she agreed to meet him out here.

"Both contracts appear to be straightforward," he was saying. "It comes down to an issue of preference. If you do decide to make a move, you should have your attorney look over the contract before you sign it."

Sophia pulled the thick blanket over her knees. She hadn't had an attorney look over her last contract, though the thought had come to mind. The waves thrashed below the inn's outdoor deck, again reminding her of how drastic a change she had made with this move.

"Cold?"

"Not terribly. I'm enjoying the night air, though I'm in danger of falling asleep out here if I stay too long."

Wade smiled. "I won't let that happen."

The kindness in his eyes warmed her as much as the crackling fire in front of them. He told her on the drive home from Los Angeles the other day how much he wanted to help her and she couldn't fathom why. But if Jackson trusted him, she did too.

"You'd be surprised by how cold it gets out here in the middle of the night," he said.

She cocked her head. "Do you walk around outside in the middle of the night often?"

"Not if I can help it. Not a heavy sleeper, though, and sometimes a walk turns out to be what I need to clear my head."

"Work keeps you up at night then."

He paused. "Work ... and other things."

He did not offer her more insight into the workings of his mind, so she didn't ask. Sophia took another sip of her hot chocolate, something she hadn't done in ... how long? Since childhood? She inhaled the heavenly aroma, noting her contentment.

"The way you smile while drinking that cocoa reminds me of my niece, Sadie. She loves the stuff, too."

"A woman after my own heart then."

"She's four."

Sophia laughed out loud, nearly spilling the contents of her mug onto the inn-issued blanket covering her legs. "Well," she finally said, "I guess she's a *girl* after my own heart then."

"That she is."

"Thank you for discussing these contracts with me. I've been meaning to ask ... how do you know so much about garment manufacturing?"

"Well, I can't say that I know that much about it—but enough to assist." He leaned back in his lounge chair, lines on his face softening. "My sister worked for the California Mart— actually, it's the California Market Center now. She lives in the valley but drove to downtown LA for several years to work there as an event planner."

"And now?"

"And now, she's a busy mom of a four-year-old."

"Sadie's mother!"

He nodded, his smile beaming in the firelight. "Indeed."

"You two are close then?"

"We are. She's my little sister and her daughter is her mini-me. They're both spoiled rotten."

"By you?"

"Guilty."

"So sweet. I hope I'm an auntie someday. I suppose I'll have to talk to Jackson and Meg about that." Her face grew warmer. She searched her mind for another subject to discuss. "On another note, I am still thinking about whether to make the manufacturing move from New York."

"You mean because of sales being up in the air?"

Sophia nodded her head, agreeing. "Such a guessing game, right now. All of it."

He kept his eyes on her. "Sophia, it's important to be ready for growth so that when it happens, your company will not crumble under the weight of it." He leaned forward again, this time resting his forearms on his lap. "I think you are doing the right thing considering your options."

"I hope so. I think I am too." But she also knew there were variables, that the marketplace could be fickle. What buyers liked today they could hate tomorrow. Was she ready to take a risk?

Wade's husky voice derailed her thoughts. "May I ask if you plan on staying in California for good?"

She considered his question, knowing she did not have a ready answer. "Right now that is another issue that is up in the air."

He was quiet a moment. "Well, let's hope you are convinced to make a decision very soon."

A half hour later, Sophia wandered into her room, less drawn to sleep than when she had first taken a seat in front of that outdoor fire pit. She pulled a light blanket from the foot of the bed, wrapped it around her shoulders, and padded out onto the deck.

The shudder of waves greeted her as did a gentle sweep of wind. She lowered herself to the cushioned lounge chair and tucked the blanket beneath her bare legs, allowing her thoughts to careen and churn with the waves. Romance lit her soul whenever she thought about this move to California. She'd start fresh in a new place, family by her side, sunlight and blue sky her daily companions. For the most part, all that she had imagined had transpired.

Yet a sense of being adrift in uncharted waters clouded her days. She didn't know what to make of it, or know how to fix it, but it had been her constant companion since day one. She breathed in deeply and sighed, allowing her body to sink into the lounger. If it weren't for the dip in the temperature, she might have stayed curled up out here all night, allowing morning's light to wake her.

She wasn't sure how long she'd been outside when she heard the unmistakable scrape of Christian's slider door open, then shut. Had she been asleep? Or simply lost in thought? She pulled the blanket tighter around her, the fabric cold to the touch. Her eyes had been closed, so she lay there and allowed them to adjust to the night sky.

Christian stood at the edge of his balcony staring into the night, his silhouette visible. His hand rubbed his bearded cheek, yet he continued to concentrate somewhere ahead of him. She bit the inside of her bottom lip. The inn's decks were close enough that a person could hardly avoid seeing another if they were outside at the same time. Though that were true, why did she feel like a voyeur?

A chill ran through her and Sophia pulled the blanket even tighter around her body. Doing so must have stirred up a sprinkle of dust—and she sneezed. And sneezed again.

She recovered in time to see her neighbor's arms dangling over her side of the balcony, his hair as lopsided as his grin. Though she knew it wasn't polite, Sophia started to giggle.

"Something funny?"

This only made her giggle more. *What in the world?* A grown woman with a fledgling career as a designer and innkeeper and she found herself ... giggling?

Christian attempted to take on a stern expression, but to her he resembled a young boy who hadn't gotten his way. He couldn't have been funnier if he'd tried. Or cuter.

"You know, Ms. Riley, I feel it is in your best interest to inform you that stalking can get you time in the slammer."

"Sl-slammer?" She laughed so hard that tears fell and she had to use the end of the blanket to wipe them away. "What's a slammer? Do you mean jail?"

"Jail. Pen. Pokey. Big house ... "

"You are just making all that up!"

"I'm a writer. We're not allowed to use the same word twice."

"Ah ha ha. That's hi-hi-larious."

Christian frowned. "Wait. Are you really cold?"

"F-fr-freezing."

"Then what're you ... never mind. Hang on." He disappeared and seconds later returned with a giant comforter. He tossed it over his railing and onto her lounge chair. As she wrestled to come out from under it, the entire deck shook when something landed on it.

Christian stood inches from her.

Sophia tucked the comforter beneath her chin and peered over the top of it. "You jumped over the railing?"

"Sshh," he said, tucking the folds of the blanket around her. "Don't tell the management."

She watched as he pulled up a chair next to her, his bare forearms seemingly unaffected by the frigid exhale of the sea. He reached out and put a hand on the comforter that now embraced her. "Feel better?"

"Much." She'd stopped laughing but couldn't quite remove the smile. "What were you doing out here in the cold?"

He peered at her. "I could ask you the same."

"I had a blankie."

His face broke out in a grin. "Oh, a blankie. I see. And now you have two."

"It would appear so."

He inhaled a deep breath and let it go with an audible sigh. "You told me once that designers get stuck too. Remember that?"

"Mm-hm. Is that what is happening to you tonight? Writer's block?"

He raked his beard, as if the motion helped him form words. "It's not that so much. The story is, well, it's in here. I can feel it." He put a fist to his heart.

"But you are having trouble putting it to paper."

"Strangely, no. In fact, since I spoke to you about this last, the words have poured out so fast I've had to keep a towel handy to sop up the spillover."

She tipped her head, examining him. "You have an interesting way of saying things."

"From your mouth to readers' ears."

"Is that why you were stargazing tonight? So you could think about your story while looking into the vastness of the sky?"

How could he explain his writing process to her without sounding like an idiot? That he waited around for his muse to show up, like a dog sought a lap? That when she did, he threw himself headlong into the story she whispered to him, until his fingers and back ached and he emerged sweaty and in need of a bath, unsure of how many hours had passed? Instead he simply said, "Speaking of arranging words, I like the way you said that."

"Thank you."

"And to answer your question, I was." He eyed her. "Do you ever think about how things might have been in your life if you'd made different choices?"

More than once Sophia had questioned herself, her choices, her lack of decisions. When she learned of her father's existence, why hadn't she insisted on spending more time with him? Of flying to California and meeting her only brother? But the minute she found herself running down the path of "whys," she also discovered that she would only pick up more questions, like tumbling waves picked up seaweed

When she didn't answer him right away, Christian dropped his chin to his chest and brought his clasped hands to his forehead. Then he caught eyes with her again. "I'm sorry. Something about the night and the stars make me terribly philosophical. Writing has stirred up my brain, I guess, making deeper thoughts difficult to avoid.

"I would like to read one of your books," Sophia said, struck with the sudden thought.

He was quiet for several seconds, his chin now resting on those clasped hands. "And I would love to know what you think."

"Oh, I don't know ... I can be fairly critical."

He cracked up.

"You don't believe me."

He leaned back in his own lounge chair and reached to her, resting his hand on her arm through the layers of blankets. "I don't think you are capable of being critical, no. Nor mean or nasty—even if you did nearly report me to airport security."

"You called me m'lady."

He yawned, his voice drifting. "Yes, because that's what servants call royalty."

A giant sweep of a wave bellowed as it landed onto shore. Royalty. Never in Sophia's life had she felt anything close to such a revered title. Another wave landed, this one with no less intensity. The sound of it washed over her, both a comfort and a tremendous force. What would it be like to be considered worthy? To fall freely into one's purpose? Another wave caused the earth to tremble, the night breeze to swell with the kind of melody that brings forth dreams.

CHAPTER 7

*T*he chatter of a sparrow woke Christian from slumber. He shivered, which was par for the course when you've slept all night without a blanket on a lounge chair next to ... royalty.

He scratched his beard then rubbed his eyes, noting the coldness of his nose on the way up. The sun's glow, coming from somewhere behind them, caused him to squint. A good sign that today was gonna be a good one.

He took her in with one swipe of his gaze, her hair a rumpled mess, part of the comforter tucked up around her neck and the other half dusting the ground. Christian scooped up the tip of wayward comforter and pulled it over his legs, then settled back with a yawn.

The sea had quieted some after last night's concerto, though the wind and water could still be heard mixing it up just a few yards off. He'd come out here to download after a strange day followed by an even stranger evening in the restaurant. Jackson's usual banter appeared to be laced with the barbs of a stingray—tiny yet sharp, painful.

On the other hand, Sophia had seemed pleased that he'd painted her well.

Sophia stirred, then sighed. He watched her, then looked away. What right did he have to be here on this lounge chair as she slept? He should go. He'd crossed the line, staying here all night. Besides, if Jackson discovered him, he might come to the wrong conclusion and throw him out. Then where would he be?

"Chris?"

He turned his head. She'd never shortened his name like that and he liked the sound of it. "Morning."

She rubbed her eyes and brushed back her hair with a hand. "You must be freezing." Her voice was groggy.

He patted the section of blanket that barely warmed his legs. "I managed to get some use from your castoff."

"Hmm. Nice of me to leave that for you."

He chuckled. "Thank you, your highness."

"What were we talking about last night again?"

"You mean, what was I saying that bored you enough to fall asleep during our conversation?"

"I believe you fell asleep first. So ... maybe you were boring yourself?"

"You're one of those early risers, aren't you?"

"Guilty."

His eyes traced the shape of her face. He enjoyed teasing her, but the more he grew to know Sophia, the more she rose to the challenge of his humor. A part of him wondered how many challenges she'd rise to where he was concerned. He took one last breath of cool sea air. "I should go."

"Wait." She threw off her blankets and they landed on him in a heap. "Let's have coffee first. I'll make some."

He swallowed back any kind of resistance. He wasn't an idiot. Nor would he allow himself to fantasize about this moment—she'd offered him coffee, and nothing more than that.

Still, a niggling that began the night he'd scared the heck out of her at the airport had grown with each encounter of Sophia. Christian sat up. He leaned his elbows on his knees and dropped his gaze to the ground, allowing the raw pain of a good stretch to help him with perspective. His own choices had brought writer's block upon him, and until Sophia's arrival, he'd been experiencing a full-blown attack. He'd seen improvement since then, though he hadn't attributed it to anything—or anyone—specifically.

Until now.

He gulped. Her approaching footsteps caused his heart to knock ferociously in his chest.

"I hope you like it black." She handed him a cup. "It's the best way."

He took both mugs from her, steam rising from them. "I'll take your word for it."

She slid back onto the lounge chair and pulled the comforter over her. After Sophia settled against the backrest, she reached for her mug and took a sip. "Mm. Perfect."

He too took a sip and ... winced. "Wow. Strong."

She smiled. "I know. I doubled up the pods. You know, because a certain someone told me how bad the coffee was." She paused. "You're welcome."

He gave her a half smile. Yeah, he'd said that, hadn't he? "So your antidote for bad coffee is to have more of it. Interesting concept."

She gave him that cute laugh again. "Sometimes you don't know what you're missing."

That pounding of his heart revved again, only this time it made an enormous loop, like the roller coaster at Disney's California Adventure.

Sophia squared her eyes on him. "Are you okay?"

He swallowed, settling both his thoughts and the erratic jostle inside his chest. He'd never been the guy to hold back, to keep from saying what he was thinking when he thought it. So why the hesitation now? He took another sip of the dark brew that turned into a gulp. When he pulled the mug away, his eyes found hers. The morning light cut a soft swath across her makeup-less face. Her eyes sparkled when she watched him, and somehow he found courage to tell her how he felt about her, something he only now had begun to realize.

"Sophia," he started ...

A song played from somewhere inside her guest room and she jerked a look over her shoulder. "Raven?" She slid a worried glance at him and threw her legs over the side of her lounger and stood. "Sorry. That's my rep on the phone. Must be urgent for her to call me this early in the morning. Will you excuse me?"

"Of course." He downed his last sip of coffee with the hopes of stilling his heart, though he knew that the load of caffeine he'd ingested very well may have the opposite effect.

Sophia emerged from her room, mouth open, eyes wide.

Christian stood up. "That doesn't look good."

Sophia pressed her hand into her cheek. Her eyelashes fluttered as she looked up at him, those eyes still wide. "That was Raven, my rep. She's three hours ahead in New York," she said. "There's a post ... on Instagram. Liddy posted it. Of me."

"Liddy?" Christian said.

Sophia's eyes found his. "Meg's good friend. She ... she was her matron of honor."

"Ah. I think I remember." He didn't, but he was trying.

Sophia lowered herself into her lounger, her expression dazed. "The post has started to go viral, Raven said."

"What was the post about?"

She snapped a look at him. *Man, she looked beautiful in the morning ...*

"A photo ... of me." She dropped her gaze to her phone then darted a look back up at him. "I don't have Instagram on my phone. Do you?"

He patted his pocket, surprised to find his phone there. It hadn't buzzed all night. He thumbed through his apps and found Instagram, which he hadn't opened in a year? Two?

Sophia peered over his shoulder. "RyterMan? That's ... clever."

"I was young when I signed up."

"Hmm."

He laughed and pulled his phone away. "Don't 'hmm' me!"

She reached over him and tried to tug the phone back. "So sensitive. Can you find the post?"

He scrolled with his thumb. "Do you know her account name? Or her last name?"

"Quinn. It's Liddy Quinn."

She crossed her arms and rocked side to side next to him, antsy.

"Oh. Wow." Christian leaned closer to her so they could both see his screen. "This is it," he said, pointing to her picture.

"Really?" It wasn't the one she feared would draw attention, the one with her and Meg. It was another one that she didn't recognize. She stretched the picture on the screen with her thumbs. "I was afraid of something like this," she whispered.

"Afraid? You look ... you look *amazing* in that photo." His heart did that harsh pounding thing again. Liddy had captured Sophia in a contemplative moment, her hair upswept, a glance over one shoulder. But the color struck him more: red. A sort of translucent, rosy red. He took in the photo again, unable to remove his gaze from her face, nor could he dispel the desire of wanting to know every detail about what was running through her mind the moment the photo had been snapped. *Pull yourself together, man.* Finally, he said, "I'm not surprised it's got so many likes. But what has that got to do with your rep?"

Sophia had that dazed look in her eyes again as she gazed out to sea. "She says her phone is ringing off the hook. Buyers are asking for that dress."

"I see."

"Do you?"

"Not really." He scratched his chin, still not clear on the problem. He didn't know much about the dresses she designed, other than they were usually lightweight in muted colors, but he felt certain she had the ability—and creativity—to design something similar to what she was wearing that day. Or wait— was that akin to plagiarism?

She sighed, the sound of it like a cry, and lowered herself into to the lounger. Christian's former publisher and ex-agent had both urged him onto social media, which he had done, but begrudgingly. Signed up for everything but found all that posting and cross-posting too mind-bending to keep up with, so he'd quit all but a couple. It wasn't the interaction with people that had driven him to jump off the never-ending internet highway, but the constant competition for higher numbers. More followers. More likes. More views. At one point he'd asked himself a simple question: At what cost?

Maybe that was the crux of Sophia's reticence in rejoicing at the moment. He pulled the comforter up around her and tucked her in, then sat on his own chair, facing her. "I think I understand a little of what you're going through. But you can hire people to handle social media for you. It doesn't have to be so overwhelming."

She smiled weakly. "Thank you. I know I can—Wade has told me that too."

Punch to the gut.

"But that's not the issue," she said, continuing. "I ... that dress is quite old. Out of style. Liddy and Meg saw it with my things and begged me to put it on. I don't design like that anymore."

"You designed it?"

"Yes, of course."

He knew it. Wanted to jump up and punch the sky. They'd given him such grief at the restaurant last night when he'd dared to suggest that Sophia's color palette shouldn't be limited to black and white. From the moment he'd spotted her at the baggage carousel, she reminded him of a watercolor painting that once hung on his parents' wall at home. Ethereal. Intimate. A blend of color and space.

A tear slipped down her cheek, and he reached for her hand. "Hey."

"I'm sorry you are seeing me this way. Probably tired from sleeping outside all night."

He brushed a second tear from her cheek, surprised by the intimacy of the act. It was not yet 6 a.m., but a boldness began to barrel through Christian, and at this moment, he wasn't sure he could stop it if he tried. He'd come here to get away, but in meeting her, he'd found a sense of home. Lightness and air seemed to follow her around, sweeping him up in it. He wanted more of that.

He enveloped her hand in both of his. "Sophia?"

The shrill of her cell phone startled them both. An arrow lodged in his chest, blocking his airway.

She removed her hand from his and answered her phone.

Wade.

Seriously? At six in the morning? Sophia continued to talk to him about the Instagram post and who-knew-what-else, so Christian stood, shoved a hand in one pocket, and headed for the handrail. The sea had turned churlish and yet he reminded himself that it was going to be a good day. The stars aligned last night and the sun arose this morning, casting a perfect glow.

But the more Sophia smiled and nodded and spoke words of affirmation into that blasted phone, he wondered ... had he read everything wrong?

~

"THIS IS WHAT YOU WANTED!" Wade downed his second espresso of the morning. "We have to jump on this, Sophia. Would have been better if you already had your own account, but we can make this work with Liddy's."

"But I don't even know if that's okay with her—"

"Let's offer her a cut."

"A cut of what?"

"Of sales. Oh, I don't mean anything particularly large, but let's offer Liddy an incentive to put up more posts. We also need to find people who will share the original post. I'm working on that now. When did you say Liddy would be joining us?"

Sophia felt lightheaded. Her mind spun. Liddy had agreed to meet with them this morning, though they hadn't talked about it, but honestly, Sophia's reaction when Liddy did walk in could go one of two ways: hug her tight or slug her. Good thing she never had a propensity for violence.

"When will you be able to get the dress into production?" Wade's question crashed into her thoughts.

"I am still thinking about it."

Wade smiled. "Spoken like a true artist, but Sophia, you need to act quickly."

She exhaled and snapped a look at him. "Wade, I appreciate

all of this, but first, let's talk about your fee. Because it is likely that I cannot afford you."

"Afford me? Listen, I knew your father. I'm already being paid handsomely by the inn. Let me do this for you on my own dime. I want to."

She swallowed a sip of water. "Why?"

Wade went silent for a moment, one pregnant moment. His dark brown eyes penetrated hers before he finally replied. "Is it enough to say that I enjoy spending time with you?" He paused long enough for her to admire the trim silhouette of his chambray sport coat, his cream shirt open at the collar, contrasting the rich color of his hair. And the way he continued to stare at her.

His voice sank deeper. "You are creative and talented, and I would love to see your designs on every woman who walks through the inn's entry doors."

Sophia enjoyed spending time with him too, though she'd not yet dared to admit it. Wade brought a calm presence into the frenetic memories of her past. Structure. Safety. And a hope for better things to come. She bristled at the idea of being a damsel in distress, though. She would need to make that clear.

"You are much too kind to me. I appreciate your help, Wade. I-I enjoy spending time with you as well."

He gazed at her a beat longer than usual, which made her heart make a surprise flip. She caught her breath and allowed it to fill her again, then said, "But I insist on paying you back."

Wade frowned and began to speak, as if in protest, but Sophia stopped him with one palm in the air. "And I'll start by buying you your morning gallon of espresso."

He was laughing at full throttle as Liddy arrived at their table, a boxy indigo diaper bag dangling from the crook of one arm and a baby with flyaway hair over her shoulder. Wade stood to pull out her chair for her, but first she bent and gave Sophia a peck on the cheek.

"Phew. Sorry I'm late. Still getting used to having to be presentable before 10 a.m." Liddy took a seat and glanced up at Wade. "Thanks." She plopped Beau Junior onto her lap.

The baby squirmed and Sophia held out her arms. "May I?"

With zero hesitation, Liddy plunked him into Sophia's waiting embrace. She blew a breath that dislodged several strands of hair from her face and laughed. "Thank you for the invitation. Now, what can I do for you?"

Sophia cuddled Beau Junior and nodded at the menu. "Please. Order breakfast first, and then we will explain."

The waiter swung by and took Liddy's order just as Meg pulled up a chair and sat down. "Ryan, I'd like a gluten-free blueberry muffin and a matcha tea."

"Right away," Ryan said.

"So what are we all meeting about?" Meg asked.

Liddy gave her a mock scowl. "I believe this is a private meeting. Were you even invited?"

Sophia gasped. Neither woman looked all that upset with the other, though. She could never tell with these two. "Liddy," Sophia interrupted, "a post of yours has gone viral. Have you seen it?"

Wrinkles appeared on Liddy's forehead and she scrunched her nose. "On my account? Shoot. I haven't looked at it in days —how do you know?"

"Raven called. She's my rep in New York, and, well, she's been getting a lot of calls from buyers. She traced their interest to your post."

Liddy gasped, covered her mouth, then splayed her fingers wide in the air. "Oh my gosh! The picture I posted of you in that ravishing dress?"

"What picture?" Meg asked.

"You weren't invited," Liddy quipped.

Sophia nodded. "Yes, it was a photo of me."

Liddy lifted her chin to the ceiling and sighed. She recovered. "I don't think I ever remembered to send it to either of you. I was scrolling through my phone while nursing Beau Junior in the middle of the night and found a *gorgeous* pic of Sophia. So I posted it without thinking."

Wade cut in. "Well, you must've been thinking like a marketer, because you used her name—and now there are buyers clamoring for her designs."

"Well," Sophia said, "for this design, in particular."

Liddy laughed. "I'm a genius."

Meg rolled her eyes at Liddy. "Oh shut up." She then sat back, smiling. "This is great news. Have you told Jackson?"

Sophia shook her head.

A server appeared with their dishes and beverages. He disappeared as quickly as he had come.

Wade picked up his mug, but before taking a sip, he cut a concerned look Sophia's way and said to everyone, "She's still taking it all in, I think. We're here this morning to strategize the best way to make that post grow even more—so that all that interest will actually generate sales. Second, she needs to get the dress into production right away."

Liddy gave her a half-smile, half-worried frown. "That won't be too hard, will it?"

Sophia hugged little Beau tighter still. "I don't know."

Meg touched her arm. "Sophia, honey, for someone whose design company may be about to take off, you don't look too excited. Is everything all right?"

"It's just ... that dress. I'm not sure it fits my line, exactly."

"Oh but it does. You looked so smashing in it, Sophia. Really, you did. And I'm sorry I didn't show you the picture first." She turned to Meg. "Seriously, if you ever do the same thing to me, I'll kill you." She swung her gaze back to Sophia. "But I can't say that I'm unhappy at the way it's turned out!"

"I'm glad you're saying this," Wade said, "because Sophia doesn't have an Instagram, so I'm hoping you'll be willing to post a few more photos for her. I have a strategy to try to keep the momentum going all the way until Fashion Week."

"In New York?" Meg asked Sophia. "Are you going?"

Sophia shook her head. "No, no. Raven will go. She always does that for me. My booth is small, but it works well enough. She'll be there to take appointments and process orders on the spot."

Liddy released a wistful sigh. "I love New York. Will be a long time until we can go again. You know, with the baby and all."

Meg clucked her tongue. "For heaven's sake, you can take a baby to New York."

"Uh, five hours in a cramped metal can with a poopy baby? The other passengers would love us. No thank you."

Meg shrugged. "Just pass around some of those apology baggies that other parents bring on the plane. Those are always a big hit."

"Yeah, until the first gut-piercing cry when there's still half of the flight time left."

Wade scowled. "So will you help, Liddy?"

"I can pay you," Sophia said.

Liddy snapped out of her fake fight with Meg and turned to catch Wade's even gaze. "You have to ask?" Liddy waved him off. "Of course. I'll do anything—and everything—that I can to help. And don't even think of paying me anything." Beau Junior started to wail so Liddy reached over and plucked him from Sophia's arms.

If only she could shut her eyes, pull Christian's comforter back over her, and fall asleep to the sound of waves following their course. But this was real. She had come to the Sea Glass Inn not knowing if her fledgling design company could be revived. If she were honest, Sophia wasn't sure she even wanted that. Her designs had brought her a smile in her darkest moments, but now, her hobby-turned-business had sprouted wings that she had neither designed nor foresaw.

She had always worked hard to create an aesthetic pleasing to the masses. Something tried. And true. She'd decided long ago that experimentation was for others—not her.

Until, that is, Meg and Liddy had spotted the dress she'd toiled over for herself years ago. Her stepfather had been right —it was too short. Too loud. Oh, but how she loved slipping the soft fabric over her frame that first time. She'd stood in front of her mirror, the one leaned up against the wall of her bedroom, and examined it at all angles so she could pin those places that needed work.

"So do you think you'll be able to get it into production quickly?" Meg's voice interrupted her memories. Her sister-in-law watched her with anticipation.

Sophia licked her lips, thinking. Could this be the answer to the inn's problems? If what Raven predicted became true, her long-discarded dress had the potential to be her biggest seller yet. She didn't dare to dream of numbers, but maybe, just maybe, the little red dress could help her brother in ways she had not imagined.

The idea centered her, and the tension that she had carried with her all morning began to dissipate. Perhaps it was providential that, at the last minute, she'd taken the long-forgotten dress and tucked it into the suitcase she'd brought with her. Not to mention the very real surprise that the dress still fit her so well.

She smiled at her sister-in-law. "It will take some work to re-create the pattern, but yes, I think I can do it."

Meg lunged toward her and grasped her hand. "I want to help in any way I can—I'll do whatever you need, so please use me."

Sophia glanced around the table. Three willing faces—and one precious baby boy—met her gaze, giving her the motivation to start again.

CHAPTER 8

A week ago, Christian found himself shivering on Sophia's deck, awakened by the surf. The thought of that night warmed him to his toes. Except for the occasional whir of a sewing machine, he had hardly seen or heard from her since. Christian glanced over to her suite, knowing what he'd find, yet hoping to be wrong. Sure enough, Sophia's deck lay empty. As far as he could tell, her slider door had not clicked open once all day. Maybe in days.

Less than twenty-four hours after his spontaneous campout with Jackson's sister, Christian had wandered out here with his laptop and imagination, keen on stirring up the creativity that he'd found in abundance only a short week ago. Unfortunately, he'd found himself vexingly empty ever since.

Christian looked up, scanning the horizon, desperate for a sighting of ... anything. But all he found was ... nothing. He pounded the glass table, rattling his computer and further jostling his thoughts. Where had she gone? The sea creature who had swum through his thoughts and onto the page had, for whatever reason, chosen not to surface again.

He ran his eyes over his manuscript, scrolling up and back down again, landing on the dreary vastness of white space. If she doesn't show soon, he thought, he'd be stuck with a story that had no end. Christian drummed his fingers on the table-top. A grunt left him and he fired up some music on his computer, attempting to set the mood. He pictured her in his mind's eye, a matriarch of sorts from an underwater land. She was about to surface. He could feel it.

But first ... Facebook. Marci had apologized profusely for her slip. The publisher that had once employed her had released new covers regularly and without fanfare. It hadn't occurred to her that he, as an independent author now, might have something different planned—a big reveal. How could he stay irate with someone who had the best of intentions?

Still, Marci had promised to take down the cover right away, and though he'd meant to double-check, he'd been distracted until now. He pulled up her page, scrolled down, and ... *check*—no cover anywhere in view.

He was about to sign off and get back to work when something familiar caught his eye as he scrolled by. He scrolled back up.

"What ... how?"

His cover, the same one that had been removed from Marci's page, appeared on the screen with an ad below it—and he'd been tagged.

CJ Capra is back! The Burns Golden Agency is pleased to announce our association with the bad boy himself, bestselling author CJ Capra. Coming soon: Is she real or legend? Find out in The Spell.

Christian pushed himself from the glass deck table, his chair falling behind him. If raking a hand through one's beard could draw Facebook's attention to an egregious post, that "ad" would be gone by now. His jaw clicked as he unclenched it.

He picked up his phone, a string of words not fit for tender ears at the ready. Though his fingers hovered above the number keys, he stopped and slammed the phone back down on the table, thankful not to hear glass cracking as he did.

Burns knew he would call—knew he'd react with a tumult of emotion. He'd be there on the other end of the line, too, with his own string of words, ready to strike back.

Well. He wouldn't bite. Not this time. If his time in seclusion had taught him anything, it was that self-respect flourished in the soil of self-control. And though his confidence had been battered as of late, he was in no deficit of self-respect.

The familiar ring of his phone jerked him from his rumination. *Burns.* He smiled. The man couldn't take the waiting, apparently, and had called from his office's second line—the one Christian hadn't blocked—to gloat. He listened as the phone rang and rang, but he made no move to answer it. Instead, Christian grabbed his laptop, turned on his heels, and headed through his suite and out the front door—leaving his cell phone behind.

He found a shady spot beneath a midsize queen palm to write, far enough from the screams and plunges of the inn's swimming pool, but close enough to sense the lightheartedness of families playing in the sun. Christian needed something to buoy his otherwise glum countenance.

He opened his computer. In his mind, he saw her swimming in a looping fashion, readying herself for the battle building onshore. She drifted onto sand, the moisture from her magnificently long body wicked away. She stood strong and beautiful, her eyes like lit celadon.

"Can we talk?"

Christian's chin jerked up. "Hey, Jackson."

Jackson sat on one of the cushioned chairs across from Christian. "How's the book coming?"

"Good. I'm pleased."

"So it's helped, you being here."

"I'd say. Definitely."

Jackson nodded, his eyes not quite focused. "I suppose you'll be moving on once it's finished. Have you figured out where you'll be going yet?"

Christian paused. They had never talked about when he might leave. From what he understood, he'd had an open invitation to stay at the inn for as long as he needed. But, of course, he didn't want to take advantage of his friend's generosity ...

"We've been friends a long time."

"Yep."

"Know things about each other that neither should probably repeat."

"And I never have."

Jackson cracked a smile, though it did not appear to reach his eyes. "Nor have I."

Christian's brain scrambled, trying to come up with something meaningful to add to this cryptic conversation. Between his agent's threats and his need to finish this book without interruption, he didn't have a lot of brain power left to force out of Jackson whatever it was that needed cajoling.

But he tried anyway. "Is everything okay with you? Have you been working through the issues with the hotel? I've seen your, uh, consultant around." He almost used the word "lurking" but thought better of it. "So, I hope that's a good sign for you."

"Wade's been a tremendous help in us getting our footing again. Having him come onboard has been a sobering—and humbling—experience."

"How so?"

Jackson sighed and sat back. "Like I said, you and I have been friends for a long time. You know how I was as a college student. Cocky, impatient, full of myself ..."

"Go on."

Jackson cracked a half smile. " I've grown up, not by my own choice. Have had to learn some things in the hardest way." He speared Christian with a look. "Do you understand what I mean?"

Christian set his laptop aside. "We all have things in our pasts we regret. So, yes, I think I do."

"Good. Good. To answer your question, having Wade here has taught me that it's okay to get help, to not rely on myself to have all the answers. I've benefitted from his years of experience."

"I'm glad to hear it."

Jackson jabbed him with another pointed look. "Wade has become like family and I hope to have him around here for many, many years to come."

"Sounds cozy."

"Why is everything a joke to you?"

Christian cocked a brow toward his friend. In a few short sentences, Jackson had reiterated the length of their friendship and pressed Christian about his departure date. Then he waxed poetic about his father's former business consultant. Was he the only one that found this at least somewhat comical?

He sensed, however, that this was not the time for laughter. "Just trying to lighten the mood. Sorry things have been so ... intense around here lately."

Jackson pursed his lips and nodded, but added nothing else to the conversation. Though Christian felt certain his friend had much more to say.

SOPHIA LOOKED up from her worktable, noting the myriad boxes spread across her parlor room floor, their top flaps open.

She had intended to purchase temporary shelving, unpack everything, and set up the perfect workspace.

There had been no time for that. Not after Liddy's post had, as they'd all suspected, gone viral. How many views now? Ten thousand? Twenty? She'd lost count. All she knew was that Raven's phone continued to ring with potential buyers wanting information. Would she be at Fashion Week? What is the price point? Size range?

And the bloggers. Several wanted interviews and permission to share photos. They wanted the dress in different colors, too. The recognition of her high-spirit dresses had thrown a hook around her recent obscurity and tossed her into the public arena more than ever before, flapping unsteadily as sure as the hem of a skirt lofted on an updraft.

Sophia let out a breath that she had been holding. Several times a day this week she'd had to remind herself to breathe.

She'd started this project with much uncertainty, but as she found her grounding and her focus, confidence grew. Starting with day one, when she'd laid the old dress on the wide and long table that Jackson had given her to use. The pattern no longer existed, so she would need to create one. She started by pulling pattern paper from one of the shipping boxes, allowing that familiar smell to fill her senses. It smelled like work and creativity ... home.

Carefully, she pinned the seams of the dress then laid muslin on top of the fabric. With chalk, she rubbed the pattern onto the muslin and then laid the muslin over the pattern paper. Using a tracing wheel, she transferred the pattern onto paper, then took measurements and made appropriate adjustments.

In between the recreation of her pattern, she'd had to shop for fabric and other supplies and, well, eat. She'd even had to borrow Meg's garment rack. But now, as several samples of her dress hung on that rack in the middle of her room, a mixture of pride and gratefulness came over her. And hope. While she continued to fight off a niggling of dread, of revisiting the past, she also came to think of the production of these dresses as a way to help her family.

That fact alone helped her press on.

Sophia straightened in her chair, wincing at the tightness of her lower back and the tension in her shoulders. On her feet, she padded over to the slider door and flung it open, allowing the day's sea breeze inside. She breathed in a potent combination of salt and air and earth, the freshness of it renewing her muscles, her nerve endings.

She glanced over toward the deck off of Christian's suite and rose onto her tiptoes. Empty. Disappointment whisked through her, though she hardly knew why. She had no time for small talk anyway, not with deadlines shining their glaring spotlight on her every move.

When her phone rang, she nearly ignored it. *Wade?*

"I'm glad you picked up," he said.

"Just taking a break. A small one."

He chuckled. "You're allowed that."

"But it's back to work for me now."

"That's why I called, actually. I'm going to be leaving LA soon to head back your way, and I thought I'd coax you out for a late dinner."

Sophia peeked at herself in the mirror. Tendrils of her hair hung in disarray having escaped a hastily affixed hair tie. The half circles beneath her eyes betrayed her lack of sleep. And when had she last worn shoes?

"I-I think I will have to pass tonight. Too much work awaits me."

"Sweet, Sophia. You cannot keep up this pace, especially if you're not eating well. They say that stepping away from one's

art for a time is the best way to stir up creativity." He paused.
"Have I convinced you to meet me yet?"

She stole another glance in that mirror. Could she spare the
time to pull herself together?

"Are you still with me?"

She inhaled, aware of the hollowness of her stomach. "Yes,
yes. Okay. I will meet you, but I cannot promise how I will
look—or that my shoes will match."

He laughed. "You're beautiful no matter what shoes you
decide to wear. I'll see you in a couple of hours."

Wade's call gave Sophia the motivation to whip off her hair
tie and run a brush through her mane. She smiled, thinking of
how he had pulled her out of that place that all artists go, the
retreat of the mind. While the mind could be a fertile place full
of rich soil and lush growth, she'd found hers could be rather
dark. Dreary. Hopeless.

She cleaned up her workspace for the evening, taking care
to have a plan in place for the next day's work. Then she pulled
herself together with fresh clothes, makeup—and shoes. The
more she readied herself, the louder her stomach's cry. She
arrived in the restaurant right on time and found a table near
the window.

Her waiter approached to pour her water from a pitcher.
"Will someone be joining you tonight, Sophia?"

"Yes, Ryan. Wade Prince should be here shortly."

He poured another glass of water and set it across from her.
"Would you like an appetizer? Spinach croquettes? Scallop
carpaccio?"

Her stomach leaped. "I would love the sliders."

Ryan broke out in a smile. "Absolutely."

Sophia took a sip of water and watched waves breaking in
the distance. She wasn't unhappy Wade had talked her into
this, though she did wonder if he'd be arriving soon. Unfortu-

nately, in her haste to make it downstairs in time, she had forgotten to bring her phone.

Ryan arrived with the sliders—she hadn't realized there would be four on a platter. She breathed them in. *What was keeping Wade?*

"Been stood up?" Christian had appeared at her table, an iPad in one hand, the other hand shoved into a pocket.

"I sincerely hope not."

Christian slipped a look over his shoulder at the door, then swung his gaze back to her. "I was kidding, but if some guy's left you to sit here alone eating those delicious Kobe beef burgers, then he's a chump."

"Join me, won't you? I'm sure he'll be here soon."

Christian slid into the chair across from Sophia, his smile quirky and questioning. "His loss is, well, you know." He paused. "You've been hiding lately."

"I could say the same about you."

"Me? I've been here. But I haven't seen or heard anything from your neck of the hotel lately."

"That is a relief. I was worried that my sewing machine may have been bothering you."

His lips parted in recognition. Light from outside the window highlighted flecks of burnished gold in his beard. "So that was you whirring?"

She wagged her head, trying not to laugh too loud. "Not me —my sewing machine."

"They have you sewing the drapes now? If you want, I can talk to Jackson for you."

She cracked up. "Now you know the real reason I've come to live here."

He grinned widely at this. "I stand corrected."

Sophia lifted the small platter of sliders. "Hungry?"

His eyes caught hers and held them for a beat. His Adams

apple bobbed and he dropped his gaze to the burgers. "I could eat."

She nodded. "Please."

The restaurant was beginning to come alive, the din growing. Each bite of food brought Sophia closer to feeling like herself again, and more than once, she'd forgotten—albeit briefly—about the stress that had driven her all week.

Sophia sneaked a look at Christian. He had a ruggedness to him. Translucent sea blue eyes notwithstanding, even without his scruff, she thought him rugged. Wild. Though how a man like he could sit for hours on end and dream up stories, she didn't know. At the very least, she would have thought his novels would be action-adventure tales of swashbucklers and maidens, sword fights and freedom from oppressors. Or maybe crime thrillers with cigar-chomping detectives and bloody scenes of misdeeds followed by justice delivered.

She was surprised—intrigued, more like it—to discover his love of fantasy, fairytales, and ... magic.

Perhaps for this reason she had found him easy to like, yet difficult to know. She froze on that thought. She wanted to know Christian. What made him devote his life to writing? Why, really, had he come here, to a suite at the inn, to write his next novel? And ... how did he earn that scar on his face?

Embarrassed, Sophia swallowed her questions along with a last bite of a slider. She sipped her water and hoped he could not read her mind. She searched for something ... anything to fill the space between them.

Sophia relaxed against her chair and played with the napkin in her lap. "I was wondering if you would tell me about your book."

"*The Spell?*"

"I didn't know that was the title—it's, wow, I love it. Sounds beautiful." She froze again. "I mean, intriguing."

He laughed. "You could use the word beautiful. I'm a guy, but I can take it."

"I'm relieved to hear that. What has been happening with your book?"

He pursed his lips, his head tilted slightly to the side. Had she said the wrong thing? Asked an invasive question?

Finally, he said, "My agent is suing me."

Now, that ... that was not what Sophia had expected to hear. She frowned. "Why?"

He wadded up his own napkin and pitched it onto his plate, his smile rueful. "Honestly, I have some doubt that he'll pull the trigger, but he appears to enjoy making trouble for me." His sigh sounded weary, almost defeated. He caught eyes with her. "It's made this week rather distracting."

"I don't understand. Are you writing something that he did not approve? Did not agree upon?"

"No, no, nothing like that." He flashed a look at her. "Do you know why I'm here, living here?"

She didn't. Sophia shook her head to that effect.

He nodded, closed mouth. If she had to guess, the expression on his face told her he was about to lay it all out for her—no matter how it sounded. That defeated look in his eyes had suddenly turned defiant. "To put it succinctly, I came here to write without the encumbrance of my ex-agent's influence. Life had taken some detours, and your brother offered me this place to start fresh. But then ..."

"Yes, what then?"

Christian dropped his chin and sighed. He lifted his eyes to hers. "Though we had parted ways, he inadvertently got wind of the fact that I am writing the book that he and I once talked about. Our ties had been severed, and there'd been no chance of a contract for this one—and I had come to terms with that.

But he decided, once he learned that I had revived the story, that he should be entitled to his share."

"Because you and he had spoken about it together?"

He sat back and she thought he might end the conversation. "'Fraid so."

"Does he have a contract? What I mean to ask is, an enforceable contract?"

Christian shook his head. "No. Nothing like that. Listen, I'm not afraid of him. I don't think he has anything to stand on regarding my book, but it's a hassle."

She nodded. "I can see that. I've turned off my own phone much of this week, so I do understand how important it is to leave all the distractions behind."

He smiled at her, the blue of his eyes a distraction of their own. "I'd love to see what you've accomplished this week while ignoring me."

"Christian—"

"Kidding." His smile turned playful. "But seriously, don't be a stranger."

A ripple of something ran through her, like a charge. She didn't respond—but didn't have to. A comfortable silence sat between them, as if they had been close for many years. Finally, she spoke. "Are you feeling a little better about it all now?"

He nodded. "I am, but I haven't told you the latest."

She felt both of her eyebrows raise in anticipation.

"Burns—he's my former agent—Burns announced on Facebook that he's representing my book. Even posted the cover." That rueful smile was back. "The plot thickens, eh?"

She tightened her hands into fists, unexpected anger rising. It hit her like a hurricane. "Why would he do that?"

Christian shrugged. "Who knows why jerks do what they do? Could be anything. He might think that by doing me a favor—offering some pre-order promotion—that I'd come running back to his agency. Or, he might be fishing for a contract. He's already said that one publisher who originally passed on it is suddenly interested. All I know is that he's made it mighty hard for me to extricate myself—and my book—from his clutches. At least in the public's eye."

"But you won't allow him to represent you, right?"

"No, I won't. But once something's on the internet, it's there forever."

"A distraction of a different kind."

He nodded, their eyes engaged, that sad smile shaping his mouth. "Exactly."

"Promise me you'll fight him."

Both his smile and his eyes lit. "Look at you, little fighter!"

"I'm very serious." Even she did not know exactly what it was that created the storm inside of her. All she knew at this moment was passion ... for justice. "You fight this, Christian. I will be the first one to buy your book. I promise."

He laughed into the air. "For you, a free copy."

"Will you sign it?"

"You mean so it'll be worth *less*?"

She frowned.

Christian reached across the table and laid his warm hand on top of hers. "Thank you for pulling me out of that deep dark place of self-loathing. I needed it."

Sophia couldn't bear to pull her hand away until he did. His touch enveloped her, ignited her, surprised her. She longed for their hands to linger there entwined, a thought that surprised her as much as the simple act of his touch soothed her.

Another human rushed up to their table.

"Very sorry to have kept you waiting." She pulled her hand away just as Wade bent down and kissed her on the cheek. He smelled of high-end cologne and hurry. He reached over and shook Christian's hand. "Thank you for keeping her company."

Christian's manner was the epitome of calm, yet beneath the scruff of his beard, she detected a hardness to his jaw. He slid out of his chair and stuck a hand in his pocket. "No problem."

Wade took the seat that Christian had vacated. "Glad there's something left." He singularly focused on the remaining slider. "I'm starved."

Sophia gave Christian a little smile, but he only nodded and walked away.

CHAPTER 9

*A*fter Christian's odd exchange with Jackson the week before followed by his encounter with Sophia—and Wade—soon after, he found he needed a change of scenery. A hard truth to explain should he have been asked. Because as breathtaking and accommodating as his suite at Sea Glass Inn was, staying there to write had proven a distraction he didn't need. Nor one he could afford.

Besides, he reasoned, eating, sleeping, and working in the same small space—no matter the view from that space—could have a crippling effect on creativity. He felt certain of this. So he had spent a few days writing from various sunny spots throughout the city, including a courtyard shop that served up coffee and acai bowls and a brewery with Wi-Fi. He'd made such great progress, that after another day of wandering, he finally found himself ready to stay "home" for a while.

Laptop in hand, Christian strolled back into the inn through the front doors, sending a nod to Thomas at the bell desk as he did. After days and hours spent writing off-site, he welcomed a little human interaction—not enough to pull him completely out of the story in his head, but enough to give his mind and body a respite.

"Afternoon, Christian," Trace said. The concierge desk, which had been surrounded by guests this morning when he'd strolled out, had quieted considerably. "Chef's serving yummy strawberry shortcake in the cafe today. They grow the strawberries near here, you know. You should stop in."

He patted his stomach. "You trying to make me fat?"

She rolled her eyes. "Oh, up-lease. Guys don't have to watch their figures the way we women do." She took another bite of her dessert, which she'd been hiding beneath the counter, and shook her head. "World is an upside-down place."

The concierge phone rang and Trace stashed her shortcake back into its hiding place. The clip of Meg's heels stormed up behind him. "Christian, have you heard?"

"I ... heard what?"

Jackson's wife was petite and powerful in her fitted suit. She carried a clipboard and wore a worried frown.

"Excuse me, Meg?" Trace leaned across the desk, her hand over the mouthpiece of the phone. "There's a phone call for you. She says her name is Priscilla. You two met in, uh, somewhere in Italy."

"Priscilla?" Meg glanced from Trace to Christian and back again. "Please tell her to hold just a moment." She swung a look back at him. "I need to take that, but talk to Sophia, if you haven't already. You're an artist—you can help!"

He hesitated as she jogged in those heels around the concierge desk, took a seat, and answered the phone. No, he hadn't spoken to Sophia today. In fact, other than an occasional wave from his neighboring balcony, he hadn't seen the elusive fashion designer all week.

He huffed a sigh. The real reason for his need of a change of scenery exposed. On his way to the bank of elevators, one of which would take him to his temporary home, he pivoted and headed to the bar instead. Christian slid onto a barstool, ordered up a bowl of the seasonal shortcake that Trace recommended so highly, and spent some time avoiding ... her.

Johnny served him his dessert followed by a shout to someone behind him. "Hello, Mr. Riley. What can I get for you?"

Jackson took the stool next to Christian's and gestured to the voluptuous bowl of strawberries and cake and fresh whipped cream in front of him. "One of those would be great. Thanks."

Christian didn't turn, but lingered on a bite, swallowing it slowly. Jackson's presence turned on a proverbial light bulb in Christian's mind, especially as he replayed the implications from their last conversation.

"Come here often?" Jackson asked.

"I pay my bills, if that's what you're asking."

Jackson scoffed. "Good thing."

"What's up?" He refrained from asking if he knew what had spooked Meg where Sophia was concerned. If Jackson wanted to tell him, he would. Still, curiosity clawed at him, leaving his insides raw.

"I assume you've spoken with your neighbor recently."

Christian gulped his water, washing down a large bite of cake. "Can't say that I have. She's a busy lady, I hear."

Jackson squinted. "What's wrong with you?"

Christian took another bite and ate it slowly. He swallowed and wiped his mouth with a napkin. "Guess I could ask you the same question."

Johnny served Jackson the cake, conversation between them silent. But instead of taking a bite, he said, "She's my sister. Maybe I should have thought out the implications of ... of everything."

"You mean like housing your jailbird friend next to her?"

"Knock it off." Jackson placed both forearms squarely on the bar in front of him and swung a look at Christian. "She's vulnerable. And beautiful ... and somewhat naive."

"Is that why you've set her up with Grandpa?"

"You really are a jerk. You know that?"

Christian smiled evenly. "So I've heard."

Jackson groaned. A dollop of whipped cream slid down a massive strawberry, but he ignored his dessert. "For the record, I haven't set her up with anybody, Wade included. Though, I'm not opposed to that."

"Of course you aren't."

"She needs someone stable. Especially after all she's been through, but I didn't bring her here to play matchmaker or to run her life in any way."

"But you want her to stay here, in this town."

"I hope so. I want that—Meg wants that too. We don't have a ton of family, either of us."

"I wouldn't hurt her, you know."

Jackson gave him a pained look.

Christian stabbed his dessert, which was quickly becoming a melted swirl of cream and syrup. "I'm not a monster."

"You have a temper."

"You don't think a person can change? Can learn from their mistakes and rewrite their future?"

"I thought you had."

And there it was. The root of Jackson's conflicting behavior where Christian was concerned. He may have been a hothead when he was younger. Jackson had certainly seen that in him. But he had changed and his life showed that. Or it had until he made a serious misstep and clocked that ignorant reviewer. He'd had his reasons, and he'd paid his dues. But how many chances did one person receive?

Christian gave him a pointed look. "Are we all destined to wallow in our failures, in your opinion?"

Jackson seemed to ponder this, to weigh Christian's words, perhaps in light of his own life. He rubbed his forehead with his hand and leaned into it, as if holding himself up. "You know what's really weird?" he finally said. "Sophia has managed to bring out something in me that I didn't even know existed."

"Yeah?"

"Yeah."

"Well, you know what? I could say the same thing about your sister."

Jackson stared blankly toward the back of the bar. His jaw clicked several times, and for the briefest of moments, Christian understood. Or at least he thought he did. Why wouldn't his old friend be protective of the sister he never knew? Of a woman who shared his DNA yet had not been given the privilege of sharing in that knowledge until recently?

And what if he had not taken such a stance?

Christian knew what he would have thought about that— he would have wanted to shake his friend for that error in judgment. He swallowed down a bite of dessert along with his pride. "Jackson, I'll honor your wishes," he said, quietly. "I'm not going to now, or ever, expect anything more from Sophia than friendship." Even as he said the words, his gut twisted.

"We may be new to each other, but she's my sister. I want to protect her. She may overrule my opinion and do whatever she pleases. But I appreciate you steering clear so she doesn't have that option where you're concerned." He swung a look at Christian. "I'm sure you understand, under the circumstances."

Christian flipped a glance at his old friend, elbow on the counter, spoon dangling over his half-eaten dessert. He looked like a drunk who had just bellied up to the bar and spilled his guts. He pitied him.

Despite the promise he'd just made to his old pal, one he intended to keep, a very real part of Christian hoped that what pleased Sophia included ... him.

~

SOPHIA SANK INTO BLACKNESS, the song of the sea her lullaby, the caress of salt air her embrace. She submerged into the void, sensing herself letting go, her fingers uncurling, releasing from the tether of self, creation ... ridicule.

"Sophia?"

She hardly knew she'd been drifting until his familiar voice interrupted her descent. Sophia lifted a corner of her sleep mask and peered out.

Christian.

With one strong arm as a brace, he hopped over his rail onto her deck. Always scared her half to death to see him do that way up here, so far from the ground.

He pulled the other lounge chair closer to hers and sat. "What's been happening?"

She frowned. "I suppose you already know."

"If I knew, I wouldn't be asking you."

She stared at him for a beat, then gave her head a tight little shake, reaffixed her sleep mask, and crossed her arms across her midsection.

Christian lifted the mask from her face. "Sophia—hey, is this a gel mask?"

She smirked. "Yes."

"Fancy," he said. "Are you going to tell me what happened?"

Sophia pulled the mask off her face fully and flung it onto the small glass end table next to her. The glare of daylight accosted her, so she covered her face with the back of her forearm. One "woe is me" joke and she'd be throwing him out. Or maybe just asking him to leave. "This isn't my best moment, Christian."

"Well, if we're going to be friends, you're going to have to invite me to your pity parties on occasion. I can pout just as well as any of your friends."

"Men don't pout."

"Really. Is that what you think?" He swung his legs onto the lounger, laid back, and scratched his beard, as if giving thought to her words. "Maybe you're right. Maybe I don't pout. But I can brood with the best of them. Might be helpful for a while —but too long and I find it impossible to pull myself out of it." He turned his chin toward her and nearly whispered, "Friends don't let friends go down that road."

Sophia turned onto her right side, knees bent to a nearly fetal position. The sun made her eyes squint. "Everything was going so well. The samples are done. The line sheets have been revised. Raven helped produce a press kit and emailed it to hundreds of bloggers."

"And?"

Her eyes clouded into puddles. "I received the worst review ever. It might possibly be the most scathing review I have ever seen for a design." She didn't want him to see her cry, did not care to elicit sympathy, so she flipped over onto her back, her eyelashes fluttering. Regardless of her struggle, a tear slipped out of her eye and down her cheek.

"I'm sorry."

She closed her eyes. What else could he say? He couldn't fix this—nobody could. A blogger had actually called her design childish. Ill-fitting. Ugly. Not worthy of a fraction of its price tag. That alone could cut to the deep, but the words rang eerily close to words written long ago, by someone she loved. She sniffled, forcing back more tears.

Sticks and stones ...

Words will never hurt you ...

Lines from the old rhyme from childhood rang in her mind.

"Sophia, look at me."

His eyes caressed her face in a way that told her he cared. Blue and open, with faint crow's feet, they held her steady.

She said, "You don't have to say anything."

"I've been where you are. Artists produce for others, yet what we produce is personal. The accolades roll in and we promise not to allow them to go to our heads. But no matter how well our work might sell, or how many glowing reviews we see, the mean-spirited ones carry the clout. That said ... I haven't read a review in more than a year."

"How is that possible?"

He blew out a deep breath, myriad emotions alive in his face. "Stubbornness. Experience. I refuse to look at the bad ones any longer—or the good. I've learned that either one can mess with my head."

Admittedly, she had not read his work. She had heard that his first book was a runaway hit, that readers loved the adventure and magic of his stories. Others followed. Then ... writer's block hit him and he had come here to clear his head. In a way, she had been "blocked" too, and coming here had already released her to design again. The difference between them, though, was she had been stalled ... frozen with fear after a particularly harsh review by a blogger.

She rolled her neck, breathing in deeply. "I wish I could be like you, Christian."

He gave her a full-mouth smile at that and hung his head, as if embarrassed. He raised his gaze to hers again, a mischievous glint in it. "I haven't always avoided reviews." He pulled his phone from his pocket and began scrolling with his thumb. "In fact, I have something to share with you."

"You don't have—"

He raised his pointer finger. "Ah ah ah. Trust me here."

She smiled for the first time all day.

"A writer named Jeffrey Robinson said that critics are to authors what dogs are to lampposts. Now, settle back and prepare to be shocked and amazed ..."

"Are you taking me to the circus?"

He winked. "Sort of. Okay, I've found what I was looking for on my phone—I actually saved these to my notes. Motivation, if you will."

She had no idea what he was talking about but began to relax, the cadence of his voice soothing.

"The characters inspire one emotion only: disgust."

She lifted her head from the lounge chair. "What?!"

"I'm just getting started."

"The story is hokey." He glanced at her during a pause. "At best."

She made a shushing sound and gave him a single laugh.

"Predictable, boring fluff ... not worth reading ... too expensive ... a waste of beautiful trees ... cartoonish characters that made me groan out loud."

She pressed a palm to her cheek. "No."

He continued. "This book is slower than a Jane Austen read."

"I happen to like Jane Austen!"

He guffawed before reading the next one. "I'm going to sell this book on eBay, but I already feel sorry for the sucker who buys it from me."

"Ha ... I hope these aren't reviews of one of your books."

He raised one eyebrow.

"Oh, Chris! I'm sorry ... wow, those are bad."

He set down his phone. "Then there are the ones accusing

me of having an agenda, or of writing like an eight-year-old. One guy even said his dog could write a better story."

"That's terrible. How can people be so cruel?"

Christian shrugged. He wore a rueful smile and she suspected that the reviews he carried around with him hurt more than he let on. "I didn't read those to you to shock you—well, maybe a little. But I didn't do it to trivialize what you're going through right now. I wanted to show you that life goes on. People have their opinions, and some can be unkind, but in the end, it's just one person's opinion. For every blogger who decides they don't like something, there are hundreds more who decide they do."

She drew in sea air and started to feel silly. Why had she allowed that blogger to get to her? Surely she could overcome one person's words. If that was the case, then why had she allowed her stepfather's letter to affect her for so long?

"Do you believe me?"

She nodded. "I do, of course, I do. I just wish I were not so fragile."

"Is that what's bothering you?"

"It scares me. How can I be a good businesswoman if I fall apart over every harsh word?"

"The fact that you care so much is refreshing. That's one of the things I first noticed about you, actually."

"When you first noticed me? Do you mean in the airport? When you approached me all stalker-ish?"

"I don't believe stalker-ish is a real word."

"But it conveys my meaning."

He grinned. "One hundred percent it does. But that's my point. Even though I had given you every reason to believe I was a deranged maniac, you apologized to me for mistaking me for—"

"A deranged maniac?"

His laugh came through deep and hearty. She sneaked a look at him. With that beard cut close to his skin like that, and his touchable wheat-colored hair, he could be a model for a designer ad campaign. The scar gave him an edge, in her opinion. Made him slightly less pretty. Dangerous, even.

His eyes held hers and she looked away.

"Do you still think I'm deranged?" A tease laced his voice.

"I do remember apologizing to you. You didn't look like a stalker to me."

"What does a stalker look like, exactly?"

She smiled. "Thankfully, I've never met one, so I can tell you that I was tired after my long flight. Plus, moving brought on so many new emotions. I wasn't sure if I had made the right decision to come here." She turned up her palms and gave him a small shrug. "Can I ask you a question?"

"Anything."

"How did you get the scar?"

His smile faded. She had taken him off-guard. A first for her, for sure. "I'm sorry. Maybe that was too personal."

"There you go apologizing to me again."

She broke the tension with a slight laugh. "I really need to work on my manners, don't I?"

"I'm the one who said you could ask me anything."

"Yes, but it's obvious you'd prefer not to talk about it." She didn't dare tell him that his scar had begun to turn that familiar red, its intensity only serving to pique her curiosity more. "Let's change the subject."

"Not necessary, darlin'." He was smiling at her. "If talking about my past foibles helps to take the focus off of your blogger from the dark side, then I'm a willing sacrifice."

Sophia could not remove the smile from her face. How could he have this effect on her? Her phone rang and she gave it a glance. "I better take this." She flicked a glance at Christian, who peered over her in an apparent attempt to shield her from the sun's glare.

She swung her legs over her lounge chair and sat up. "Hi, Wade." She sensed Christian pulling away and held up a hand to stop him. He was already on his feet, one hand in a pocket, but he slowed his retreat. "How are you?"

"The question is—how are you?" Wade said.

She tucked a strand of hair behind her ear. "I'm fine. Really."

"I know you, Sophia. Don't let this slow you down, all right? Listen, I have some strategies to discuss with you."

"What kind of strategies?"

"We're going to nip this now. Let's call on other bloggers to bury that review. Do a whole blitz. Do you still have the other photos? Have they been edited and optimized?"

"Not yet."

"Okay. I'll contact Liddy and ask her to get them to me ASAP. Can you meet to discuss?"

She slid a glance at Christian who had edged perilously close to his own balcony.

"Sophia? Did you hear me? Let's meet to discuss all of this—I want to help you."

"Th-thank you. I know you do. I can't meet right now, though." She searched her mind for a time that she could stomach hashing through this incident. "But I can see you for breakfast in the morning. Will that work?"

He hesitated and she thought maybe he would decline. Instead, he said, "Sure. See you at eight in the hotel's cafe."

She hung up and stashed her phone on the glass table. "You weren't going to leave without saying goodbye, I hope."

Christian turned, hair flopping forward. She fought back the urge to reach up and smooth it back.

"I've kept you long enough."

Her heart grew heavy in her chest. "I suppose you have a lot of writing to do."

He licked his lips and gave her a brief nod. Yet he did not make any move to hop back over that railing.

Sophia lowered herself back to her lounge chair. "Before you go, will you read more of your rotten reviews?"

He chuckled and whipped out his phone. "It would be my pleasure."

As he began scrolling, Sophia relaxed against her cushioned lounger. She slipped the eye mask back on, and as Christian's husky voice began to speak, she couldn't deny the emergence of a smile on her face ... nor the lift to her heart.

CHAPTER 10

*C*hristian had begun to think he really was deranged. Why else would he drag himself here before he'd had his coffee just to see her with *him*?

Deranged maniac.

Glutton for punishment.

Loser.

All three monikers described him at this moment as he kept his distance from where Wade and Sophia had been seated.

At the restaurant's bar, Christian downed his second cup, trying to ignore the animated way in which Wade spoke to Sophia over their omelets. Not to mention that he'd worn another high-priced suit to the inn—didn't that guy know they were at the *beach*?

Christian's mind burned slowly. He'd been up since early in the morning pounding out words, thankful for the rush of story that had ignited within him again. The mystical being had surfaced around 4 a.m., and from his deck he'd watched her frolicking, her playfulness helping him to conjure the scenes he'd pour out onto every page.

A server named Jenny spun by. "Can I get you anything else? Will you be ordering breakfast?"

He shook his head. Though he'd had a productive night, hunger eluded him. That's when he heard angry words cutting through the restaurant's morning din.

"How could you let me be so stupid!"

"Did you see them together or something?"

"They were talking up on her deck!"

"Oh my gosh—no!"

Christian frowned. He leaned toward the end of the bar, his empty stomach sinking further. A spattering of tables clustered right around the corner from where he sat perched on this stool. Were Jackson and Meg here? And were they talking about ... him?

"It's not funny."

Meg was laughing. "Kidding."

"You should've seen this coming!" Jackson was saying. "He's a guy, Meg, a guy!"

"He's your friend. How could I possibly see anything coming?"

Christian bit back the harsh words that tap danced on his tongue. Couldn't believe it. Hadn't he already told Jackson he had only the best intentions where his sister was concerned? That he would not pursue anything beyond friendship? Did he really think he hadn't learned a thing from his public screw up?

"I'm sorry," Jackson said, presumably to his long-suffering wife. "This isn't your fault—I didn't mean that. I should've thought this through, should've considered that Christian's been a brooding guy for a while and that maybe giving him a room next to my sister ... Well, maybe that wasn't the best idea."

"Honestly, I think you're worrying over nothing."

Sweet Meg to the rescue. Christian barely held his sarcasm at bay.

She continued. "You've told me from the beginning that you think Christian got a bad rap, that he's a good guy that let his emotions get the best of him. If you really had any serious thought of him being trouble, it would've come to your mind when you were booking Sophia's room."

Christian's nerves had gone cold. He slid off his stool and turned the corner where Jackson and Meg were sitting together in a booth.

Jackson looked up but kept his expression in check. He neither smiled nor frowned. "You're here early."

"Been up all night," Christian said. "Writing."

"Of course."

Meg gave him a tentative smile. "Sit with us."

He shook his head. "No need for that. I just wanted to let you know that I'd be checking out as soon as I can pull my things together. Shouldn't be long."

Meg's expression fell.

"Hey, guys!" Liddy pulled up alongside Christian with Beau Junior on her hip. "Did my invitation get lost in the mail or something? Never mind. I forgive you all for having breakfast together without me." She laughed happily at her own joke.

Meg slid over in the booth and reached for the baby. "Let me take him."

Liddy's sigh dripped with drama as she handed over her child to Meg. "Please do. He weighs a ton!" She touched Christian's shoulder. "You doing okay? You seem a little stressed."

No sense in dragging Liddy into this mess. Christian turned toward her as she took a seat in the booth. "Was just letting my friends here know I'd be leaving the inn soon."

"What?" Liddy said. "No way. Where're you going?"

"Haven't decided yet."

"Then stay." She swung her chin energetically from Jackson

to Meg who was bouncing Beau Junior on her lap. "Convince him for me, will you?"

Jackson gave her a pointed look. "Do you two have something up your sleeves?"

Christian cut in with a snort.

Liddy rolled her eyes at Jackson. "Christian, you have no idea how much you helped Sophia yesterday. Or maybe you do, but honestly, I need you to stick around until her ad campaign is done."

Jackson kept his eyes focused on Liddy. "What exactly did Christian do that helped my sister?"

"He made her laugh. I could barely coax a word out of her yesterday, but then all of a sudden she called me last night with this great attitude. Said Christian was responsible."

Jackson looked him over. "Really."

"Oh shoot. I just realized the time." Liddy scooted out of the booth and reached for her son. "I'm supposed to meet Wade and Sophia to talk about our next steps."

"Let me keep him while you meet with them," Meg said.

Liddy eyed her curiously. "You sure? I know he loves his Auntie Megsy, but he might need a diaper change soon."

She hugged him close. "No worries. I bet his poop smells like flowers."

Liddy cracked up. "You've lost it, girl, but whatever. I'm not going to try to change your mind about that one. I'll come for him in a half hour, okay?"

Meg followed her out of the booth, the baby on her hip as if he were her own. She leaned in to give Liddy a hug, her voice raising in pitch as she spoke in tandem to both Liddy and her baby. "Sure thing. You'll find us in my office, won't she? Yes, yes, won't she find us playing in there, Beau-Beau?"

Jackson watched after them, his expression comical until he swung back toward Christian. "Have a seat."

"Gotta go."

He growled. "C'mon, I know you heard us talking about you. Sit down."

This move to the inn was quickly devolving into a reality show, and did he want any part of that? Did he really care what the man had to say? Then again, maybe he needed to say his piece, to state clearly his defense.

Christian dropped into the booth like a stone. Jenny stopped by with a fresh mug. He watched in silence as she filled it to the rim, dropped two half-and-half capsules onto the table, and took off for the next customer.

"How'd you do it, exactly? Make her laugh, I mean."

"I read her my reviews."

"What does that mean, you read her your reviews?"

"That's what I said. I read her some of the worst reviews my books have ever received."

Both of Jackson's brows rose. "And that made her laugh? Man, you play dangerously."

"Those ugly words were good for something. Happy they made her forget about her problems, even if it came at my expense." He knew Jackson had been alluding to more with that "dangerously" comment, but he didn't care to bite.

"That's all it was."

Jackson gave him a succinct nod. "I'm sure. After all, you promised you'd never want for anything more."

"Never said want."

"Semantics."

"Right. Well, if we're done here, I need to get going ..."

"Don't leave."

Christian set his jaw. "Why?"

"Because you apparently make her laugh."

"Apparently."

"I never suggested you can't be her friend."

"I don't get you, man. Two minutes ago you were questioning everything about my presence here at your home away from home."

Jackson looked away, his eyes downcast. "Well, it's been a rough couple of years." He shrugged. "Doesn't matter anyway. Wade and she have been hitting it off. He's a good guy—"

"Right. So conversation over."

"Is your book finished?"

"Working on it."

"So that's a no."

A thought struck him like a fish tail slapping the water. If he were to leave Sea Glass Inn, would his muse follow? He could not, of course, tell anyone else of his concern—they'd think him nuts. But he had found his groove here at the inn, was joyfully close to finishing his first independent novel. Now his residence rested on precarious footing.

Worse, he didn't want to go.

And it had nothing at all to do with his book.

"You know, I thank the good Lord every day for Meg," Jackson said, breaking into Christian's thoughts. "Couldn't have managed all the stress without her."

"She definitely married beneath herself."

Jackson let out a rumbling laugh that reverberated through the dining room.

"Don't check out."

"Why not? Like you said, it doesn't matter anyway. Sophia's ... " He couldn't bring himself to say the words: Sophia's with Wade anyway—or soon to be, by the look of things.

"It's more than that," Jackson said. "If you leave because of my outburst, Meg'll kill me. Or worse. She thinks I'm gruff when I'm tense."

"You are."

Jackson gave him a pointed look, eyes glaring. "Help me

132

prove her wrong. Think of it as research for your next book about a hero that works as a marriage counselor by day and saves the underworld by night."

Christian pursed his lips, weighing Jackson's plot summary. "I don't recommend you quit your day job just yet."

"Fine. But I was serious about the marriage counseling gig."

"Understood. I'll be here until the book is complete." Christian stood. "Which, as your luck would have it, should happen very soon."

A voicemail was waiting for Christian when he returned to his room. He recognized the area code. New York.

"Hello, CJ. This is Lisa Caldwell calling from Median Publishing. I hope you are well. I understand that you and Burns Golden have been chatting about your upcoming release. CJ, regardless of where you are in your conversation with Mr. Golden, I would like the opportunity to talk with you, in person, if I may. Please return my call at your earliest convenience."

A couple of years ago, one well-placed punch took opportunity down and Christian had been licking wounds of his own ever since. He'd done more than nurse his wounds—he'd bound them, watched them heal, then exposed them to daylight again, despite the naysayers. He never expected to hear from his past ever again.

But now that he had, and in light of his current precarious situation, Christian wondered if he should consider letting bygones be bygones.

SOPHIA WAS BEGINNING to think she could pull this off.

"Those numbers are fantastic," Wade said, the hush of wind

and water spiraling between them. "You should be proud—and thrilled. Are you?"

Since the viral post that had moved Sophia's designs into the spotlight, she had been pulled into a whirlwind. Ups, downs, sideways, and up again. Now as she and Wade walked along the beach in front of the inn, she allowed her new reality to settle into her mind. "I-yes. Yes, I believe I am ... thrilled."

Wade took hold of her fingers as a wave careened toward them then sputtered onto land. He laughed as he drew her away from the ripple of water. "You should be!"

She returned his smile, grateful for the water's coolness as it filtered between her toes and the warmth of evening air as it brought on the night. He let her hand go and they walked lazily side by side, her heart and mind as calm as the sea.

"You probably already know this, Sophia, but I am very proud of you, too." Wade beamed as he walked beside her with her sneaking glances as he spoke. "I know this is not what you expected ... to come here and immediately find yourself digging back into your design company. You could have turned away from interest in your designs—but you didn't. And look at you now."

She glanced toward the inn. A lone figure on a balcony stood out among the others. She knew that Christian watched the sea for inspiration, and likely, this was what drew him out here tonight as well. She raised her hand in a wave, but as she did, Christian turned and retreated inside.

Sophia lowered her hand, wrapped her arms around herself, hugging her body. He probably went back inside to write about what he had seen and how it had inspired him.

"How do you feel about the progress on the sale of Sea Castle?" Wade said, snapping her back into the moment.

She returned his gaze. "I will be honest—I haven't had a lot of time to think about it. Jackson has kept me updated with some of the details, but"—she laughed now—"I have not had much brain space available, I'm afraid."

Was that how writers' brains worked as well? Could they handle myriad details while also writing a story from scratch? How did they keep it all straight?

"Think about how the Florida sale will help you," Wade was saying. "The additional dollars will not only help Jackson pay off debts, but you'll have the funds you need to turn your attention to remodeling the inn. Of course, none of this will be possible until after Fashion Week—I know you will be thinking of nothing else until then."

"True."

"Are you sure you won't consider attending yourself?"

"Oh, no. I have Raven for that. She's a pro at Fashion Week, so I will happily leave all of that to her."

He nodded. "Spoken like a true introvert."

"Guilty."

"Nothing to be feeling guilty about." He smiled and reached for her hand again, enveloping it in his. "You know yourself. I respect that."

She allowed him to pull her along on the beach, her hand comfortable in his, a sense of calm warming her. Safety. He was right about the sale of the Florida property too, though a tinge of sadness over the entire ordeal zinged through her. "I still regret that the Sea Castle must be sold, but I can't say that I don't agree with moving forward. It is the right thing to do, especially if I finally begin to see fewer lines on my brother's face."

"I agree. A decision that will affect all of your futures." He reached for her other hand and swiftly gathered her to himself, kissing her lightly on the lips. She did not resist, though she'd been taken by surprise. His voice held a certain breathlessness. "I promise to let you get through Fashion Week before I lose my mind completely over you ... but after that, I want to talk to you more fully about your future, Ms. Agli."

Wade would make the perfect husband. Handsome, caring, smart ... though her body hung heavy with fatigue, and her mind had cramped from an overload of information, Sophia began to grow fond of the idea of Wade Prince—with her.

She nuzzled close to him as the afterglow of the sun disappeared and the temperature of the night began to drop. When they reached the path, they each slipped their flip-flops back on. He then walked her back toward the inn, one hand looped around her shoulder.

"There you are!" Trace said. The concierge ran toward them as they stepped along the winding path that edged the cliff. She held a note in one hand and clutched her heart with the other, her shoulders heaving.

Sophia put an arm around Trace's shoulders. "Are you okay? What's the matter?"

"I've been running all over the grounds looking for you," Trace said. She thrust the note into Sophia's hands.

Must speak to you ASAP - Raven

Sophia looked from the note to Trace, concern gripping her. "Did you talk to her yourself?"

"I sure did. She said it's urgent. You *have* to call her tonight. That's why I ran all over this place looking for you."

Sophia whipped a look at Wade. "I'm sorry. I'd better take this. I hope you understand."

"I do indeed. Duty calls." He walked them to the inn's glass doors and gave Sophia a gentle salute. "I'll give you a raincheck on dinner." Then he kissed her on the cheek and disappeared.

"He's a cutie," Trace said after he'd gone. "Kind of old for you, but I wouldn't pass on him either if it were me he was mooning over."

"Trace!"

The concierge laughed and patted Sophia's arm. "I was going to ask you not to tell the boss, but then it hit me—you kinda are the boss!"

Sophia shook her head, laughter filling her. "Thank you for flagging me down, Trace. I do appreciate it."

"Right-o! Now go and answer that girl. She was *frantic!*"

What could be so urgent that Raven could not wait until tomorrow to call? Sophia furrowed her brow while waiting for the elevator, which seemed to be stopped on the fifth floor. With a quick pivot, she entered the stairwell instead and hurried up to her room.

Inside, she found her phone plugged into its charger. Five missed calls.

"Sophia! Thank God you finally called me back!"

"Is everything okay, Raven? What has happened?"

"I can't believe that I'm having to tell you this, but I cannot attend Fashion Week for you."

Sophia lowered herself to the bed. It was either that, or pick herself up off the floor. "I don't understand. Are you leaving me for another client?"

"Not exactly. It's just—I've landed my dream job. I'm leaving fashion to take a public relations director position with Hayes Hotels."

Sophia couldn't breathe. She sat there, deflated, knowing she should find some way to offer Raven her congratulations— but she *needed* her!

"I don't know what to say, Raven. Of course, I'm thrilled for you, but ... is there any way you could begin your new position after New York?"

"I had hoped to, but the company has an all-week manage-ment meeting scheduled for that same week in Seattle. They specifically hired me now so I could be there for training—I swear I didn't know about it when I was interviewing. Shoot,

Sophia, I thought this job was a long shot for me anyway. Truly."

"I see. Dream job?"

"I'm really sorry, but hey, you love New York, right? Now you can go back in my place."

"Me?"

"Or maybe hire an assistant to go with you? I can probably find somebody in my contact list to assist."

Even as she said it, Sophia knew finding someone at this late date was less than ideal. The strongest candidates were already booked. And those who weren't would be too green to learn what they needed to know in such a short time.

"When do you start?"

"Next week. That means I can give you a whole week's training before I leave. Oh, except that I had planned to take Friday off for a three-day getaway, but that leaves four days!"

Four days to finish last-minute details on her designs ... and learn everything she needed to know about her biggest selling event of the year. She hung up and continued to sink into her bed, longing to yank the soft comforter over her head so she could sulk properly.

Friends don't let friends go down that road ...

Christian's admonishment from the other night, when she'd been allowing herself to sink into the abyss of despair, rose to her mind. Liddy would know what to do. Meg would have some ideas too.

Before she could take action on that enticing comforter, Sophia knew she had better make some phone calls.

∽

"SO THE PLAN is that I'll handle things up until New York, then you two"—Liddy shot her pointer fingers at Sophia and Meg like she'd just pulled them from a holster—"wing it to the City. Have I mentioned how thoroughly jealous I am?"

"Only like a dozen times already," Meg said.

Liddy leaned against the vinyl criss-crossed deck chair, pouting. "You know I'd go in a heartbeat."

"But you don't want to leave the baby. We get it, Liddy. Stop apologizing!" Meg turned to Sophia. "How are you doing with all of this?"

"Well, I'm worried, nervous—a little petrified." Sophia removed her sunglasses and looked at them both. "Oh, but I am so grateful to you both for helping me. Thank you very much."

Meg gave her sister-in-law a side hug. "Wouldn't have it any other way. Plus, I love New York so much. Hopefully there'll be some downtime so we can pop into some of my favorite restaurants. Maybe even a show."

Sophia adjusted the floppy hat she'd worn, trying to hide doubt from her face. She had attended Fashion Week a couple of times, but only for certain shows and never as her own representative. If everything she had heard from Raven was true, they'd be on their feet all day—and curled up in their hotel room beds as soon as they stepped off the showroom floor and out of their heels.

"Tell me where we are with the Instagram photos, Liddy. Have they all been posted?" Sophia asked.

Liddy wrinkled her forehead, her smile comical. "For someone dating a social media wizard, you sure are unworldly. Do you even have a Facebook account?"

"Hold up." Meg leaned toward her sister-in-law, her mouth agape. "You're dating Wade?"

"N-no, it's not—well, we are close friends, but ... who said we are dating?"

Both women looked at Liddy, who sputtered and lifted her hand in surrender. "I didn't come up with this on my own.

Trace said you two looked quite cozy the other evening. Said you'd been on the beach together and that Wade was, uh, getting handsy."

"Oh!" Sophia's face inflamed—she could feel it..

"Sophia, honey, why didn't you tell me that you two had been getting so close?" Meg said. "Wade's a great guy—I just didn't realize how you two had, you know, progressed. Jackson will want to know—can you tell him soon?"

"But it was his idea, wasn't it?" Liddy shot back.

"Jackson, a matchmaker? I love the man, but he can be quite clueless." Meg laughed. "I mean that in the most loving way."

"I don't know," Liddy said. "If I were a betting woman, I'd put my money on little brother being behind this one."

Sophia watched the two women banter, her cheeks no doubt scarlet. She wasn't a prude, but she had always kept her private life private. Growing up with a sister like Gia to undermine her efforts at life and love—and everything in between—she had learned to set boundaries. And still, look at all the upheaval she'd managed to cause.

Perhaps this was the reason she had not mentioned to anyone how fond she was becoming of Wade.

"Wade and I are not officially dating. But if that changes, you two will be the first to know." Even as she said it, his words from the night before ran through her mind. *I promise to let you get through Fashion Week before I lose my mind completely over you* ... "Now," she said, "shall we continue?"

For the rest of their meeting, Liddy and Meg let the matter rest. Even after they'd gone, Sophia lingered by the pool that overlooked the ocean. How had she ever preferred the grittiness of the city to this? Two children—a boy and a girl—each took turns jumping into the pool, climbed back out again, and jumped in again, all the while crying out, "Daddy, Daddy, look at me! Look, Daddy!"

A typical scene that she could never quite remember from her own childhood. Not that her stepfather had ignored her. He helped her with math and stood in the gap when Gia was being a pest. He loved their mother, and though he traveled for work often, she could not remember a time when he hadn't returned home with gifts and stories from his travels to the States.

If only those arrivals home weren't followed by his drinking ... to excess.

"I'm such an idiot," she murmured.

"Come here often?"

Sophia looked up to find Christian watching her.

"Not as often as I'd like." She nodded at a chair. "Please, join me?"

He gave her a half smile and pulled out the chair. "You looked lost in thought," he said when he'd sat down.

"My mind had wandered, yes." She ran a quick search, but couldn't exactly recall what she had been thinking about when Christian interrupted her. "But I'm glad you brought me back to the present. I have so much to prepare for today."

"Really? I thought you were nearly done." One of his eyebrows rose, his eyes watchful, lucid. If he weren't a writer, Christian could be a cover model for some rugged, outdoorsy magazine. She pictured him in the jungle with a machete ...

"Sophia?"

She blinked. "Sorry, sorry. I received some news yesterday. My rep, Raven, abruptly quit."

Both of those brows rose now. "What does that mean for your presence at Fashion Week?"

"It means that I will have to attend."

He nodded. "So you're going home."

She smiled regretfully. "It appears so. Thankfully Liddy has jumped in to help me prepare, and Meg will attend the show with me. I don't know what I would do if they had not agreed to step in."

"I think you'll do great. No one knows your product better than you."

She swallowed back a response that would likely have been negative and forced a smile. Though she believed what he said in theory, the thought of selling the brightly colored dresses caused her to sweat. She fanned herself with a napkin, the effect less than adequate. "Sorry." She gave a brief laugh. "It's awfully hot."

He winked. "I often have that effect on women."

She laughed, embarrassed.

He added, "Of course, they are usually menopausal women, but hey, I'll take what I can get."

Sophia continued to laugh and fan herself. He'd made her forget about her problems, a feat he had accomplished regularly since the moment they had met.

"I want you to know that I'm not stalking you, Sophia."

"Why would I think that?"

"Because I'm going to New York myself. I'll be there the same week as you."

"But you hate the City."

He sat back and chuckled. "Hate is a strong word. I'm just not as *enamored* with New York as some people. You, for example. But, who knows, maybe this time my experience will be different."

For the second time this morning, Sophia sensed her spirit lift. First when Liddy and Meg agreed to step in after Raven's abandonment, and now, inexplicably, from the knowledge that Christian would soon be in New York as well. She folded her arms on the patio table and leaned toward him. "I guarantee it will be different because I'm going to show you around."

"Won't you be somewhat preoccupied?"

"Meg has agreed to be the face of our booth. I'm sure I will have some time to show you why you need to love New York as much as I do."

He gave her a doubtful smile, but said, "I'm willing to give it a shot."

"Good. Now, why will you be in New York?"

"Haven't I already told you?"

She tilted her head to one side. "No, I don't think so. Unless ..."

"Unless?"

"Is it because you are following me there?"

He grinned and leaned onto the table as well until they were nearly nose to nose. "How can I convince you, beautiful Sophia, that I am not the stalker that you think I am?"

She stared back at him. "I would help you out if I weren't so terrible at witty comebacks."

"Oh, I don't know. You've caught me off guard more than once."

"I doubt that—I'm pretty slow."

He frowned and pulled away slightly. "Why do you do that?"

"I don't know what you mean? What do I do?"

"Criticize yourself."

She gave him a laugh and waved him away. "I was kidding, of course."

He rubbed the back of his neck and watched her, his forehead knotted. It unnerved her how he seemed to parse her words, as if reading more into them than what she'd meant. Maybe that's what writers did, though.

"Promise me you'll treat yourself better—you deserve it."

She glanced away, the direction of this conversation uncomfortable. She swung a look back at him. "You never did tell me why you're going to be in New York during Fashion Week."

A smile broke across his face. "Well, that's coincidental, I assure you. Actually, I've agreed to meet with my former publisher about the book I'm working on."

"So is this why you've been to New York before? To meet with your publisher?"

"Exactly."

"Well, then, that's the problem. You don't strike me as a suits and silver type of guy, and I presume that's what you have encountered while there. Right?"

"Well, right, but I'm not sure I should be happy with your assumption. I do know how to wear a suit, I'll have you know, and I am quite comfortable using silverware."

"Quite?"

He slapped his forehead with his palm. "I can't win."

Relief that they had returned to their usual, casual banter filled her. "Be that as it may," she said, unable to stop smiling, "I promise to sneak out and show you some of my favorite places. Promise me you'll keep an open mind?"

He returned her smile. "I promise."

CHAPTER 11

Sophia counted through the layer of black skirts stacked on her bed. She bit her lip. Reached for one more skirt, this one a dusty gray, added it to the top of the pile, thought better of it, and quickly removed it.

"Knock, knock." Meg entered the suite wearing a chocolate-brown suit that fit her petite frame and curves as if an artist had painted it on. "How are you doing? Almost packed?"

"I'm doing my best to keep it simple." She flopped onto the bed. "So much to think about!"

"I hear you. And if you're anything like me, you like options, which makes packing difficult." Meg peered over her shoulder at the stacks of clothing piled up. "Then again, you've pretty much decided on a color scheme—black—so that should make it a little easier. Though, won't it be rather hot for all that ... dark?"

"The summer is stifling, but it's quickly turning. I've already checked. Plus, we will mostly be indoors during the day hours —sorry to tell you that."

"No need to apologize, Sophia. I'm going for you, remember? Now, have you chosen shoes?"

Sophia pressed the back of her hand to her forehead. "Not yet. I haven't been on my feet all day in years, so I need more time to make footwear decisions."

Meg laughed. "I'm guessing slippers wouldn't go over well in the booth."

Sophia gave her a pointed frown.

"Okay, I get it. Just thought I'd ask." She laughed more. "At least I can assure you that these feet of mine have stood on high heels daily for years, so you won't hear any complaining from me. Now, do you need any more help getting our supplies together?"

Sophia pointed at several large boxes. "I don't think so. Despite the sudden flood of interest in my dresses, we are a low-priority company. We will have to somehow get all the samples and racks into the showroom ourselves."

"I've done trade shows for years, so I'm happy to be your lackey." She flexed her bicep like Rosie the Riveter. "I've been working out to prepare."

Relief cascaded through Sophia and sudden tears pricked the back of her eyes. Meg plunked down on the bed and hung an arm around her neck. Though Sophia had grown up alongside a half-sister, she had never had a moment like this. And never was such a long time ...

"I'm with you, girl," Meg said. "We got this—you and me. You'll see."

Sophia nodded, no words forming. Just a deep and abiding gratefulness that both Jackson and Meg had become such integral parts of her life.

"Bless you."

Meg kissed her swiftly on the cheek and stood. "I'm off to

finish my own packing. Is there anything else you need before I go?"

Sophia glanced around. "No, not really. I mean, I feel like I'm forgetting something but can't think of a thing."

"You'll probably feel like that until we're back at the airport and ready to leave New York. Okay, last call before I go ... maybe I should send up dinner for you?"

Christian appeared in the doorway. "Just what I was stopping by to ask."

Meg turned to him. "Great! So you'll drag her out of here for a break and get some food in her?"

He leaned his lanky frame against the doorframe, crossing his arms. "Sure thing."

Sophia waved a hand in the air. "Uh, hello. I'm here too and can speak for myself."

"I'll let you two duke this out," Meg said. She gave Sophia a warm smile and headed out the door.

Christian unfolded his arms and stepped inside, glancing around. "Looks like a bomb went off."

"That's a cliché, and I thought writers were supposed to avoid those."

"Except when they fit ... like a glove," he deadpanned.

She laughed hard for the first time all day. He walked toward her and offered her a hand, which she used to haul herself up.

"Hungry?"

"Famished, but I need to make this quick." Adrenaline had kicked in, burning up calories and creating a hole in her stomach. She hadn't worked this hard and this long without food in ... well, had she ever?

"Okay by me," he said.

They grabbed the elevator down to the restaurant. There was

no host when they entered, so Johnny waved them toward a table by a window. She exhaled some of her stress as the bartender slid two menus onto the table. "What'll you have to drink?"

She looked at Christian blankly.

"After you," he said.

She thought a moment. "Better make it coffee, Johnny."

Christian smiled. "Make that two."

Sophia took a quick peek of the placid sea, feeling her nerves unclenching. She hadn't looked outside of her window, or stepped out onto her deck, all day.

"Are you ready?"

A ripple of worry scurried through her, but she squelched it. "I believe so. We'll see how it goes."

Johnny brought coffee and cream to the table, took their food orders, and left them in the quiet.

"A toast." Christian lifted his mug. "To New York."

"Agreed. And to a few minutes of thinking about something other than New York."

They laughed and clinked and drank their coffees while sitting in relaxed silence, except for blissful moments of small talk. A server delivered their salads—Cobb for her, steak for him—and they settled into more silence as they ate.

"Sophia?" Wade stopped midway between the bar and their table, a quizzical expression on his face. "What are you doing here?"

Unease crept into her shoulders, erasing the relief she had just achieved. Her mind spun. She hadn't made any promise to Wade, so why did she suddenly feel called out—almost as if she were cheating? Or wait... had she said she'd meet him tonight?

"Wade ... we're just having a quick dinner. Will you join us?"

He closed the gap and put his hand on her shoulder. "Did you do the interview already?"

148

Sophia's airway constricted and she put a hand to her chest. "Oh, no."

"You didn't forget, did you?"

Abruptly, she stood. "Oh, no. I did. I forgot all about it." She patted her pocket, searching for her phone. "Maybe it's not too late ... oh, I'm such an idiot."

Wade shook his head. "Calm down. I'm not sure how you could have forgotten—but don't worry. I'll take care of it."

"How will you do that?" The tone of her voice rose.

"I'll make a call. Tell her agent you've been so swamped—" he stole a glance at Christian as he said this—"and see if her blogger can talk with you when you land tomorrow."

"Tell her I'm sorry." Sophia lowered herself back into her seat, stunned. "If only I weren't so stupid ... how could I forget such an important interview?"

Wade held his pointer finger to his lips, and she closed her mouth. He walked away, barreling into the phone, "Hello, Leann! Hey, yes, yes, mixed signals. Absolutely, she can call your office when she lands in New York. I'll remind her twice." He laughed like they were old friends, then hung up the phone and approached their table again.

"Wade, I'm so sorry."

He bent down and kissed her cheek and sent another glance toward Christian. Sophia tried to relax, but a thousand details wrapped themselves around each other in her mind.

"It's handled," he said. "Until next week is over, I'll be in damage control mode. I promise you."

Christian rolled his hand into a fist and pounded it on the table. "Whoa, do you hear yourself?"

Wade gave him a startled look. "Excuse me?"

"Damage control? Like she's a constant screw-up?"

Wade gave him a puzzled smile now, though his chin appeared to have hardened. "What does that mean?"

Sophia shook her head and looked from one to the other. "Christian, no—I don't think Wade meant anything by that."

Christian pinned her with a stare. "You are *not* an idiot, Sophia." He turned his attention on Wade. "She's not stupid, but you stand there and let her talk to herself like that. Didn't even say a thing."

Wade didn't move. "I've never called Sophia anything like that, nor would I ever."

"Right, because she's too busy beating herself up. Instead, you let her—and then show up on your white horse to save the day."

"Christian, please," Sophia said. "What are you saying?"

His eyes zeroed in on her, like spheres. "I'm saying beating yourself up all the time is a bad idea, Sophia. And *this* guy is also a very bad idea."

"The claims you are making are ridiculous," Wade said. "They're baseless. I want nothing but the best for Sophia and her company." He turned to her, his eyes imploring. In them, she saw how much he cared. "You know that, I hope."

She nodded. "Of course, I do. And I'm so thankful to you ... for everything." She frowned at Christian. "What's gotten into you, picking a fight like this? Can you stop that right now?"

"Picking a fight?" He dropped his gaze to the table as if reloading, then shot her another look. "You are a beautiful, kind, and talented woman, Sophia. But you are also your own worst enemy. I know that's a cliché—but I don't care."

"I agree with how you described Sophia—everything except her being her own worst enemy. She made a mistake and I helped her through." Wade's steely glare did not waver. "If you're her friend, why would you see anything wrong with that?"

"You're twisting my words."

Wade placed a hand on Sophia's shoulder and continued to

look at Christian like he'd been out in the sun too long. "I think you'd better go."

Christian's gaze shifted, staying with her. "Is that what you want?"

Sophia pressed her forehead with her hand. She blew out a sigh. "I'm leaving in the morning for the biggest week of my career, and this is all ... too much." She inhaled and squared her shoulders at him. "Yes, I think you'd better go."

Christian stood up from the table, dropped two bills onto its surface, and walked out of the restaurant.

HE ALWAYS BOOKED AN AISLE SEAT, but on this particular afternoon, Christian wished he had secured a spot by the window. He had forgotten about the lengthy circle the pilot would make around the bay before landing. Always reminded him of a game of "psyche." Passengers would sit, cramped and bound to their seats, the airport in view, when—whoosh!—the airplane would pass the coveted airstrip at JFK and fly out over the water, toss a wave to Lady Liberty, and tease its inhabitants with another approach to land. If he were by the window, he could at least pass the time by staring out at the sights, instead of brooding over his confrontation with Sophia—and what's-his-name.

He bypassed baggage claim, pulling his carry-on behind him, and skipped the snaking cab line too, opting instead for Uber. His driver mistook his silence for a desire to know more about Manhattan. Accordingly, he yammered on through Jamaica and Queens and through the tunnel until they finally reached Lower Manhattan. "You stayin' in Midtown?" the guy had said when he'd been offered an address. "Man, that's the best area—in my opinion. The best."

Christian hopped out of the car and shut the door behind him before the driver could point out one more must-see venue. A bellman took his name and his bag, and within minutes, he was checked in to a room with a view of Rockefeller Center.

He checked his phone. A voicemail from Lisa and a missed call from Burns. He blew out a breath. It was Friday and he'd agreed to meet Lisa over the weekend because she'd be leaving on vacation soon. But Burns had no part in his plans. Wasn't invited nor was he kept abreast of Christian's travel details. He'd made Lisa promise him that.

"Welcome to New York, Christian. This is Lisa Caldwell. I trust you have arrived and are enjoying the sites of our impressive city. I would like to meet you tomorrow for coffee. I'll take a train into Manhattan and meet you at Espresso Hub on 38th at 11:30 a.m. sharp. Looking forward to it, Christian. Goodbye."

He tossed his phone onto the bed, grateful she hadn't wanted to meet tonight. He needed a shower and a decent night's sleep before he could find the temperament to converse like a professional. The street below his window teemed with people—tourists, laborers, executives—all going somewhere. Maybe even buyers and designers strolling around in couture as they readied themselves for another iconic week of fashion.

Christian stood at the window a moment longer, ran his hand along his beard, and let out a low growl. No matter that his brain was a befuddled mess after that confrontation with Sophia—or that he'd come all this way to meet with Lisa Caldwell—Christian had a book to finish. With some reluctance, he pulled his laptop from his bag, set it up on the hotel room desk, switched on the light, and got back to work.

SOPHIA'S HOTEL sat midway between Central Park and Times Square, her room on the forty-fourth floor offering her a glimpse of the gaudy lights of the latter—even in the morning. Her phone buzzed.

Ready to set up? I'll call a cab.

She answered: *Call one with a big trunk!*

Though they'd stayed up late in Sophia's room watching a rom-com and eating far too much mini-bar chocolate, Meg had insisted on booking—and paying for—her own room. They each needed their beauty sleep, she'd reasoned.

Considering Meg had fallen asleep twice during the movie, while Sophia had watched every minute with eyes wide open, she knew which one of them would be needing a second coat of foundation today.

She slipped into a pair of Adidas and waited for the bellman to arrive with two carts to help her haul the boxes downstairs. Two bellmen loaded the cab with boxes.

"Wish we could take those two with us," Sophia said.

Meg looked out the back window. "Oh, honey, I think they're too young for you."

Sophia laughed, thankful for the break in tension. An impressive wall of windows greeted them as their driver pulled over to the unloading area. Her lungs constricted and Sophia gasped for air, one hand on her chest and the other on the seat back in front of her.

Meg had already exited the vehicle, but ducked her head back inside "What's wrong? Are you okay?"

She didn't answer, instead reminding herself to breathe. After prying her fingers from the seat back, Sophia pushed herself out the door. "I'm fine—I'll be all right."

Meg stuck an arm through hers. "Of course you will be! Let's get in there."

For the next few minutes, they worked quickly to unpack a

couple of dollies and load up their boxes. More than once Sophia sensed her knees buckling at the amount of money those plain cardboard boxes held. The samples alone had cost her, but if sales would be a fraction of what Raven had predicted, she'd more than make back the money she'd laid out. More than that, she would make enough to help her brother out of the red.

As expected, Sophia's label was assigned a plain white table in a plain white corner. Even though she was not situated near the bank of windows that overlooked a magnificent skyline, she could see it from afar. That was good enough for her. For now, anyway.

For the next two hours, she and Meg worked quietly along-side each other. Representatives from other brands had begun to dribble in, most with severe faces, walking at fast clips, their arms laden with supplies.

"Isn't this great?" Meg turned side to side to point out what she wore.

Sophia tried not to laugh at the hot pink tool belt her sister-in-law had strapped on. She bit her lip.

Meg put her hands on her hips. "What?"

"It's just that I don't often include that type of accessory with my designs."

"It's a gift from my dreamboat."

Sophia snickered.

"Hey, look over there."

Along the bank of windows where lengths of white tables were positioned end to end, where women and men hustled to display their wares in the best light and layout possible, stood a lone mannequin.

"Doesn't it look like she's wearing a halo?"

Sophia turned her head, eyeing it like an art critic.

"Well, she certainly does look angelic over there. When I

was a little girl, I always loved to walk along the street and look in the windows at the mannequins all dressed up."

Meg stepped up next to her. "Where I'm from, you have to go to an indoor mall to find much of that, but I know what you mean." She threw an arm over Sophia. "Florence had windows I could have stood in front of for hours. Swoon-worthy."

Sophia smiled. "I had forgotten about your time there. Would be wonderful for us all to go back and visit together sometime."

"Oh and to see Domenic and Elena!"

The dear, sweet people who had been instrumental in helping her find her family again ... Sophia exhaled, trying to refocus on the work in front of her. She thumbed through her dresses and took another glance at the line sheets she had prepared with specifications for her garments. The space was basic but clean and colorful. The colors of her dresses alone—raspberry, blueberry, kiwi, and lemon—had changed the feel of her collection from last spring to now, and a fresh lift washed over her. The memory of her stepfather's note had dimmed the more she toiled over this collection the last few months, giving her a sweet sense of renewal and hope. She blinked away tears of relief.

"If you don't mind," she said to Meg, "I'd like to take a walk and get my bearings. Are you okay here?"

"Absolutely. Enjoy yourself."

She began to wind through the crowded showroom, dodging an influx of people and garments and rolling racks. Creative energy buoyed her steps. Within the walls sales-minded people with an appreciation for great design moved swiftly, earbuds attached to phones, mouths moving. She'd been fearful to come here, not sure what to expect having always relied on Raven to face her buyers. But something worthy and wonderful swelled inside of her as she took in the variety of garments and leather bags and shoes—oh the beautiful shoes!—that lined the walls and hung on racks.

Sophia moved through the building sure of one thing: She was ready. She smiled a greeting here, offered a nod there, as she made her way back to her section of the showroom.

As she turned a corner, a flicker of something caught her eye. She looked again, more closely this time, the sight familiar —yet not the same. The mannequin with the halo was no longer wearing her birthday suit. Sophia's heartbeat began to accelerate and she changed directions. She no longer moved toward her own space, but instead, she headed for the dress-wearing mannequin. Steps away now, sweat sprang through her pores as if she had contracted a sudden illness.

Sophia now stood toe-to-toe with the mannequin that wore a dress so similar to her own design—she could have sworn she had created it herself.

SOPHIA FOUND a spot away from the crowd in the corner stairwell. She holed up there to think things out, but instead, she was thirteen again, in her room, piecing together a satin blouse from a pattern she'd created on her own.

Her stepfather opened her bedroom door and stuck his head in. "You up here all alone again?"

"Yes, Papa."

"C'mon down. Sun's out, and you should be too."

She had turned around to see his face. She'd know if he were earnest just by looking at him.

Eyes bloodshot.

Mouth hanging open.

That wide crevice that developed between his eyes whenever he was cross.

Nothing earnest about him tonight.

"Better yet," he said, "you run on downstairs and help your mother with the dishes, you hear?" He drew out every utterance of the letter "s" a beat longer than was normal ...

THE SHOWROOM STAIRWELL door swung open with a bang, pulling her out of the memory. A couple of set-up guys grunted in her direction, bounding around her to the next floor. Their footfalls reverberated through the stairwell.

Tension shot through her back and she dialed up Wade.

"Sophia! How is the showroom? Are you all set up?"

"Not exactly." She explained what she'd encountered—a dress so much like hers, like the one she wore in the photo. "I'm not sure how to handle this, Wade. I'm not prepared ... I never considered that someone would do this. The showroom opens in a couple of hours. What should I do?"

"Hmm. This is quite typical. There are snakes in every garden. I'll put a call in to Liddy so she and I can brainstorm over how to fix this."

She bit her lip and tucked a wayward strand of hair behind her ear. "You think that will work? What else can I do?"

"Move on. After this show, people will have moved on anyway and you'll be able to start fresh on a new ad campaign for your next line."

But she didn't want to move on yet. She'd worked hard on *this* line and something inside of her wanted to defend it.

"It's business, Sophia. And this kind of thing happens all the time. Next time we'll be more prepared for this type of thing. Maybe we'll embed something hidden in your clothing, something no one knows about. You'll see."

"Yes, okay. That sounds like a ... like a good idea."

"Feel better?"

"A little."

"I thought so. I'll get on damage control over here—will ramp up your presence over the next few hours. You'll get through this, Sophia. Trust me."

She wanted to trust him, but how could she when she didn't quite trust herself?

hristian held the wet razor in front of his face. The man eyeing him warily in the mirror was still somewhat of a stranger, though in the past year or so they had become better acquainted.

He puffed out his bearded cheeks then released his breath. His father used to lather his face on Friday evenings before he escorted his mother out on their weekly date night. Always thought that rather formal, but as Christian spread old-fashioned shaving cream over his newly trimmed beard—he'd trimmed it first so it would be simpler to shave all the way off —he realized that his father had been on to something. *So chivalrous, you are!* His mother had always said that when his father would emerge from the bathroom, his skin as soft as a baby's behind. He smiled at the memory.

His phone rang. *Jackson.*

Not the most convenient time, but whatever. "Hey," he said when he picked up, careful not to smear his phone with too much shaving cream.

"You're in New York?"

Christian hesitated. "I'm here for a meeting, yes."

"A meeting. Right."

He ran the razor under the flow of water and tapped it on the edge of the sink. "Didn't realize I needed to inform you of my plans."

"When they involve my sister, I suggest you do."

"I'll remember that."

"Are you kidding me? You expect me to believe that you happen to be in New York—during Fashion Week—and it has nothing to do with Sophia being there too? Johnny said you and she were toasting to the trip!"

Christian sighed, exasperated. Spies everywhere. "Hey, yeah, I know it sounds strange, but you don't know what I've been up against with my book lately. My old publisher called for a meeting, so I decided to come out here and deal with a situation before life got more complicated."

"I know all about complicated." Jackson swore. "You promised, man."

He heard the pain in his friend's voice, a distinct sadness mixed with frustration. Christian hated to be a part of it, yet also knew that his motives where Sophia was concerned were pure. Even from the beginning. "It was coincidental."

"Right. Listen, I told you ... Sophia's been through a lot. We all have. Leave her alone."

"I haven't seen her ... and I don't plan to." He didn't mention that he and Sophia weren't exactly on the best terms right now anyway. Not after she'd chewed him out for deigning to tell her not to criticize herself so much.

"One more thing. I think it would be best if you moved out of the inn. I hope you understand."

Christian nodded and a dollop of shaving cream dropped onto the counter. After his infamous and very public dust up, the media had painted him as a volatile, tortured artist. It was

160

all baloney, but journalists—at least those who followed him around in the days following the incident—didn't care. B.S. sold.

But Christian had believed Jackson when he'd said he knew that everything had been blown up out of realistic proportion. He thought Jackson had seen through the haze of half-truths and rumor, but apparently, he was mistaken.

Christian forced himself to hold still. "I couldn't agree more. Now, if you'll excuse me, I was in the middle of something."

Jackson was saying something when Christian hung up the phone. He stared a beat more at his white lathered face in the mirror. He looked ridiculous. Like an angry Santa Claus.

He grabbed a clean washcloth from the counter, soaked it in hot water, and scrubbed every square inch of the shaving cream from his whiskers. He had changed his mind.

LISA CALDWELL REMINDED Christian of myriad older women who had worked in the attendance office at his high school way back when. Her silvery hair was short and wavy, her face powdered in white, her lipstick a shade brighter than what a much younger woman likely would have chosen. And like those women he remembered, she spoke her mind.

She fanned herself with a Playbill and talked nonstop about the humidity at this time of year. "I had purposely chosen this particular coffeehouse for its air conditioning, but it has woefully disappointed me," she was saying.

They sat in white leather-look chairs that swiveled to take advantage of both the view of the coffeehouse's modern aesthetic and the sight of a bustling West Village through the windows. Regardless of the existence of AC, the soaring open ceilings and manufactured cool air were no match for the last vestiges of summer.

"The lobby of my hotel is small," Christian said, "but I believe the temperature is much better. It's about a five-minute walk. Would you like to go there?"

She flashed him a frown, her gold-rimmed glasses slipping down her nose. "Heavens, no. Five minutes in that humidity and I will be reduced to a puddle."

He took another sip of his coffee, tempted to ask the barista for a couple of cubes of ice—something he had always regarded as sacrilege. They had been talking pleasantries for a half hour or so already—travel, coffee, the weather—so that Christian began to believe this meeting had been a big waste of time. Originally he was supposed to have met her at the publishing house's headquarters. He expected sweet talk and pressure, but now, he wasn't sure of anything.

"Let me cut to the chase," Lisa said, finally. "Median Publishing would like to make you an offer on your new novel."

"The same book you passed on last year."

Her eyes flashed. "I'm aware. You realize, of course, that it was *your* actions that caused the pub board to pass on your last project initially."

The blame game. He wasn't falling for it.

"May I continue?"

He nodded. "Please."

She pulled a contract from her bag and laid it on the round table between them. "Here is the offer in writing. We, of course, will have to include Burns in this as he is the one who initially brought you to my attention."

The swig of coffee in Christian's mouth turned bitter.

"This includes a healthy raise in your advance and royalty percentages," she continued, "for which I'm sure you will be pleased. The language in the contract is standard, except for the clause about behavior." She paused to flash him a look above her glasses. "The pub board has added some specific language as it relates to you, my dear."

Lisa really did remind him of those women who kept teens in line during high school.

"Now." She stood the pages on end and gave them a good stack on the table. "Take a look. If you sign today, I have been authorized to offer you a bonus—something self-publishing could never offer you."

He downed the last of his coffee. If he were to take this offer, he could relax a little, not worry about his next steps, but focus solely on writing instead—at least in theory. He knew that the publishing house would certainly make demands on his time outside of the actual writing of the book, though it would be helpful to him to have their team supporting his efforts.

But her comment about the addition to his contract also meant reopening the sins of his past. How would they handle the probable pushback from the most esteemed reviewer of his genre? Did they have a specific restitution in mind? He glanced at the pages, the clause about his "behavior" tempting him to read through the entire document at this moment without stopping.

"Of course, you will have to rethink the whole mermaid angle. Mermaids are out, my friend." She picked up that Playbill again and began whipping it closer to her face. "Witches are still in, though. We'll have one of our editors take a look at that aspect and advise you accordingly."

A trickle of sweat broke out on Christian's forehead. He took the stack of papers and slid them into his satchel. "I'll look this over and get back to you."

"Burns Golden has already publicly announced your

project. Unless he is publishing it himself, I think you'll want to have a reputable publishing house to back you."

"As I said, I will take some time to ... consider your offer."

"It expires at midnight."

Christian forced himself not to roll his eyes, her Cinderella-esque routine annoying. He stood and offered her his hand. "I have your number. It was a pleasure."

Lisa stood as well, her expression unreadable. She took his hand, pumped it once, then walked out quickly ahead of him. Christian considered his options. He sat back down to review the contract while in his current frame of mind when a familiar figure hurried past the coffeehouse windows.

Sophia.

He slumped in his chair, though it took every ounce of willpower for him to do that. Every nerve ending screamed for him to run outside and stop her.

But she wasn't speaking to him—and he was still angry about it.

Wasn't he?

And he'd made a promise to Jackson.

Then again, had he? He'd said he had no plans to see Sophia while in the city, and given the unlikelihood of running into her in a place of this size ...

"Christian?"

Her eyes were red, the skin beneath them swollen, yet no tears. Her expression reminded him of a wild animal, both broken and fierce—like she might slay the next giant that stepped onto her path.

"Fancy running into you here."

"Not in the mood, Chris." She spun around and headed back out into the humid city.

He rolled his eyes and went after her, against his better judgment. But though her body language screamed furious, she had shortened his name—something she'd done on her own and only in their most heartfelt, intimate moments. He couldn't let her just leave.

Christian caught up to her, grabbed her by the hand, and gently tugged her back toward him. Inches apart now, he tucked a strand of hair behind her ear, his thumb a light touch on her cheek. Her eyes shone. "What's happened?"

"I'm not speaking to you. And no jokes!"

Slowly, he let her go and jammed his hands into his pockets. "We really going to stay angry with each other?"

Her eyes flashed. "We were having a perfectly nice dinner when you had to pick a fight with Wade. What do *you* have to be angry with?"

"You gave him the last slider."

She grunted into the sky and turned her back to him. "I have to get out of here."

He watched the rise and fall of her shoulders but said nothing. Nor did she go anywhere. They stood as a clump on that sidewalk, people filing past them at dizzying speed, her back still to him. When she didn't make a move to leave, he guided her around to him.

The tears then began their tumble. "I'm an idiot."

He shook his head. "Tell me what happened but without the name calling." A flash of something skittered across her face. Anger? Frustration?

Her eyes closed now and she tucked her chin low. She was working hard to keep her emotions in check, it appeared.

He lifted her chin with his forefinger and she flicked away a sprinkle of tears with the back of her hand. Her eyes snapped open, wide and clear. "You're here."

"I am."

"Why?"

"Had a meeting, but we're talking about you right now, though. Tell me what has you so upset."

"Someone has stolen my design. They are not doing anything to hide it—it's out in the open on a mannequin!"

The words came at him like she'd sprayed them with a firefighter's hose. The Sophia he knew was quiet, almost shy. Enjoyed a nice laugh, though even her spontaneous ones had a gentle finish. This Sophia had fire—and he rather liked it. No, to be honest, he loved seeing this passion coming from her—though not the reason behind it.

Her brows plunged. "What're you staring at?"

He held her hands, not only to calm her, but to keep himself from getting pummeled. "I'm, well, I'm shocked for you, Sophia. Disappointed. Sad." He wracked his brains for more adjectives that described how he felt. For a writer, his vocabulary was seriously sucking right now. But she, on the other hand, with her set chin and red lips, was decidedly enticing. He hated his own guts right now.

Her eyes implored him. "I-I don't know what to do."

"What did Meg say?"

"She—I haven't told her."

"Then ... where is she?"

"I left her there. I was just so ... so shocked that I ran out. Then I called Wade."

Christian kept his expression bland. "What could he do?"

"Oh, he's going to try to fix it, he said, by increasing our social media presence." She shrugged, as if she didn't have a lot of hope.

"Then I ran again."

Right into him. In a city of more than eight million people, Sophia Agli Riley ran out of a designer's showroom—even after calling what's-his-name—and into his arms. Something poetic about that ... though he'd have to keep that to himself.

She let out a sob.

Had he lost his mind? This wasn't about poetry, nor about the calling of his own heart. It wasn't about this mystical, magical moment that impossibly brought their two souls together.

This was about Sophia's livelihood, the resurgence of a calling lost in the muddle of the past year's struggles—and he wasn't about to let her give up now.

"You're too much of a fighter to give up now, Sophia. Let's go back."

"That's where you're wrong. I'm not a fighter. Just the opposite." She sniffled, her cheeks blotched and beautiful. "I sew and I design because I've spent so many years hiding from the things I could not change. That dress ..."

He waited, listening.

She huffed a breath. "That dress caused me a mess of problems. I should have thrown it away years ago."

"But you kept it for some reason. Why?"

She looked away.

"C'mon, it can't be that bad."

She swung her gaze back to him, offering only a slight shrug. "Because it reminded me of both the best time in my life —and one of the worst."

It wasn't what he had expected her to say. He didn't know what he expected—he'd really only wanted her to open up. Now he longed to know more, to understand the story behind her words, to know, in essence, *her*.

And if he were to be unequivocally honest, she had shaken him. Could he want to be reminded of both the best times and the worst in his life, even if they were one in the same?

"Sophia, you may not realize this now, but you are stronger than you think. You don't need anyone else to fix this for you. I have every confidence that you, and your sidekick, will figure out a way to woo people over to your booth." He paused and offered her his arm. "Let me walk you back."

Though the expression on her face told him she was still miles away, Sophia hooked her hand into the crook of his arm. They walked on silently through the summer heat, navigating the throng and the occasional stench emanating from below the city streets. As they approached the showroom, they passed a public trash can.

Christian carefully extricated his arm from hers. "Wait here a second." He jogged back several paces, wiped the sweat from his forehead with the back of his hand, and tossed the contract Lisa had given him into the garbage. He exhaled a relief-filled sigh and rejoined her. "Ready to go?"

Sophia snapped a look up at him, a new resolve—absent a smile—on her face. "Ready."

~

"BADGES?"

Sophia lifted hers for the guard's inspection. "He's with me," she added.

The security guard stationed at the entrance held firm. "No one gets in without a badge."

"But he's here to help me with my booth. I'm sorry. I don't have a badge for him."

The guard shook his head

Christian said, "Go in and find Meg. I am confident that when you two put your heads together, you'll figure out what to do—even if that's nothing at all." He pulled out his phone. "I know you're not sure yet if you're speaking to me, but I'm sending you my hotel information right now anyway. Call me later."

He was right. She wasn't speaking to him yet, exactly.

Though she could not deny the thought that running into him on a crowded sidewalk in the City had to have been some kind of divine setup. He was right in another respect too—this was not his battle to fight. She, with Meg's help, needed to huddle together and think this new development through.

Sophia stepped back inside and into the maze. The bustle of people had grown into a throng. She realized that getting out into the fresh, though humid, air had helped her step back in here with new perspective. Maybe ... maybe the discovery was for the best. At least she knew what she was up against. It was just a dress, she reminded herself. She had buried it once, along with a memory that should have stayed covered, so perhaps this moment in time would serve as its last hurrah. The simple, colorful dress that had drawn her stepfather's ire for reasons she would never know had now been knocked off. So, in a way, it could no longer be attached to her, like a weight that continually dragged her down.

Sophia turned the corner, fully expecting a heavy weight to drift from her shoulders when she again took in the view of what, for all intents and purposes, was her dress—in someone else's display.

Of course the very first person she saw when she stepped into view of the offending display was Meg. Fuming mad Meg.

"Where've you been?"

She cringed. She had made her sister-in-law angry and inwardly started to curse herself for the way she'd run off without telling a soul, but then she heard Christian's voice in her head. *"Don't talk to yourself that way, Sophia!"* So, instead, she simply said, "I needed a walk. I'm sorry I upset you."

Meg pressed her lips together in a sort of frown. "You didn't upset me. I knew you had gone for a walk."

"Oh. Then why the fury toward me now?"

Meg stole a look behind herself and then grabbed her by

the arm, pulling her close enough that she could hiss in her ear. "I think someone has copied your design. I'm so sorry."

"I know."

"What? You know? How ...?"

"I saw it when I was leaving for my walk."

"And you didn't come right over and tell me? Sophia! We need to strategize about this."

Sophia exhaled and rolled her shoulders. "I don't know what we can do. It's difficult to prove that something's been knocked off. They only need to make three differences in their design to make it their own—in a court's eyes, anyway—and those could be simple things."

Meg blinked her eyes several times, her nearly black eyelashes beginning to shimmer. "I hate this."

"Doors will be opening to buyers in an hour. There is nothing more we can do."

Meg straightened, an almost-sinister glint to her eyes. "Oh yes, there is!"

"You're scaring me ... a little."

Her sister-in-law grabbed her by the arm and pushed her toward the space they had set up with all of their samples. Meg thumbed through the rack of dresses and plucked out the raspberry dress.

Sophia shook her head. "No, no, that doesn't go there. Remember? That's the original dress, not one of the samples." She laughed ruefully. "Nobody wants that."

Meg held the dress's hanger by the crook of her forefinger, her elbow jabbed into her hip. "Are you kidding me? Nobody wants the dress that you were wearing when your picture went *viral*?"

"But you don't understand. I made some modern updates to the stitching, and also to the bows on the back ..."

"Put it on."

Sophia tilted her head. "Excuse me?"

Meg swung the dress in front of her. "You will wear it. You're the one who was in the picture ... so you're going to wear it like you did that day—and wow those buyers."

"I'm not a model, Meg."

"You are today. We will have our own mini-runway." She thrust the dress at her. "Do it."

Though Sophia sensed her lungs closing up as rapidly as the time ticked away, she obediently grabbed the hanger carrying her years-old dress and headed for a nearby restroom.

SOPHIA SLIPPED out of the restroom, bloodied and raw. Figuratively speaking, that is. When had her creative outlet turned into such a cloak-and-dagger affair? Into something that had begun to cause her daily worry instead of a shower of blessings?

Still, Meg's call was brilliant and Sophia had taken it a step further by upsweeping her hair in a similar fashion to the way she'd done it in the picture. Rare for her, but she had been told in the past that an updo reminded people—and the wearer—of times past.

"Perfect," Meg said when she'd re-entered the showroom. "If this fashion design gig doesn't work, you could turn to modeling."

"Hush!"

Meg laughed. "I'm serious, except you'd probably have to wear heels since you're just under the mega-height requirement."

"Please."

Meg's face lit up, and Sophia realized she was looking past her. "Welcome," she was saying.

The woman looked Sophia up and down. "Spin around," she said, making a circle with her pointer finger. "Hmm."

Meg motioned the woman to come closer to the rack of samples. "The dress Sophia is wearing is the prototype. Here you'll find new and modern twists, as well as a variety of colors to choose from."

"They are lovely," she said.

Meg continued. "These dresses have a past, really they do. My sister-in-law designed them all. She grew up in Italy, you know."

"No, I had no idea."

"Oh, yes. You could say that these dresses were inspired by the Italian countryside ..."

"In summer," the woman added, with a laugh.

"Absolutely. Quite hot in the summer."

"Oh, don't I know it!"

"Sophia toiled away in her small studio. Her mother and an Italian neighbor taught her to sew when she was quite young. Years later, the family moved back to America, the land of Sophia's birth—and that is where she found her success."

"A true American success story!"

"Yes, truly. Dresses made right here in New York, on American soil!"

The woman slapped her leather folio onto the counter. "I'd like to place an order. I have six stores to fill."

Sophia stood speechless as Meg deftly handled the woman's orders, chatting like they were longtime friends. She did the same thing many times over, each buyer leaving with a new friend in her sister-in-law. Meg never stopped moving and talking, admittedly embellishing Sophia's upbringing here and there to the point that Sophia herself felt homesick.

The visits from hungry buyers made her dizzy. So many questions!

"Can I touch the fabric you're wearing?"

"Do you have all sizes?"

"What is the fabric made of? Is it a blend?"

When the last buyer had left and the din in the showroom had dimmed to a whisper, the enormity of it all—the viral post, the sudden and lavish interest in her designs, the last-minute scrambling after Raven's departure—all of it began bearing down on her until she could no longer stand.

Meg frowned at her. "Sit down, Sophia. Here." She reached beneath the table and handed her a bottle. "Have some water. You look like you're not feeling well."

Sophia downed the water like a woman who had just traversed the desert. "I'm feeling great. Overwhelmed. Happy ... but exhausted."

Standing next to her, Meg bent to give her a side hug. "Aw, my beautiful, sweet, introverted sister-in-law. I read once that extroverts gain energy from interaction with people. While introverts—"

"Not so much," Sophia cut in, laughing. When her laughter had died down, she said, "I owe you so much, Meg. Thank you."

Meg squatted to her side and put her hands on Sophia's shoulders. Her eyes glistened. "I'm so, so incredibly proud of you. And ... and I'm forever grateful to have found you."

Sophia blinked away her own tears. "Now you've got me started!"

Meg smacked a kiss on her cheek. "Let's get this place cleaned up. I'm ready for a nap."

"Okay, and then we'll do dinner. My treat—of course."

Meg touched her hand to Sophia's cheek. "If you don't mind, all I really want to do tonight is get into my jammies and slip under the sheets."

"You sure?"

Her sister-in-law nodded. "Don't worry about me. After a good night's sleep, I'll be all ready to tackle this again."

Sophia threw her head back and gasped, more laughter spilling from her. "Oh, that's right—tomorrow. We're coming back here again tomorrow."

CHAPTER 13

*C*hristian considered the purple of twilight that fell across the sky. He'd been standing at his eighth-floor window for several minutes, his mind skipping from topic to topic. He had a book to finish. A home to find. And an ex-publisher to inform about his decision regarding her offer.

Yet his mind continued to land on the same question: Had Sophia dealt handily with the offending brand at the showroom?

Something told him that, once she learned of the issue, Meg wouldn't let Sophia sweep it under the sales rack, so to speak. He hadn't known Jackson's wife too long, but from what he'd observed, she was no shrinking violet.

Not that Sophia was either, but she had a gentleness about her that made him thankful for Meg's solidarity with her at the booth. Sophia could not have survived her odd upbringing or lighted a candle this bright for herself if she had been overly timid. Yet, like him, she had found solace in hours upon hours of creating her art while alone, with only the thoughts of her mind as distraction.

A ding from his phone announced an incoming text.

Hello CJ! Britt Jones here from Fifth Avenue Books. I heard you are in town and wondered if you'd like to stop by the store and sign some stock. Hope you don't mind the text, but you are welcome to come in anytime. I hope you do! Thanks!

"That was ... unexpected," he said aloud.

His phone rang in his hand, startling him. Lisa Caldwell's name flashed on the screen and he pressed the answer button.

"This is Christian."

"Hello, it's Lisa Caldwell calling."

"It's not midnight yet."

She laughed roughly. "I'm not twenty anymore, Christian. Beauty sleep is calling. Have you made your decision?"

A picture sprang to his mind of watching the pages of that contract fall into a city garbage can. Seemed like days ago, his mind focused fully elsewhere ever since he'd made his decision.

"As a matter of fact, I have."

"Fabulous."

"I thank you for the offer, Lisa, but I have decided not to accept it."

She paused before answering. "I see."

"I will also be informing Burns that my project will be independently published, as I have previously stated. I expect you will be seeing a retraction post soon."

She laughed uproariously at this.

"You have something to add?"

"I thought you were kidding."

"Far from it, Lisa. Your offer was generous, and I thank you for it, but I meant it when I said that I will not be publishing my book with your company."

"Oh, I know that. That's what I'd hoped you'd say."

"It is?"

"Christian, we can't give you what you want. That story ... well, it's gutsy, and that's not something I, as your editor, can support. But as your fan... I fully believe in it."

He paused. "I'm surprised to hear you say that. You pressed me pretty hard."

"Yes, well, I'm good at my job. Off the record, though, I'm proud of you. Go blaze your trail."

He rubbed the back of his neck. "Much appreciated."

"But don't expect Burns to back down nicely." She cackled again. "It's going to take some doing to pry his boot off of your rear end. I'll be watching it happen from afar, though. Mark my words."

He laughed now—whether from the imagery she'd created or the relief at closing this door, he wasn't sure. After they'd hung up, he wandered back over to the picture window that provided a view of the Empire State Building. The purple evening deepened into an inky sky, and tonight the powers that flipped the tower's nightly light switch had decided on the color blue. Rich, cascading blue. The colors of that tower changed regularly, always a surprise to him. Sophia probably knew the meaning behind the color key, if there was one.

His desire to discover how Sophia fared continued to gnaw at him. He hated to admit this, but he hoped she would call him. He had received zero promise from her that she would, though, and now the walls around him had begun to close in.

The growing gap in his belly reminded him to eat. He could wander the streets of the city that never slept or call room service, but the latter would mean staying in this suddenly oppressive room. Neither of those options cheered him much. Agitated, he ran his hand across his face, startled. He'd meant to shave that off. Whatever.

He checked his phone again, but a rapid knock on his door caught his attention. Early for turndown service ...

He threw open the door and blinked. "Sophia?"

She stood on the threshold, breathless, flushed, beautiful. Her long hair upswept, lips berry-red, and a dress that followed each and every curve with perfection.

"I-I ..." She struggled to get words out, as if she had run all the way up the stairs to the fourth floor. "I wanted to tell you what happened."

He opened the door wider now and ushered her in, the sweet and citrusy scent of her perfume trailing behind her, that eerie oppression lifting and quickly being replaced with something heady and altogether ... different.

SHE DIDN'T KNOW why she had come, other than a pulsating desire to tell Christian ... everything. She stopped and whirled around. "This is your room?"

He nodded, a quizzical look on his face. "It is."

She turned away and took in the view of the Empire State Building from his corner suite. It blushed in the color of blue, mesmerizing her. The tower lights had been around since she was a little girl, although not as many variations existed back then. Whenever they were in New York, her stepfather would ask her and Gia to guess what color the building would be that night and he would look up their answers in the newspaper to see who won.

She stared at the iconic building, marveling at its strength and resilience, until she felt Christian's breath on her shoulder.

"I'm glad you're here," he whispered.

She steadied herself with a breath of her own and curled a

gaze over her shoulder. Oh, he was tall. "Thank you. Um, you gave me your hotel info and I thought, well, I thought I'd come here and tell you what happened. You know, since we ran into each other earlier."

"Would you like to sit down? Are you hungry? I could order us some dinner."

She was famished. Had not eaten a morsel all day, even though a tray of something yummy had passed her by several times that afternoon.

She shook her head no, though, her head too scrambled at the moment to think about food. She took a seat in one of the two brown leather-like chairs placed strategically near the corner windows. Though the room screamed upscale, this was still New York and space came at a premium. He may have the semblance of a high-end parlor overlooking the Empire State Building, but his bed took up the rest of the square footage and Sophia realized she had unwittingly stepped into his private space without an invitation.

She looked up at him. "On second thought, perhaps we should go out."

He took the chair across from her. "Tell me your news first."

She tried to control her smile, but it had a mind of its own. "My sister-in-law is brilliant! She talked me into putting on this dress. I didn't want to, but she insisted."

He leaned forward, arms on his knees, watching her intently.

"When I got back to the showroom, Meg had the idea that I should wear the dress that I was wearing in the picture that Liddy took. Like I said, I really didn't want to—I'm not a model or anything—but I slipped it on and, oh Chris! We had so many sales. Hundreds and hundreds of orders, mostly for the dress in this shade, but many in the others as well."

179

He chuckled. "A perfect idea. Why didn't I think of that?"

"Because you're a writer not a marketer." She laughed. "Meg's tough. She was calling people over, saying things like 'See the inspiration behind Sophia's line!'—I could have died on the spot, but she just kept smiling and talking and taking orders."

"You look happy."

"I'm encouraged, elated, and yes, pretty happy." She leaned back in the chair and let out a sigh that sounded girly to her own ears. "And to be perfectly honest, I am very, very hungry."

He stood and reached for her. "Dinner, m'lady?"

She snapped him a smirk. "Okay, this time, I'm in."

Despite nightfall, the sidewalk teemed with people rushing about as if it were still morning and they had long to-do lists to tackle. They wandered past restaurants overflowing with diners chatting and eating and sipping cocktails. With each doorway they passed, her stomach protested a little more.

Christian's hand found her elbow. "Let's go uptown," he whispered. "I have a place."

He flagged a cab and whisked her inside.

Their driver swore and swerved his way through Manhattan, while still able to carry on a conversation. "You goin' to dinner?" he was asking. "Lots of fine dinin' up by the park. Or Lincoln Center's good too."

"Thanks. We'll stick with Midtown."

The hostess with the plunging neckline at the entrance of the restaurant gave Christian a grin that had a language all its own. The woman barely glanced in Sophia's direction, but after a day of being scrutinized constantly, she had no complaints.

"CJ, you're lookin' fine. It's been awhile. Your regular table's open, if you'd like it."

"I was hoping you'd say that, Mara."

The woman tucked two menus under her arm. "Right this way."

When they were seated, Sophia said, "You hate New York yet you have a regular booth at this high-priced restaurant?" She paused. At Sea Glass Inn, he always wore flip-flops and board shorts and reminded her of a surfer who didn't actually surf. His casual attitude fit in so perfectly in the beach culture that she had not considered his ability to adapt to city life as well. "So much for me showing you around."

He shrugged. "You have now been to the two places that I frequented on my previous trips to New York."

"I find that hard to believe."

"Believe it."

She opened her menu, her eyes unable to focus on the elaborate descriptions. For some reason, she felt jumpy and unsettled. She lingered a moment longer, then with her choice made, she shut her menu and studied him.

"What?"

"I'm trying to decide if I should stay mad at you."

He rolled his eyes. "Give a guy a break."

Her face broke out in a smile. "I do have a question, though."

"Bring it."

"How did you get that scar? I ... I know I've asked you before, but I don't think you really ever told me."

Their waiter appeared before he could answer and took their orders for both food and wine.

"Wow," Christian said after she placed hers and the waiter had gone. "You really are hungry."

"Stop that."

He laughed.

The waiter reappeared with an uncorked bottle, which he opened adeptly, poured a sip into a glass, and gave it to Christian. Formality done, he poured two glasses of the Cabernet Sauvignon, set the bottle on the table to breathe longer, and slipped away.

Christian swirled the wine in his glass, but did not take another sip. "Okay, about the scar." He stretched one arm across the back of their booth. "If we're going to be friends, Sophia, then I'm going to be straight with you. I'm guessing your brother has never told you much about my past—and you probably don't read news rags."

Friends. Of course. Yes, he was her ... friend. She chased away a small letdown. "I've wondered about your scar, but did not want to pry." Especially since she herself preferred to keep some of her own things buried. "Jackson never mentioned anything about it to me."

Christian tapped the exposed part of it with his finger. "This is what can happen after three too many beers and a confrontation with the most egregious reviewer of one's genre."

"You had three beers?"

"Four. The first one was completely acceptable."

"Ah." He hadn't struck her as someone with a temper, let alone one that could grow large enough to cause damage. "So you got into a fight and he, uh, hit you?"

"I hit him."

"Oh. I see."

"Surprised?"

"A little." She took a sip of her wine while consuming this news. "He must have done something terrible for you to react in that way."

"Actually, he *wrote* something terrible about my last novel—

not that it's a decent excuse. Anyway, he called it disturbing, among other things."

"Such as?"

"I think I bored you quite enough weeks ago with tales of my bad reviews."

She implored him with a look.

He blew out a breath. "Okay." Christian looked into the air, as if trying to recall the exact words, then looked right into her eyes. "He suggested that readers light a candle in memory of the trees that lost their lives in the making of my novel."

"Ouch."

"Said something to the effect that the only high note was that every other crappy book on the market won't look so bad by comparison."

"Oh, my. I don't recall you mentioning this when you read me all your terrible reviews."

"I didn't read them *all* to you. I do have some pride," he quipped.

"Admirable."

His smile was rueful. "Actually, I couldn't. I knew that if I did, I'd end up telling you about that night, about this face." He flipped his hand in a way that gestured toward his cheek. "Wasn't ready to do that."

"Christian, I'm sorry. That must have been a painful night for you—in more ways than one."

"The words wounded me, but I let them. I take responsibility for that. Once I gave in to the pity party, it was over. I'd been drinking and the guy could see how his review gnawed at me. He'd been drinking too much too, and so we took our battle outside. He said something to me, then that got under my skin so far that I let him have it. Punched him first, but he bounded back up and got me. I landed on the corner of a flatbed of a two-ton truck. Spent the night in the ER getting stitches and a tetanus shot for my lack of judgment."

"Sounds like he had it coming."

Christian spat out a laugh so harsh that it was good he had not been sipping wine at the time.

A remnant of laughter was still on his face when Sophia said, "What did he say?

"I don't know what you mean."

"He got under your skin, so you punched him. So ... what was it he said that got to you?"

His blue eyes dulled, and he looked around, as if wondering if their dinner would be coming soon.

"Chris?"

With a sigh, he leaned forward, strong forearms on the table, as if bringing her into his confidence. "It's ugly, hurtful stuff." He considered her for a few more seconds, and she almost thought he would clam up. Instead, he said, "Reading your novel made me look with hearty anticipation toward my own suicide."

"No."

He sat back. "I'm sure he wrote that for his own entertainment. Probably made him laugh quite boorishly at the time."

"It's unthinkable."

The crystal blue of his eyes hooked her and reeled her in. In his watchfulness she saw care and concern and deeply felt emotion. She could hardly tear her gaze away.

"It was a matter of being at the wrong place at the wrong time."

"I see. So you mean that if you hadn't run into each other, the fight would never have happened."

"The thing is, it would have happened. A friend in college committed suicide. The reviewer knew that, so he capitalized on it." Christian leaned his elbows on the table. He pulled his gaze from hers and ran a hand across the crown of his head before looking back to her. "I wanted to find him."

"That is so much to bear, Chris. I can't imagine what you went through, and your friend's family ..."

"It's nothing to joke about, that's for sure. I had written about it in an essay, which is why the topic was public knowledge.

"What I find so especially stunning is that this reviewer knew about your friend and still wrote what he did." As she said the words, Sophia's mind slipped back to her stepfather's letter. He, too, knew how painful his written words would be to her, and yet he'd written them anyway.

Of course, she was never meant to see them.

"Chris? Do you think your reviewer is an alcoholic? Or maybe an addict?"

"It's possible."

She nodded. "Not that it's an excuse, but I've some experience with this sort of thing ... in my family. Someone once wrote something to me that ... well, I'm just trying to say that I have a small understanding of how you felt."

Christian's eyes narrowed slowly as he watched her.

She sighed and looked away. "Sometimes truly wonderful people make surprisingly terrible errors in judgment, especially after they've given in to excess."

Christian reached for his wine and took a sip. "And sometimes they're just truly terrible people to begin with."

She nodded, thinking about the way some of her brand's competitors stopped by her booth to say hello and wish her well, while at least one company sent over a scout to "spy." She understood the need for researching the competition, but if the young woman in the oversized spectacles and chic black suit would have allowed her, Sophia would have gladly given her a look at her samples. She would have shared her own story with her.

Instead, the woman pretended to show little interest even while peering over shoulders in front of her space.

"Thank you for telling me your story."

He saluted her with his glass. "You're welcome."

"I have another question to ask. If you don't mind."

"Anything. Especially if we're changing the subject."

"What did you stop and throw away on the street today?"

By the look on his face, she knew she had surprised him. Both of his brows shot up and he hesitated before speaking.

"I hope I'm not prying," she said. "It—well, you had a funny look on your face when you did it."

He was smiling and nodding at her now. "Is that right? A funny look, huh?"

She laughed lightly. "You know ... you reminded me of a cartoon character who had just had a lightbulb go off in his head."

He snickered. "What, like SpongeBob Squarepants? Is that what I looked like?"

She was laughing more fully now and waving his words away with the swipe of her hand. "No, no. Fine. Maybe it wasn't like that at all. If it's personal, I'm sorry for asking. Forget I asked!"

"Sophia, Sophia ... you could never pry." He grunted a laugh. "Okay, you twisted my arm. I threw away a contract that I'd decided not to sign."

"For your book?"

"For my book."

She swallowed. "But isn't that why you came all this way?"

"I came to hear them out, and in the end, I decided to go my own way."

"Spoken like a true rebel."

He scoffed, a glint to his eyes. A server appeared with their dishes and he waited to respond. "I could say the same about you," he said when the server had gone. "For someone as gentle and lovely as you, I'm impressed with your fortitude—and yes, your rebellious streak."

"Me? Rebellious?"

"When Meg suggested you fight back by putting on that dress, I think it blew wind on that spark that I had already seen earlier in the day. You were fighting mad, though you didn't want me to know it. I saw it in your face."

"Well, if picking up my scrappy self and defending my work means I'm a rebel, then consider me guilty as charged."

Christian leaned forward until she could see the blues in his eyes turning like a kaleidoscope. Her heart let her know of its presence, the sound of it pulsating through her ears.

"I can think of a multitude of adjectives to describe you, Sophia, but scrappy is not—nor would it ever be—on my list."

He didn't move away, but kept staring at her. She, for her part, didn't move either. The world of diners and tourists swirled around them, but she could not muster a thing to respond.

Their waiter's voice cut through the silence. "Is everything tasting good here?"

Christian's eyes didn't leave hers. "Everything's great."

THEY LINGERED on the sidewalk outside of the restaurant, the air decidedly balmy, neither of them saying much.

"I guess I'll grab us a cab." He stuck his hand out, and regrettably, a yellow car stopped immediately. He helped her in, then jogged around to the other side to slip into the back seat beside her.

He opened his mouth to give the driver the name of his hotel, when Sophia interrupted. "Lincoln Center, please."

Christian slid her a look, a smile forming.

She smiled back, her mouth dazzling. "There's something about Lincoln Center at night ... have you ever been?"

"Can't say that I have."

"Well." She tapped his wrist. "You'll love it."

Minutes later, they scampered up the wide, lighted stairs that led to a celebratory fountain in the center of the plaza. Sophia stopped, her back to the fountain's voluminous display, her gaze sweeping over the building in front of them. "Isn't she beautiful?

The Met.

He'd never been inside The Metropolitan Opera House, had never given the place much thought at all.

She took his hand, pulling him along toward the impressive building. "Look at the windows," she said. "I love to come here, especially at night when those arched windows are backlit by the chandeliers. Isn't it gorgeous?"

He took it all in, for the first time ever. "Yes. It is."

She shut her eyes for a slow moment, her smile turning reflective. "When I was a kid, my mother and I sometimes would come here late, just as the doors opened and the crowds came spilling out. She and I loved to see the men in their tuxedos and the women in their gowns. We'd ooh and aah"— her gaze found his now—"like they were strolling the catwalk just for us."

They wandered to each of the buildings that flanked the square, taking in lights and people and stargazers. For him, New York had always been the place to get things done: business lunch at his favorite restaurant, finalize the contract, sign the books—then get out. In the short time they had been here, he had already seen so much.

"I've got more to show you," she said.

"Lead the way."

They took a cab to an address on East 42nd Street. He paid the driver and hopped out. "Grand Central?" He held her door.

"So much more than a terminal!" She whisked him inside on sheer energy until they stood beneath one of the massive chandeliers in a side corridor. "Look up," she said.

They stood still, holding onto each other for support, gazing up at the spheres of golden lights that dropped from the ceiling like acrobats.

"Each of the chandeliers weighs a ton. This is one of the world's earliest all-electric buildings, so the Vanderbilt family designed those chandeliers with exposed bulbs."

"Ah. So they were showing off a little."

She swung a look at him that included a slight eye roll. "Wouldn't you?"

He cracked a smile.

She dragged him out to somewhere in the middle of the main hall and again grabbed his arm and peered up at the painted ceiling. "It's said that the constellations are backward when looking at them from this angle. That this view shows us what the Divine sees."

He took in the vast overhead mural scattered with stars. How many times had he bolted through this hall without ever having glanced up? Without knowing the presence of stars hanging overhead. He continued to hold her hand, taking in the depiction of the heavenliness, not wishing for this night to end.

She began to pull away from him. "Stay here while I go wait for you at the information booth."

Reluctantly, he let her hand go. "What ... what do you mean?"

Sophia grinned and held her forefinger to her lips. "Shush.

In a few minutes, pretend to find me at the base of that large opal clock over there."

He looked toward the massive four-sided clock that held court over the information booth and then back to her. "Is that a thing?"

But she only smiled and turned away.

Christian dug his hands into his pockets and took another look around the grand terminal. He'd been through here before—how many times, he could not recall—but only to catch a train or disembark from one. Never to pay the building's architecture much thought. Back then, he might have thought the idea crazy.

But now?

He sneaked a look toward the information booth. Sophia's eye caught his, but she snapped around and pretended to look at brochures. What was she doing?

She looked over her shoulder again, a little coyly this time, and he took that as a sign.

Nonchalantly, he wandered toward that big clock, stopping twice to take random pictures of the terminal's turn-of-the-century architecture. Playing the part of a tourist the best he could. For all he knew, those photos would be blurry and undecipherable. When he arrived at where Sophia stood, idly browsing the brochures, he tapped her on the shoulder. "Sophia Agli? Is that you?"

She spun around, those sculpted lips of hers open in surprise. She took his hand in both of hers. "Christian Capra ... oh my goodness, it's you! How lovely to see you here—of all places!"

They collapsed into laughter.

"How'd I do?" he finally asked.

She slipped her hand into the crook of his arm as they began to stroll. "I think you should stick with writing."

He gasped only for her to reply with lilting laughter. "Should we stay and spy on others?"

"Why'd we do that again?"

"Because this clock is a famous meeting place. People from all over New York meet at this very spot."

"Hmm, really? I thought they met at the top of the Empire State Building."

She paused. "Wow. You are a romantic—I had no idea!"

He quirked a grin at her. "There's a lot you have yet to learn about me, Sophia."

Sophia's laughter quieted now, a smile lingering on her face. They were walking, arm in arm, directionless, yet neither displaying restlessness.

"How about dessert?" he asked her.

Her face lit. "Yes. I have the perfect place."

"Somehow I knew you would."

Outside, he signaled for a cab, but she tugged on his arm. "I was thinking we could walk."

He nodded toward her feet. "Sure you don't mind? Are your feet tiring?"

"Or you could carry me."

He froze.

She burst out laughing. "See? I can make jokes too. Yes, I'm fine walking in my heels. Been doing this for as long as I can remember. Let's go up Lexington."

His head swirled at the temptation of her. If she'd been serious about him carrying her up the block, he would have scooped her up and found a quiet place. No questions asked.

They arrived at Serendipity III, and after ducking in and around tables and a hodgepodge of colorful lighting and eclectic, enormous clocks, they found a table in the back corner. He'd never heard of this place, but by the number of people milling about, he was in the minority.

"Would you like to share a frozen hot chocolate with me?"

"You're asking me to share the impossible with you, but sure."

She snickered. When the waiter appeared, Sophia said, "One frozen hot chocolate with two straws please."

"You are full of surprises tonight, Sophia."

"Do you still hate the City?"

"Never said I hated it."

"Well, what did you say?"

He mulled that. "I believe I said I don't care for it."

"At all."

He gave a slight laugh. "What?"

"You said you didn't care for it *at all*."

He nodded and smiled, ducking as if he'd been caught. "Right. Right."

"And how do you like it now?"

A small smile persisted. "I've gained a whole new perspective, Sophia."

The waiter delivered their chocolate-and-whipped-cream concoction, which was an ambitious undertaking, even for two. They'd been given both straws and spoons, he supposed, to use as the partaking progressed from ice-cream firmness to a pool of pudding.

"So," he said, after his second bite, "this place was in a movie and that's why you like to come here?"

She shook her head, waving her spoon around. "It's been in at least *three* movies and that's probably why I heard about it. I come here, though, because it doesn't take itself all that seriously."

He looked around. Yup, hard to stay too serious in this place. "You mentioned your mother earlier. Did you also come here with her?"

"Yes. Many times."

"What was she like?"

Sophia seemed to mull that for a moment, chewing her bottom lip. "She was ... eccentric."

"Ah, so like mother like daughter."

Sophia laughed, visibly relaxing, her smile authentic. "Actually, we were very much alike, I'd say. My mother taught me to sew—I think I've mentioned that—she was artistic, but also quite organized."

Christian scanned the fifty-year-old restaurant, a patchwork of art and kitsch.

Sophia caught his eye. "I bet you're wondering why we liked to come here." She shrugged. "I don't know, really. One day we were jumping over puddles on the sidewalk, the rain coming down in sheets, when we ducked into this place. All at once it felt warm and aglow with happiness. We stayed here a good long time that first time."

"Then it makes perfect sense that you'd want to return here often." He took one more bite, his mouth starting to freeze.

"I couldn't return, actually. Not for a few years after. But then, after a while, I wanted to come back."

"When did you lose her?" he asked quietly.

"I was fifteen."

Christian nodded, his heart heavy in his chest. If it were appropriate to wrap her in his arms right now, he would. "I'm sorry."

She gave him a half smile. "It's okay. She's in here now." Sophia put a palm to her heart. "Knowing that has helped me through many times of heartache."

She'd opened up to him, and though he knew he was treading close to territory she might deem private, he couldn't help himself. "Can I ask you something?"

"Yes. Of course."

"What did you mean when you said that someone in your family once wrote something hurtful to you?"

She dropped her gaze to the table and gave her head a little shake before returning his gaze. "You know, that is something I have never in my life talked about." She sighed. "It was a long time ago. My, uh, my stepfather wrote some things in a letter that I do not wish to repeat. Although, I was never meant to read it in the first place."

"I don't understand. Then how did you come to see it?"

A flash of something, anger perhaps, or a kind of fear, flashed in her eyes. "My sister gave it to me."

He stabbed at the soupy chocolate with his straw. "Your sister. Does Jackson know?"

She reached across the table. "No. Please don't tell him. She's given him enough grief that I've vowed to keep the hard things to myself."

Christian's eyes swept over her face. So many emotions passing across her features. He took a deep breath and asked, "Whatever did she have to gain by giving you your stepfather's letter?"

"I sometimes think she did it to get back at me for being so close to our mother." She shrugged. "That is only a guess."

"You mentioned something about addiction earlier. Was he an alcoholic?"

She leaned her wrists on the table and lifted her chin, as if to think. "He drank too much sometimes, and even so after my mother died. But he really wasn't an angry person, even when he drank."

"You don't have to defend him, Sophia."

Her eyes flashed. "Oh but I do! You see, he never meant for me to see the letter. He knew that I read his words, and that I was deeply hurt. He tried to explain why he wrote it, but I'm not sure I ever understood what he was trying to convey."

Christian studied her. She was lovely. So different from other women he had met. There were plenty who were smart and talented, yes, but kind? Forgiving? Humble yet beautiful? He couldn't name one other. "Maybe you reminded him of what he had lost. You said yourself that you and your mother were similar."

Sophia stared at Christian. Maybe she had never thought of things in quite that way before. She swallowed, blinking back tears. Or maybe he had gone too far.

He cleared his throat. "Where is your stepfather now?"

"He's gone. He passed away two years after I left. Unfortunately, I was living here and he was in Italy."

"I'm sorry."

"I'm not sure if things were ever quite the same between us." She blinked away those tears, not meeting his eyes. "It's my one regret."

He saw her back to the hotel, no awkwardness between them, yet their voices quiet. He paid the cab driver and escorted her into the building. After he knew Sophia was safely upstairs, he planned to walk the four blocks back to his own hotel to clear the webs that had formed between the thoughts in his head.

"Oh!" She spun around to where Christian stood near the hotel's front doors. "I completely forgot that I dropped off some of my bags from the showroom at the bell desk. I was going to bring them to my room, but—"

"But you were in a hurry to see me?" he quipped.

She laughed—her old smile was back. "Something like that."

He gave her a dramatic sigh. "Okay. Fine. I'll help you with your stuff." He avoided thoughts of what he would do when invited into her hotel room ...

The bell desk was unstaffed. She gave her name to the desk clerk so she could call someone to retrieve her bags.

"Sophia ... Agli?" the woman asked, but didn't wait for an answer. "I'm very sorry."

"Sorry?"

"We've had a delivery for you, but I have not had anyone available to bring them to your room."

"A delivery? I wasn't expecting anything, but it's not a problem. We can take it with us now."

"Wonderful. I will only be a moment."

Christian leaned against the front desk as the desk clerk disappeared to dig up Sophia's delivery. "Good thing I brought my considerable muscle mass with me."

Sophia gasped.

"Hey, now. No need to be alarmed by my strength."

"They're beautiful," she was saying.

Christian turned to look over his shoulder and that's when a gasp left him too. The clerk struggled beneath an obnoxious display of red roses. "Somebody die?"

She sent him a "you're incorrigible" look.

He looked away, as if bored, while secretly hoping that those roses were from Jackson—though that would be weird.

Sophia reached for the vase. "Thank you for taking such good care of them."

A bellman appeared with two bags bearing Sophia's name. "Can I take these up for you?"

"No, we can take them," Sophia said.

One of the bags was stuffed and unwieldy, like a soccer bag full of balls and cleats. The other was a simple rolling backpack. Christian bent to pick up the overstuffed bag by its handle. How would it look if he were to leave her to navigate the halls with that overly aggressive spray of flowers in her arms while he grabbed the other bag—the one with the wheels —and pulled it behind him?

He set his jaw—and reached for the flowers, noting the card

signed, "*All my love, Wade.*" Carrying Sophia's gift from another man gave new meaning to the term "walk of shame." What might putting a fist through a wall add to that phrase?

They stood in silence in front of the bank of elevators. "Are you and Wade dating?"

He had expected her to give him a knee-jerk "no." But she didn't. Instead, she took a long while to answer—a gratingly long time.

"To answer your question, Wade and I are not dating."

The elevator doors opened, and he waited for her to enter before following her inside.

"Because it seems to me that a guy doesn't send flowers like this unless, you know, there's a serious relationship in the works."

She bit her lip and tucked a strand of hair behind her ear that had fallen from her updo. "He wants there to be."

"He told you that, then."

"He knew that Fashion Week has been consuming my time." She turned toward Christian, her expression earnest. "Wade has been a huge help to me these past few months. I'm grateful to him for so much."

"So once this week is behind you ... "

She rubbed her eyes. Despite their present conversation and his drive for answers, she had to be exhausted. Even he knew she had been moving nearly nonstop all day—and would wake up and hit the showroom floor in the morning for round two.

"He's a good man, Chris," she finally said.

So am I.

Jackson's admonishment hit him in the gut: *She needs someone stable.*

Christian had spent too many years taking what he wanted, when he wanted it. Except now. Jackson knew Christian's reputation intimately. Had covered for him when necessary. Friends through and through.

He could not dishonor his friend's request that he leave Sophia alone.

And considering she had someone waiting for her on the West Coast, he may not have even been given the option.

As they walked the long hall to her guest room, Sophia changed the subject. "I can't wait to get home and sing Meg's praises to my brother. We'll all have to go out to dinner one night and recap this week."

"About that ... "

"Now, I know you still have many pages to write, but you'll have to take a break to eat, won't you?"

They arrived at her door. "Sophia, I'll be leaving the inn soon."

"Oh."

"I'm sure the inn could use one of its best suites back."

"I ... well, what about finishing your book? I was not aware that your stay had an end date."

"It didn't, but you see, I'm nearly finished, and that means it's time for me to move on." And frankly, he'd rather go than see her with what's-his-name, despite that promise to Jackson.

"When do you leave New York?"

"Tomorrow afternoon."

"That soon?"

He did not connect his gaze with hers. "It's time. But I thank you for giving me the grand tour of New York tonight."

Her expression was awash with questions. "I hope you enjoyed it ... as much as I did."

He didn't have an answer. He was beginning to find it difficult to breathe in this hot, stuffy, and altogether suffocating hall.

She nodded, as if acknowledging his discomfort. She waved

her key card in front of her door and let it fall open. He entered quickly, put the vase on the closest surface, and headed back out to the hall.

Sophia took a step closer to him. "Meg and I will be heading back in a few days. I hope that we can find time for one more sunset out on the deck." She paused before saying, "I'd really like that, Chris."

He took a step back and turned to leave, but turned around. "I'd like that too, Sophia. I would really like that too."

CHAPTER 14

*B*ritt Jones had been the manager of Fifth Avenue Books for four years. She was a rock star in the book world, having set two feet on the precarious world of printed books even as the divide between internet sales and brick-and-mortar store sales had widened.

If he had known how last night would end, he would not have agreed to stop by the bookstore.

Christian accompanied her down aisles of shelves bulging with every topic and subtopic imaginable, an anomaly in the age of internet shopping and digital books.

"Thank you so much for stopping by, CJ," she was saying. "And on your way to the airport! I was so pleased when you returned my call."

He put on his professional voice. "It's a pleasure to stop in at my favorite bookstore—even though it is in the City."

Britt laughed. "I will not be surprised one bit if one of these days I read that you've up and moved yourself to somewhere like Montana."

He mustered a smile. "Could happen. Might even inspire me to set a book on a ranch."

"That would be lovely." She led them into a room where two staff members were stacking books on a table. "Now, we've set you up here, out of the way of customers since this isn't an official book signing. Oh, I do appreciate this."

Christian took in the stack of books. There must have been dozens. He tilted a look at Britt. "What's all this?"

"Please don't take offense. If I had known you would be in town, I certainly would have placed a larger order. In fact, a secondary shipment is already on its way here."

He scanned the stacks and did a mental calculation to figure out how much time this would take. "Do you want them all signed?"

"Oh yes, if you can! Our patrons would love it. Ever since your next book was announced, we've had so many inquiries— you have no idea. At first, we didn't have many in and I wanted to say to those people—'Hey, why'd you wait so long to buy the first one?'" She had a fist pressed into her side, her expression comical.

"But then, you know, people are deadline motivated. Good job floating out rumors about the next book before even making a preorder available." Her boisterous laughter bounced through the room. "Dazzling move, that one."

He'd been called many things over the past couple of years, but dazzling wasn't one of them. For the next half hour he dutifully signed books while a staffer placed "signed by the author" stickers on covers. Muzak played in the background, providing a fertile ground for his mind. If Burns's announcement about his next book, which wasn't quite finished yet, had caused someone astute like Britt Jones to order up this many copies of his previous novel, then he'd learned a couple of things.

First, buzz came from the unlikeliest places.

And second, Burns had unwittingly done him a favor. He bristled at the likely scene his old agent would make once he learned that Christian had turned down Median Publishing's offer.

"Isn't that why you came all this way?"

When Sophia innocently asked him that million-dollar question (euphemistically speaking) last night, he'd had to face it himself. And the truth unveiled itself to him. Jackson had called him on it, but he'd rebuffed him. Said his travel plans, which mirrored Sophia's, were purely coincidental.

But the truth had smacked him in the jaw last night: He had traveled all the way from the West Coast, to the dreary City, to be close to ... her.

"I can think of a multitude of adjectives to describe you, Sophia, but scrappy is not—nor would it ever be—on my list."

How had he managed not to tick off the string of adjectives he really had for her? Ethereal, breathtaking, sexy ... unforgettable ...

"Sir?"

Christian glanced up. The young staffer across from him gave him a quizzical look. He'd been staring into the void, his pen hovering over the open page of a book.

"Thinking up a new story, sir?"

An embarrassed laugh came out. "You could say that. Sorry to keep you waiting."

"No problem. I do that all the time when it's slow around here."

He was still thinking of this exchange at the bookstore when he stepped off the gangway and into the airplane at JFK. Only instead of the memory buoying him, the realization that he'd be checking out of the inn as soon as he landed cast a rope around his heart and tugged it down into the pit of his stomach with a mighty force.

∼

THE RED-EYE SOUNDED like a good idea at the time, and even though they had gained three hours on their journey from the east to west coast, Sophia could hardly wait for a hot shower and cool bed sheets.

"You're here!" Trace's bold voice announced their presence to the lobby. She abandoned two women at the concierge desk to come around to give Sophia and Meg each a hug. "You gals are a sight! Are you glad to be back? We heard all about it— sounds like an amazing trip."

"It was, but you're right, I'm glad to be back," Sophia said.

"Me too!" Meg said. "Where's my husband?"

Trace chuckled. "That man better be out buying you flowers since he's not here to greet you."

"I'm here, I'm here." Jackson stepped up to the desk, pulled his wife close, and kissed her soundly. He reached out to Sophia, gave her a hug and a quick kiss on the cheek. "You should've let me pick you up."

Meg waved him away. "The shuttle was perfect. The driver only swore once."

"Twice," Sophia chimed in.

Meg laughed. "Okay, twice." She huffed a sigh and looked around. "I love this place."

Jackson pulled her close. "This place loves you too."

"Oh my gosh, it's getting thick in here." Trace fanned herself.

Sophia leaned over to them both. "Before you two get out of hand, I just want to thank you both for your support. I'll never forget it." She gave Meg a hug.

Meg hugged her back, tears lighting her eyes. "Not sure if it's the lack of sleep or what, but I'm pretty darn emotional right now. Love you, girl."

Thomas appeared next to Sophia, a cart full of her luggage and boxes. "I'll go ahead and take these up to your suite now."

"Wonderful. I'll go with you."

They exited the elevator to the fourth floor with Thomas leading the way. Christian's door was open. She hesitated. They had not spoken since their dinner in New York, and though the days since had been dizzyingly full, more than once she had lingered on thoughts of his plans. Maybe he should stay awhile, get the book finished, and then figure out what was next. No sense in rushing away, especially now that the summer tourist season had passed. She'd been planning to take the issue up with Jackson, but with Christian's door open, now was as good a time as any to give him her two cents.

She rapped her knuckles on the door. "Knock, knock."

A housekeeper emerged from the bathroom. "Hello, Ms. Riley."

"Hello, Mandy. I was looking for Mr. Capra." She glanced behind her. "There's no cart by the door, so didn't realize his room was being cleaned."

"Oh, it's not. I was just inspecting it for the next guest."

"I don't understand." Her mind raced with options. "Has Mr. Capra checked out?"

"Yes, ma'am. I believe he has. Too bad. He was such a nice man. Maybe he'll come back sometime."

She leaned her hand on the doorframe. Christian had checked out. Just like that. No text or call. Sophia glanced back at Thomas who was wheeling his cart toward her door. Though it took effort, she trailed into her room behind him.

"Will there be anything else?"

She shook her head. "No. Nothing. Thank you."

He shut the door behind him and she surveyed the room. Though she longed for rest, the quiet was ... unnerving.

~

SOPHIA OPENED her eyes to the telltale sign of a good time. Laughter poured in from somewhere beyond her deck. She ran a hand through her hair and put her feet on the ground, eager to chase away the grogginess of travel. More laughter reached her. She padded over to the slider door and peeked out to see two young girls shrieking and chasing each other around on the deck next to hers.

Christian's deck.

She let the curtain drop and curled back up in bed. Her phone rang and Jackson's name popped onto her screen.

"Hi," she said.

"Glad I didn't wake you."

She sat up, punching pillows behind her back. "No, you didn't. A couple of girls next door did that."

"Hmm."

"What?"

"Note to self: My sister is grumpy when she's awakened during a nap."

She let out a half laugh. "Stop."

"I really just called to check up on you. Sounds like you and Meg had a grand time without me."

"Ha ha."

"Would you like to join us for dinner tonight? I can have a car bring you over."

"To the condo?"

"Yes. I'm barbecuing ribs tonight and making my famous pasta salad. Convinced yet?"

She smiled at this. In the few months that she'd known her

brother, she had not often seen him away from the frenzy of work. "You had me at barbecue."

A knock on the door pulled at her attention. Christian? She glanced at the door. "Somebody's here," she said. "I can be ready at five. Will that work?"

"Perfect. Your driver will be waiting."

Another knock on the door.

"Just a minute." She ran her fingers through her hair and quickly walked to the door.

Wade stood on the other side wearing a sharp gray overcoat and a black shirt, opened at the collar. He smelled amazing.

"C'mere, gorgeous." He stepped into the room and pulled her into his arms.

She laughed but turned her head. "I just woke up from a nap!"

He nuzzled her ear. "You look like you just stepped out of a magazine."

She pulled back. "You are ridiculous."

"Here." He handed her a bouquet of white roses. "For you."

She peered at him over the bouquet. "More flowers? These are beautiful. Thank you."

"So proud of you, Sophia. You did it!"

He was right. A few months ago she had found herself in that place where all creatives go at one time or another: despair. She lacked creativity and focus and wasn't sure if she still had a future in design. Until she'd come here. She didn't know exactly what had happened to change her course. Other than that photo that Liddy happened to snap ...

"Listen, I have a meeting to get to, but I was hoping I could take you to dinner later. To celebrate."

"Oh."

"What's wrong?"

"Well, I've promised Jackson I would have barbecue with him and Meg."

"Tonight?"

"Yes, sorry. Sometimes I don't use my head—I should've known you would want to get together to discuss everything."

A smile broke out on his face.

"What?"

He pulled her into an embrace then held her at arm's length, his gaze brushing over her. "First, I hate that you make our time together sound like a business meeting."

"That's not what I meant!"

He laughed heartily now. "And second, I know about the barbecue. Actually, I'm the driver Jackson enlisted."

"You are not." She leaned in closer. "Wait. Are you really?"

"I'd rather have you all to myself, but if that's not possible, I can share. For at least one more day."

"Well, then," she said, "I will take you up on your offer of a ride."

He kissed her hand. "Tonight, then."

Sophia clicked the door closed behind Wade and began to search the small suite for something she could use for a vase. She had to settle on one of the large mugs she used to hold her paint brushes, then opened the curtains to let light in and put the flowers on an end table.

She looked away from the window and glanced around the room. For the first time since she had moved into the inn, she longed for home. Not the home she had come from, but one she could settle into for the rest of her life. Though her father had owned this place and gifted it to Jackson—and to her—she still looked around and saw ... a hotel room.

The simplicity of the roses on her table caught her eye. Fresh. Delicate. Alive. In her mind she could picture a home with a garden full of flowers close to the sea. Maybe hardwood floors and children's toys strewn about.

She passed by the sliding door that led to her deck and stopped. Whitecaps floated on the surface of the water out there, a sure sign of tumult on the sea. Would have inspired Christian, if he had chosen to stay at least a short while longer.

She still could not believe that he had checked out without saying goodbye. Maybe Christian never had the wild idea of settling down, as she did. Maybe he truly was a restless wanderer who was destined to find home wherever he laid his head.

SOPHIA SLIPPED out onto the deck where Jackson held court over the barbecue. He wore an apron proclaiming him *The Grillfather*. "Smells delicious. Oh, and nice outfit, by the way."

He kissed her on the cheek. "What can I say? Meg dresses me."

"I'm so happy to see you in something other than a suit."

"You don't like my work clothes?"

"That is the problem. You work all the time."

One of his eyebrows darted up. He turned over several links of kielbasa. "Not you too. Meg's on my case all the time about the workload. She actually threatened to hide my car keys."

"I applaud her, but surely you could call one of your valets to pick you up. Right?"

"Exactly what I told her. And then I pointed out that we would have to pay that person and give them mileage. So she gave me back my keys."

"Smart girl."

He gestured toward a bottle of champagne and a pitcher of orange juice. "Mimosa?"

"That sounds perfect. Thank you."

Meg and Jackson lived in his condo near the beach, a gated community with manicured lawns and shrubs and walkways that wove in and between hundreds of perfectly placed residences. All had decks or porches, but only a quarter of them had partial views of the ocean.

Sophia gazed toward the horizon, the sun looming far to the west. "Is this why you live here? Because of that view?"

Jackson glanced up from his basting. "Can't beat it." He pointed to a massive grassy area with a pair of tongs. "Park on one side, dunes on the other, and that ocean right in front."

"Where did Meg live when you met?"

"Meg? She leased a house. Bigger than this place, but since I own this one—"

"And you are near the beach ..."

He smiled and nodded. "Yes, because of all that, I convinced her to give up her lease and move here. So she moved in—with two closets-full of clothing."

"So it's a cozy existence." Sophia tried not to laugh too hard.

He pointed the tongs at her. "Because of people like you!"

"Guilty." She laughed.

"So, is Wade helping Meg in the kitchen?"

She sipped her drink. "How did you know?"

"I figured, since he likes to cook. How about you? Do you like to cook anything special?" He laughed nervously. "I feel like I'm on a date."

"Yes, I know what you mean. We went from being strangers to family without learning all those funny little nuances along the way."

Wade appeared just then wearing an apron and carrying a platter of marinated steak. "What did I miss?"

"Sophia and I were just getting caught up on, well, life."

"And Meg was just filling me in as well." He grinned at Sophia. "You were more amazing at Fashion Week than you let on."

"I do not recall saying that I was amazing at all."

He moved behind her and rubbed her shoulders. "That's what I mean. Jackson, your wife told me that Sophia made several wardrobe changes per day and still managed to keep smiling."

"I have no doubt."

"Truly, I could not have done any of this week without Meg," Sophia said. "She showed tremendous spirit when I was feeling so very overwhelmed."

Jackson was smiling and laughing and checking to see if the kielbasa was done when Meg joined them on the deck with a plate of raw, sliced vegetables: onions, zucchini, and mushrooms. "Lots of laughter out here." She set the plate down and poured herself a glass of juice. "Cheers."

Sophia touched her on the arm. "Jackson told me all about your extensive wardrobe."

"You mean he was complaining about it, right?"

Sophia smiled. "I wouldn't call it complaining. I believe he was being quite complimentary."

"Oh, right!" Meg laughed.

"Speaking of complimentary," Wade said, "Sophia's been singing your praises out here as well."

"It's true," Sophia said.

Meg wrapped her arms about Jackson's waist and rested her chin on his shoulder blade. "Oh really?"

"Hey, hey," he said, arms and grilling tool up in the air. "Don't mess with the cook."

"Sheesh! Still pushing me away, even after all this time." Meg shook her head, but a knowing smile graced her mouth.

Wade wrinkled his brow. "Should we even ask?"

Meg rested a hand on her side. "Do you know that this man actually threatened to fire me?"

Jackson lifted his chin and looked into the sky as if searching for answers. "Why me, Lord?"

"Jackson," Sophia asked, "why did you want to fire Meg?"

"That's where the error lies! I didn't want to fire Meg—I *had* to threaten to fire her." He swung around, those tongs stuck out like an officer's flashlight. "For her own good."

Meg rolled her eyes and took another sip of juice.

Sophia looked from Jackson to Wade and back again. "I don't understand."

Meg patted her husband's back. "We joke about it now, but on second thought, this might not be a good thing to bring up so soon after ... well, you know ... all that stuff with Gia." She paused. "I'm on my way back to the kitchen. Need anything else?"

With Meg out of earshot, Jackson took in both Wade and Sophia. "I threatened to fire her to keep her away from danger. But you know Meg—never afraid of a little adventure." He tilted his head when he smiled. "My delivery could have been better, I'll give you that. But at the time, I did the best I could."

Wade nodded. "Yes, I remember hearing this story. You were trying to protect her, but she fought you every step."

"Bingo."

A million thoughts jostled like bumper cars in Sophia's mind. Why would Jackson think that hurting her heart would protect her? Why not just be straight with her? She shook off her questions as best she could as Wade poured her another smidge of champagne.

"I told Meg I'd make the garlic bread," Wade said as he retreated to the kitchen. "Be back soon."

Jackson tossed the veggies with oil in a grill pan as Sophia sipped her wine. "Can I ask you something? "Did ... did Christian tell you where he was going?"

"Uh, no, not yet." He paused. "I'm sure he'll touch base at some point, though."

She chewed her thumbnail. "I was just wondering."

"I hope he wasn't too much of a distraction for you these past few months. My friend Christian is somewhat of a free spirit."

"No, not at all. I consider him a ... friend. Well, I thought we were friends."

Jackson frowned and shook his head. "I wish I would have thought more clearly about what room to book him into." He paused and pivoted to face her. "Christian and I have been friends for a long time. Did he do something to you that I should know about?"

Sophia gaped at Jackson. "No. Nothing bad. I ... I just thought he'd say goodbye before checking out. That's all."

Jackson looked over his shoulder toward the house. "Might not want to have Wade hear you say that."

"Why? Wade and I aren't, you know, we're not ... dating."

Jackson raised an eyebrow but said nothing.

"Not officially."

"But you spend time together."

She cracked a smile.

"I'm not trying to pry ..."

"But you are prying."

"Look. All I am saying is that Wade is a great guy. He'd be good for you. Our father trusted him implicitly—and if only I would have consulted him before things had spiraled so."

"We have talked about this before. You must stop blaming yourself."

"Well, all I meant was ... maybe we would have found you sooner. And that would have been spectacular."

A lump formed in her throat that she could not deny. She threw herself into her brother's arms and hugged him tight. "I love you, little brother."

"Love you too, sis."

Lovingly, he put her at arm's distance so he could speak directly to her. "I want to see you happy."

She was wiping her tears away with the back of her hand when Wade and Meg marched back out bringing with them bread and eating utensils.

Meg stopped. She began to blink rapidly. "What's happening?" She looked back and forth. "Are you both ... *crying?*"

Wade began rubbing Sophia's shoulders again.

Jackson put down the tongs and slid both arms around Meg. He pulled her close and smiled widely. "Maybe it's time we spill the beans, honey."

Meg shot both arms up in the air. "I'm pregnant!"

"What? Are you serious?" Sophia flew into Meg's arms. "I can't believe you kept this a secret during the entire trip!"

Wade gave Jackson a man hug. "Congratulations! Beautiful news, you two."

"Wait!" Sophia looked incredulous. "Was it even safe for you to be working so many hours in New York? Oh, Meg! You should've told me."

"I made her check with her doctor first," Jackson said.

"And don't you remember how I begged off going out every night?" Meg said. "That's because I went back to the room and slept!"

Sophia hugged Meg again. "Is this why you cry so much all the time?"

Jackson whooped a laugh. "I'm glad you're the one who said it." He laughed again. "Better you than me!"

As the four of them sat around the dining table, passing plates of food, Sophia reveled in her brother and sister-in-law's good news. In this moment, the trials of the past few months culminating in a successful Fashion Week slipped farther into the past. She looked at Jackson and Meg and Wade. It was as if everyone had moved on.

Move on. After this show, people will have moved on anyway ...

Wade's words to her when she had called him from the stairwell struck her now in a way that caused the air to squeeze right out of her lungs.

Is that what Christian would do once he finished his book? Move on? Where would he go? Was it even her question to ask?

And would she ever see him again?

CHAPTER 15

She yawned three times in a row as Wade walked her from the parking lot to the door of her suite.

"I bore you that much, huh?"

"You could never bore me." Another yawn overtook her, and when it ended, she laughed. "I guess I'm still recovering from the week. From the past month, really."

He left with a promise to call her the next day. After she'd taken a warm shower and slipped into her nightgown, Sophia pulled on a robe and stepped outside onto the deck. The neighboring room was dark; perhaps the family had gone to sleep.

The waves, however, had not. She recalled how surprised Christian had been her first morning here when she was trying to decide whether or not she could get used to the ferocious sound of cresting waves that crash landed on packed sand with regular precision. She allowed herself one rueful smile. He had suggested she might need medication for her reticence of the sea's roar.

Out of habit, she glanced at the neighboring deck. She

knew he had left, that others had taken his place, and yet she still half expected to find him threatening to hop over the railings. And then actually do it.

Sophia chewed her lip. Christian was a restless guy, a wandering spirit. Jackson had told her so in a way that seemed designed to let her down easy. Maybe that's why Christian left as quickly as he did—so she wouldn't grow too attached.

Only she feared she already had.

She blinked away the onset of tears, sniffling. He could have called. Or texted. Or left her a note. Instead, he had disappeared with no word of where he had gone. Had he thought about her at all? Or did he think his brief mention in New York that he'd be leaving soon would be sufficient?

She hung her head, the crush of waves filling her ears, the collision of myriad thoughts jostling tender emotions.

A thought from earlier in the evening lingered. Had her brother truly threatened to fire Meg—and had she believed he would follow through? By the sound of things, both assertions were true. He was trying to keep her away from danger, he said. But what struck Sophia was that, as he put it, his "delivery could have been better" and that he "was doing the best" he could.

Maybe she reminded him of what he had lost.

Christian's theory about her stepfather reverberated in her head. But it did not answer why he would write her a hurtful letter, one that criticized her work and cast doubt upon her future as a designer. Unless ...

She gripped the hand railing as if doing so would help her remember. Her stepfather was a kind man. Even when he drank too much, something that happened with regularity after her mother's death, he still cared for her. And for Gia. Filled their home with food. Attended their school functions.

Took photos before dances, though she hardly participated in any.

Maybe he wrote that letter to her out of fear. She had decided to move to New York with a couple of friends, and though she should have known he wouldn't want her to go, she never considered letting that slow her.

Maybe he hadn't wanted her to go.

But instead of just telling her that, he drank.

And he wrote her an angry letter.

Then he tossed it in the trash ... only for Gia, her one-and-only sister, to find it.

Sophia pressed a hand to her forehead, a sob escaping. Her shoulders shook as she cried it out, allowing the wind to sweep away her tears. Could it be that she had been focusing on her stepfather's one major slip so long that it had become her mantra?

The more she emptied herself of built-up tears, the more the truth became clear as crystal: Her stepfather had not wanted to lose her—but he told her so in one very bad and imperfect way.

IT WAS SAID THAT, in the days of old, when a sailor would be lost at sea, the mermaids would cry — and their tears would surface in the form of sea glass.

By the looks of the piles of sea glass refined by agitation and coughed up by the ocean, emotions had been running high among the mermaids along this lolling stretch of the coast.

Christian skipped the quarter-shaped green sea glass across the surface of a wave, watching it jump three times. He may have exaggerated that last jump.

Living away from the shoreline wasn't as bad as he'd thought it would be. He had rented a Shangri-la thirty miles up the coast from Sea Glass Inn, staying for the past two weeks about a mile inland in the back house of a property. Ever since, he'd kept his head down until he'd finished the book. Once he got rolling, it hadn't taken long.

The entire process both worried and startled him. Worried him because he feared leaving the Sea Glass Inn within full view of his muse would stunt his writing progress and startled him because it hadn't.

When he'd finally lifted his head from his sprint-filled writing days, he'd realized with a start how little he'd eaten in the previous weeks—though the coffee had been plentiful. But he could not stop himself from forging on. He'd sent the manuscript to his editor and checked in with Marci about the changes they'd discussed regarding the cover. He'd also hired a virtual assistant named Grace to help him with social media, advertisements, and swag.

Add to all that the fact that Burns hadn't backed off much from his assertion that he was entitled to a slice of CJ's pie, Christian had done something that made his skin crawl—he and Grace planned a full-out social media blitz.

In essence, CJ Capra had taken the leap from the traditionally published world and into the independently published one with every part of his life.

Now he found himself here on the beach, barefoot with his pant legs rolled up, walking through soft and wet clay-like sand. He ran a hand across his overgrown beard, planted his feet in that wet sand, and allowed his body to sink into it. He expected that any moment sand crabs would nip his toes to protest the invasion of their dwelling. He didn't care. The past weeks were hard fought.

He missed her.

But her heart was elsewhere. He had seen it on her face when she received those roses in New York, her expression lit with hope. He picked up a rock this time and pitched it, with force, into a wave. Sophia had already had enough upheaval in her young life anyway—even without Jackson's promise of a sound pummeling if he were to get in Wade's way.

This morning, Christian had clicked the lock on his daily rental shack, driven downtown, and rented an RV. The man at the RV rental counter told him he could park at a famous surf spot and miss the crowds of the weekend. So he'd found a place to park on this breezy and somewhat lonely length of the sea where he could get away.

Though he'd enjoyed the privacy and solace of his inland home, he had missed the smell of the sea. He trudged along, the wind tousling his beard, the sea spray refreshing his skin, and inhaled, the salt air clearing away the gray matter that had settled in his brain.

Other than a couple of old guys with bald heads and goatees jogging by with surfboards under their arms, the beach was deserted. And he liked it that way. He'd gotten used to the quiet, the new frontier of reaching readers from behind screens instead of at book signing tables in the center of a busy bookstore. Along with his bed on wheels, he had brought food, and basics, and a stack of books he'd been avoiding until all his writing was done. As far as Christian was concerned, he was set for the entire week.

He walked another ten yards or so, noting the precision of pelicans torpedoing the ocean, and realized—he didn't have anywhere to be. Nor anyone to meet. He was free to walk or not walk, to plunk down on the sand...or not.

With another cleansing breath, he continued on his walk.

Up ahead, two brown-skinned men hopped out of a pickup truck. Carbon copies of each other, except for their heights. The taller one climbed into a wetsuit and helped the younger one into his. Then the pair scrambled down the rocks with their surfboards fastened to their ankles with Velcro. He watched them, father and son, ride into the surf.

A flock of gulls flew overhead forming a "v." Always wondered how they knew who to follow—and how the leader knew to be in the lead. He watched them a good long time, till they were nearly out of his line of vision.

A wave rolled in harder, engulfing his feet on landing. The water cooled his toes, the wave pulling away the tension from his body on its retreat. If he were not upright, he might have fallen asleep right there on the beach ... and he might still yet.

And then ...

His phone rang.

Christian fought the urge to curse. He pulled the wailing hour-stealer from his pocket, his hands holding it nimbly. The only way he'd ever truly break free of the phone's constant nagging would be to hurl it into the surf.

But it was his editor calling.

"Hey, Christian. It's Bette. Got a minute?"

"I've got all day."

She chuckled. "Well, I won't keep you that long. I wanted to let you know that I've read through your novel and it's amazing. Truly." She cleared her throat.

The added "truly" had him wondering. "But?"

She let out a small but exasperated sigh. "The end!"

"What about it?" He started up his walk through the surf again.

"The mermaid just leaves ... what's with that?"

"Not sure I understand the question."

222

"For one, there's too much unsaid between her and the hero."

"I don't write romance."

Her sigh like running water filled the earpiece. "Well, you sure have a strange way of showing it."

"Anything else?"

"I'm serious about the ending. You'll have your readers slinging the book across the room if you just leave it like that. What happens to her? Why does she just swim off to oblivion? Almost makes it sound like the Avengers lost this one."

The Avengers were the victims who had risen up in the face of oppression. He stopped. "Really?"

"Now I've got your attention. The Agitators wanted her gone—and though they were mostly annihilated, a remnant remained."

"Yes, but that's so I can bring them back in book two."

"But you let them get away with too much. This ends like a cliffhanger, and you know your readers'll hate that!"

"So you're saying Nickolas ... should go after her?"

"Yes. I am recommending this for more than getting your readers to buy book two. It's because it's the right and natural thing to do. Look at their story. Two lost beings coming together despite their scars? The ugly and the beautiful all wrapped up in one?"

He knew he didn't have to take Bette's advice. But she had been his editor for several years, his no-nonsense, no-feelings-spared editor. She was tough enough to leave Median Publishing before the last layoffs and start her own gig. She had not steered him wrong in the past, so why would she now? He had to believe she knew what she was talking about.

"I'll take it under submission," he said.

She didn't say a thing for a good long half-minute. Then, "That's all I ask."

He hung up, the glow of his "staycation" duller now. Instead of celebrating, it appeared that he had one more push to give the story. He had no one but himself to blame. In some ways, he had known all along that he'd allowed his muse to intertwine with his feelings for Sophia. And when his quest for her had turned elusive, so had his muse.

But that was a mistake.

He'd confused fantasy with reality, and when he couldn't bend one, he was at a loss to shape the other.

Christian fought off a second very real urge to curse—this time at himself.

He exhaled, scanning the horizon. The blue of the water stretched into variations of itself. He needed this break, some time to get back in touch with himself—not just the part of him that churned out stories nearly nonstop.

He was, he noticed, becoming quite belligerent about his quest for a break.

After he'd walked as far as his strength would take him, Christian turned back. By now, evening had come, along with a scattering of beachgoers. They walked in pairs or groups, paying no attention to him as he passed, some holding hands, others moving in a free-wheeling pattern, freed from the shackles of their day.

He finally made it back to where he'd parked his rented RV, climbed up the rocks, and went inside to grab a beer. Outside he sat in his lone beach chair, took a sip, and wondered at the view.

A group had gathered outside of the RV parked in the space next to his. An older couple with several young adults sat around an old washing machine drum filled with driftwood that they'd used to start a fire. As soon as that sun left them, that heat would come in handy.

Christian scanned the beach. From his vantage point, he

could see small fires had begun to pop up with groups lingering. Night surfers converged on the inky waves, and lovers strolled in the coming twilight.

He downed his last swig of beer and took one last lingering glance out to sea. Though he searched for her between each crest of a wave, Christian spotted nothing.

CHAPTER 16

*M*any weeks had passed and Sophia had never been so busy. Not even when she had sold her first couple of designs to a string of boutiques in upstate New York. After her new line's debut at Fashion Week, Sophia decided to stay with the mom-and-pop manufacturer that had been with her since the beginning—and they'd been on the phone almost daily since. This meant early mornings for her, which worked out well since she hardly slept anymore anyway.

"Another macchiato, Sophia?" Jenny had become accustomed to Sophia's daily routine.

"Absolutely."

The inn had begun to pursue more much-needed upgrades, thanks in part to the pending sale of Sea Castle, but also for a reason that none of them foresaw: CJ Capra had written a book there. Once word got out via social media that Christian had written his newest novel from a suite at Sea Glass Inn, the hotel had been booked. Fresh calls came in daily. Journalists scheduled interviews. Even mermaid gazers showed up to peer from the trail overlooking the sea at the edge of the property.

She had made a decision for a change of her own but had yet to find the time to tell her brother. Or anyone else, for that matter.

Sophia sipped her espresso and answered her phone when it rang.

"Good morning, Wade."

"Is it as sunny there as it is here?"

She gazed out the window, the day's early sunlight dappling the water. "It's another gorgeous day, even in late fall. I take it Florida is as well."

"The sun's out, of course, but the view is nowhere near as beautiful as it would be if I were sitting across from you."

She smiled. "Oh, I don't know about that. I'm wearing sponge rollers and a chartreuse terry-cloth robe right now."

"You are stunning no matter what you wear."

She laughed at this. "And you are good for my ego."

"Speaking of being good for each other, I wanted to let you know that I will be flying back tomorrow, Sophia. You've been busy, so I wanted to give you time to clear your calendar." He paused. "We have a lot of catching up to do."

This was good news. She had missed talking with him, discussing some of her business issues that seemed to crop up every day. It would be good to fall back into a routine where they could meet for coffee or perhaps a glass of wine whenever the mood struck.

Liddy pulled out a chair and sat down just as Sophia hung up. She put her iPad on the table. "I hope I didn't rush you off your call."

"No, no. We were finished."

"Wade?"

"How did you know?"

Liddy gave her a little shrug. "It's a look on your face that I've seen before."

"What look?"

"I don't know exactly ... like you're happy. But also a little, how do I put this, melancholy? Are you missing him right now?"

"Of course. Yes. That's it."

"I see you're finished with your coffee. Do you mind if I order something to eat? I'm famished." She laughed. "It's a workout having a baby, I tell you."

"Please. Order whatever you like." She surveyed the dining room. "Is Meg coming?"

One of Liddy's eyebrows shot up. "Didn't you hear? The famous Priscilla is on her way so Meg was picking up some special flowers for her room."

"She's coming here? To stay?"

Liddy nodded. "I believe she'll be vacationing for a few weeks." She leaned forward, a sly smile on her face. "Meg said something about Priscilla being a CJ Capra groupie. So I'm guessing they'll be looking for mermaid sightings while she's here."

"Oh!" Sophia forced a smile to her face. While the news about Chris's stay at the inn had boosted their visibility, it had also created an uncomfortable reality for her: daily mentions, questions, and all-around comments about the elusive CJ Capra.

Elusive because he'd left the inn, and their friendship, with no forwarding address.

Liddy laughed and held up her iPad. "There's an interview with Christian online. Would you like to read it?"

She hesitated.

Liddy waved a hand. "I'll just send you the link to read later."

"Okay,"

Liddy's eyes lit in recognition "You're here!" She stood and hugged Meg, who was beginning to thicken in the middle, albeit slightly.

Meg gave Liddy a hug, then leaned over to kiss Sophia on the cheek, all while carrying an enormous vase full of sunflowers.

"For heaven's sake, Meg, give those to a bellman to deliver," Liddy said.

Meg set the vase on the table. "Oh no, I'm fine. I want to deliver them myself, you know, so I can make sure everything's perfect for her arrival."

Sophia smiled. "And you haven't seen her since Italy, right?"

Meg shook her head. "No. So much has happened since our serendipitous meeting. Feels like a lifetime ago, really. I'm excited to see what she's up to. You will both love her!"

Jenny stopped by the table. "What can I get you?"

Meg ordered an omelet, bacon, two slices of toast, a side of avocado, and a bowl of fruit.

Liddy leaned forward and stage whispered, "She's eating for two."

Jenny giggled. "I got that. And you?"

"I'm trying to get rid of my baby fat, so just a bowl of fruit." She nodded at Meg. "And her leftovers."

Sophia leaned over and squeezed Meg's wrist. "You are simply glowing."

"I'll say." Liddy reached into her purse. "Here is a bottle of those prenatal vitamins I told you about. Throw out that garbage you're taking. Trust me."

"Yes, ma'am." Still laughing, Meg said to Sophia, "Did Wade tell you the transfer is almost finalized?"

"He called this morning, actually. It's a relief, isn't it."

Meg nodded. "Really, it is."

For the next half hour, they ate their breakfasts and caught up on life. After weeks of business calls, some for the inn and many for Agli Designs, Sophia needed this casual banter. Even more so with an impending change she had decided to make.

"Meg! Oh my goodness, it's really you!"

All three of the women turned around.

Meg was the first to get up from the table and rush over to the woman with a long slim nose, pale skin, full lips, and red hair. "Priscilla!" She hugged her tight and then slipped an arm around her waist and introduced her to Sophia and Liddy.

They were all seated at the table, and Priscilla ordered a mimosa with just a splash of orange juice. She glanced around, taking in the wide ocean view. "It's just like we're back in Cinque Terre, isn't it, Meg?"

She threw back a laugh. "Oh, yes, *exactly* like that."

Priscilla's eyes grew wide in mock surprise. "You find it so very different out here on the West Coast?"

Liddy spoke up. "You should ask Sophia. She grew up in Italy."

Priscilla turned to her. "You don't say! That's marvelous." Jenny delivered the mimosa, and Priscilla picked up her glass in a toast. "To living the exotic life."

Here, here!

She continued, "And to finding mermaids at Sea Glass Inn."

Liddy sat back, dissolving into laughter. "Word really has traveled far and fast!"

Priscilla gave a fun little shrug and wink. She took another sip of her mimosa. "I was already determined to come out here and see Meg again, but when I read about the mermaids in Mr. Capra's interview, oh! I knew I absolutely must make my plans soon. Who knows? Now that I have finally received a well-deserved settlement from my ex, the scoundrel, maybe I will discover that California is more to my liking than Virginia."

Meg nodded. "I'm so glad to hear this, Priscilla. Great news!"

"Now." Priscilla turned in her chair so she could see Meg more fully. "Let me see that belly!"

Meg's face turned pink, but she proudly patted her middle, which hadn't grown much yet.

Priscilla smiled with every part of her face. "You will make a wonderful mother."

"Thank you," Meg said.

Slowly, Sophia pushed back her chair. "I am very sorry to have to leave you all, but it's about time for a conference call." She turned to Priscilla. "It has been a pleasure."

Sophia hated to leave the party, but with Wade flying home tomorrow and expecting some of her time, she had to get moving. As she strode through the lobby, she ticked through the to-do list she'd made earlier: conference call for her design company, view initial mockups of the ballroom remodel, sign the lease on the apartment she'd just rented ...

"Sophia!"

Jackson held the side door for her, wearing a quizzical grin. "By the look on your face, I thought you were going to barrel right through the glass."

She slowed. "Sorry. Just a lot ... a lot on my mind, I suppose."

"Wade's coming back tomorrow."

Yes. She *knew*. Why was everyone telling her this? She inhaled. "He told me."

"Good news?"

"Yes, hmm. Very." She paused. "I have promised to make a call soon, but do you have a few minutes?"

"Of course." He led them to a bench along the path. "This good?"

She nodded. "I wanted to tell you that I've found an apartment, and I'm going to sign the lease today."

Jackson gaped at her.

"It's downtown," she continued, "but still close enough to walk to the beach and shops."

"Wow, Sophia. I think that ... sounds perfect for you."

"You do?"

"Don't you?"

She nodded. "Yes, I really do. I've loved my time here at the inn, but it's time I make myself a home somewhere. Are you surprised?"

"I didn't expect you to stay here forever."

"But I've insulted you."

"No, no. You could never. I'm actually relieved." He gave her a crooked smile. "I wasn't sure you would stay in California at all."

She tilted her head. "Honestly, I wasn't sure if I would be staying either."

His brows lifted. "But now?"

She looked her brother in the eyes. "You and Meg are my world. I can't imagine ever going very far from you."

Tears glistened in Jackson's eyes and he pulled her into his embrace. "I love you, Sophia. And I hope you're happy in your new home."

"I believe I will be." She pulled away, but not before kissing his cheek. "Will you help me move?"

Jackson laughed now. "Of course. Anything you need. You know that."

She glanced at the iPad in his hands. "May I borrow that?"

"It's yours." He handed it to her. "Consider it a perk of being the co-owner of one of the premier hotels for mermaid sightings on the West Coast."

She giggled at this, unable to help herself.

HE WAS TIRED OF HIDING.

With new resolve, Christian began the arduous task of removing the thick blanket of whiskers from his face, careful not to further scar his skin. The altercation, as he had come to think of it, had done plenty of that. On occasion, he winced when the scraping sound of the razor reached his ears. When he finished, Christian wiped his face with a warm, wet wash-cloth and gave himself an honest assessment.

Like his father's skin before him, Christian's was soft and shiny after a shave. Unlike his father's, Christian's had the addition of a long, skinny, rambling scar that might fade in time, but would likely never disappear altogether. Kind of like certain events in his life.

Still, the scar's presence did not bother him half as much as the first time he had examined it. Nor the hundredth time. And it occurred to him that any worry he may have had about Sophia seeing his scarred face in all its glory had disappeared.

ARMED with a copy of *The Spell*, Christian strode into the lobby of Sea Glass Inn. The first one to spot him was Trace.

"Oh my word!" She came out from behind the counter. "Well, there's a sight for sore eyes if I ever did see one."

"Hi, Trace." He glanced around. "Looks like some new things are happening around here."

"Yeah, like mermaid watchers showing up all the time. Sheesh, Christian, you've brought all the crazies out."

Leave it to Trace to tell him like it was.

"I loved the story, by the way."

He quirked a smile at her. "Read it already?"

"Oh, yes—in one weekend! That ending made me all swoony. Loved it!"

He bit back a laugh. He'd taken Bette's advice and had put his head down to write a new ending. His hero's journey had come to a natural conclusion, and his heroine? No longer elusive.

If only his reality was closer to his fiction.

Trace broke into his thoughts. "Are you here to see Jackson?" She glanced at the book in his hand. "Ooh, is that a signed copy?"

"It's a gift for Jackson and Meg, yes." Trace didn't need to know that he had something—or someone—altogether different on his mind.

She had already picked up the phone. "I'll get them out here right away." She stopped mid-air. "Meg's got a friend in town who'll want to meet you too."

He stood in the center of the lobby, the place he'd called home all summer and beyond, sensing the detachment that had begun two months ago. This place had never really been his home, but just another stop along the road of his life. He'd had many of those in his adult life, and as Christian took in the walls and glass and sea beyond the windows, he felt grateful. Thankful to have been given this gift of a place to find renewal.

But he also knew that it was time to move on again, this time to a real place that wasn't filled with corporate touches and items that others believed he needed. He had decided to find a place to make a home.

"I'm so sorry, Christian," Trace said. "Having a little trouble locating him right now."

He laid the book on the desk. "Not a problem. I'll just leave this here with—"

She hung up the phone. "There he is!"

Jackson strode toward him, the clip of his designer shoes echoing with each step.

Christian looked over his shoulder. "Hello."

Jackson smiled, but stress lines traversed his forehead.

Christian extended the book to him. "A gift."

Jackson's gaze snapped toward the book in genuine surprise. He reached for it. "It's tremendous. Thank you."

Christian nodded. "Consider it an olive branch."

Something much like relief passed across his old friend's face. He shook his head, dropped his gaze to the floor momentarily before looking up again. "I'm sorry, man. Didn't mean for things to get so out of hand."

Meg rushed toward them, pulling Christian into a hug. "It's so wonderful to see you!"

Christian kissed her cheek. "Beautiful as always."

"We've missed you, Christian."

"I've missed you too."

A woman joined them, her luxurious red hair cascading down one shoulder. Christian had never seen her before, or not that he recalled, but she seemed comfortable enough to make their group of three a foursome.

Meg's face lit up and wrapped an arm around the woman. "CJ, I'd like you to meet my friend, Priscilla."

The woman blushed, yet she was no shrinking violet. She reached out and pumped his hand. "Mr. Capra, I am a huge fan of yours and have been for some time. I have to tell you, though, that *The Spell* is absolutely my favorite."

He tilted his head in acknowledgement. "Thank you, Priscilla."

Truthfully, though, he hadn't expected to hear that. In fact, this new world of releasing a book without the umbrella of a publicist, publishing company, and agent had served to further highlight the sheer contrast between writing for months to the sound of one's own muse versus the cacophony of voices that wanted to discuss that work.

He was grateful.

He was exhilarated.

He was ... not ready. Because the only thing he'd thought about since releasing his novel—and every day before—was coming back here to find Sophia.

Meg slapped Jackson on his rotator cuff.

He shrank back. "Ow."

She slapped him again, her eyes wide, her index finger jabbing toward the window to the path that wound around the outside of the hotel and abutted the sea. The same path Christian and Sophia had wandered along together.

Priscilla's eyes flashed. She clapped her hands and leaned forward. "Well, I'll be ..."

All three had turned toward the window, along with a few tourists milling about the lobby. He followed their line of vision and that's when he saw ... them.

What's-his-name wore a suit, which he supposed was acceptable since it was nearly Christmas. Sophia ... well, she was beautiful. Graceful. Her hair hanging loosely about her shoulders, knee-length leather boots wrapping her legs, a chocolate-brown dress hugging her shape ....

Then, the unthinkable. Wade took her hand and knelt to the ground, expensive suit and all.

"He's proposing," Meg whispered.

Priscilla sighed. "That is it, y'all. I'm moving to California."

When it appeared that she had said yes, the lobby erupted in cheers. Meg squealed and turned to anyone who would listen. "I'm calling Liddy. She's going to be so upset that she missed this!"

Meg hurried away from the lobby, pulling Priscilla along with her.

Though he willed himself to keep a poker face and for his gaze to steer clear of that blasted window, he couldn't help himself. Christian watched, helplessly, as Wade pulled Sophia into a bear hug, leaving him to stare, frozen by the wayside, like an incidental forest animal. He resisted the urge to slither beneath a wide leaf.

"I know you love her."

Christian turned to Jackson, his old friend's voice surprisingly sympathetic.

Jackson's eyes bore into his. "I read your interview."

Christian swallowed. Instinct told him not to stand here and do nothing. This was the warrior's chance to show himself, to conquer his enemy, leaving him vanquished. He would be her knight and she his lady and ...

"Despite all that, I am asking you to let her alone." A faint mixture of something played out upon his face. What was it? Anticipation? Worry?

Jackson continued, perhaps unnerved at Christian's lack of reply. "She wants to make her life here ... she just told me this. You're too much of a wildcard, Christian. Always have been." He sighed, his voice weary. "Let her just ... be happy."

"And how is it," he said finally, "that you don't think she'd be happy with me?"

Jackson raked his hair with his hand. "Please."

"Maybe you're the one who wouldn't be happy if Sophia and I ended up together. Could it be that you are protecting yourself more than your sister? That if she were to choose me, she might also follow me?"

Jackson squeezed his eyes shut and shook his head. "That's enough."

Resignation. That was the emotion Christian had tried to identify earlier, the one that had settled on Jackson's face.

A commotion outside drew both their attentions. Meg and a small entourage had joined the happy couple, mouths moving, smiles forming. The three women embraced and took turns gawking over what, he surmised, was a ring. *Probably something gaudy.*

Jackson's eyes never wavered from the window. "She looks happy to me, Christian. Don't you think?"

Christian turned, putting his back to the scene. "I think you see what you want to see."

"Most of her family is dead. Her sister is quite estranged." Quietly, Jackson added, "My child needs to know his or her auntie."

Christian let that sink in. "You're pregnant."

He cracked a small smile. "Well, Meg is. She'll be pleased that you didn't notice that she has begun to show."

Christian stared at him for a long beat. "Am I that much of a monster to you? That you think I would keep Sophia away from her family?

Jackson took in the view, once again, through that window. He flicked his chin toward the commotion outside. "I don't imagine that it really matters what I think anymore."

Christian turned and watched as Sophia grasped Wade's face in both of her hands and gave him a heart-stopping kiss. He knew then, without doubt, that it was time to go home.

SOPHIA FELT Wade's lips on hers, his cheeks in her hands. She wanted to cry.

Meg, on the other hand, was all smiles and suggestions. Liddy had joined them—news traveled fast. And their new friend Priscilla stood nearby, taking it all in.

What a spectacle they must have been. Sophia feared what she might see if she were to glance toward the inn's large window, the one that offered a view of the sea—and the path they stood on now—from the lobby. Surely Wade's proposal had been witnessed by many.

"I hope you'll be married in the inn's chapel." Meg was already in planning mode. "Do you have an idea of the date?"

Liddy shushed her. "Of course she doesn't! She only got engaged three seconds ago."

Meg snapped a look at Liddy. "I was only asking."

Liddy touched Sophia's arm. "Don't mind her. She's in sales director mode." She paused. "You do *you*. No pressure to move too quickly here."

Sophia noted the caution on Liddy's face, and though it may have been meant as a warning of some kind, that look gave her immeasurable comfort. All of this was moving too fast ... including her answer to Wade. She glanced around. Jackson had joined them now. He slapped Wade on the back, and then reached for her, pulling Sophia into a hug.

Wade spoke. "Thank you for the offer of the chapel, Meg, but"— he glanced at Sophia and gave her a wink—"I think we may be looking for something a bit grander."

The ball of tears that had formed at the base of Sophia's neck doubled in size. She had kissed him hard moments ago, but while everyone else seemed to believe she was celebrating her engagement to Wade, she was actually saying ... goodbye.

CHRISTIAN SHUT the entry door behind him, his footfalls the only sound in the room. He glanced around at the small guest house—a studio apartment, really—that he'd made home for the past couple of months. It had offered him a sanctuary of sorts, a place to finish what he'd started.

And he had.

He plopped into the well-worn recliner chair positioned in

front of an ancient, non-working fireplace. A list of unread emails greeted him as he opened his phone and began to scroll.

He sat up when one caught his eye. Grace, his VA, had forwarded him the email with the subject line: URGENT (Possibly).

Dear Mr. Capra:

I am reaching out to you today to discuss the possibility of a movie option for *The Spell*. I have attempted to reach your agent, Burns Golden; however, no response has been forthcoming.

Please respond at your earliest convenience with the appropriate phone number for your representation so that we can discuss our offer.

CHRISTIAN SCOWLED. For some authors, this would be a welcome inquiry. But for him? It only complicated things. He stood and paced, re-reading the email. Would he ever rid himself of Burns and this notion that he, somehow, represented him? Grace had quite capably kept all Burns-related matter, claims, inquiries far from him. Except this one, of course. He made a mental note to ask her if he had received anything else from his former agent that he should be aware of. Otherwise, the term "blissfully unaware" could change to "utterly complicated."

In a way, though, this news was a welcome interruption. Instead of licking his wounds from the spectacle that he'd just witnessed at the inn, he very well might have a new endeavor on which to focus. Not that assigning movie rights to one's novel could ever compare with losing the love of your life to another guy. He screwed up his mouth, thinking about it, a groan escaping him. How laughable he was to have thought that he could swing into that hotel like a swashbuckler ready to scoop up his fair maiden.

He ran a hand across his face, expecting to feel the scrape of whiskers. Instead, the start of new growth greeted him, his hand raw from the sensation. He swallowed and shook his head. Keep moving forward ... just keep going.

Christian touched open his phone, scrolled through his contacts, and finding Lisa Caldwell's cell phone number, he hit "call."

She answered right away, her voice as gruff as ever. "Heard the news, I suspect."

"Hello, Lisa. What news are you referring to?"

"That at sixty-two years old, and after thirty years with the same company, I'm now a statistic. Part of the unemployment percentage along with just about every millennial in Manhattan."

He frowned and dropped his gaze to the ground. Not the news he had expected. "I'm sorry to hear that. And no, I had no idea."

"Then what were you calling about?"

He had to bite back a chuckle. Always to the point. "I was hoping for your advice."

"Well, given that I have all the time in the world right now, I'll see what I can do."

He hesitated. "I'm looking for an agent who can advise me on subsidiary rights to my book."

"Ah. And now that Burns is out of the picture, you have questions."

One of his eyebrows rose on its own volition. "What happened to Burns?"

She cackled. "You are kidding me, right? Boy, you must have been writing from a cave all these months."

"Are you going to tell me or do I need to call up Google?"

"He's out. Taken down by sexual harassment charges. Promised women book deals in exchange for, you know ..."

Christian closed his eyes, not that anything would shock him anymore. Especially where Burns was concerned. How ironic. It was the "teeth" that Burns put into his negotiating skills that had drawn Christian—and hundreds of other writers—to him in the first place. He clenched his jaw. If he ever saw that guy again ...

"What kind of rights are we talking about?" she said, breaking his concentration.

Christian crossed his arms and looked up to refocus his mind. "Movie rights. I received an email from what appears to be a legit source. I have no interest in dealing with them myself, however."

She let out a lengthy, angst-filled sigh. "Artists!"

He smirked. "So can you recommend anyone?"

"You're talking to her, you idiot."

He couldn't help it this time and chuckled in response. "You're hired."

"Fabulous. Send me what you've got. And for heaven's sake, let me in on your next 'undisclosed location,' will you? I'm not interested in chasing you all over hill and dale when I'm ready for you to sign your life away."

He grunted a laugh. "I'm thinking of going north for a time."

"North, huh? I don't think you're going to find too many mermaids in Alaska, my friend."

That's what he was going for. "Montana," he said. "You'll find me on a ranch in Montana."

CHAPTER 17

*T*hey would all find out soon enough.

After the proposal, Sophia had asked to be alone with Wade. Meg and the others had all given her a "knowing" look, but reluctantly gave them their space with a "promise to meet up later for a celebratory drink!"

Back in her room now, Sophia curled up on her unmade bed and shuddered. The look on Wade's face at what she'd had to say, well, she would not forget that for a long time.

"I don't understand," he said to her as they stood on the beach. "Is it the ring? Did I do this wrong?"

She shook her head, that heavy lump of tears making it difficult to speak. "Wade, no. I ... care for you very much. I've missed you for weeks and was so looking forward to seeing you today."

"But not marrying me." His handsome jaw had set firmly, his mouth pressed into a line.

Her voice was a harsh whisper now. "I didn't expect this, Wade. I am just now finding my way here and I had hoped to get to know you better."

He nodded but hurt marred his face. "I've already learned all I needed to know, Sophia. I love you."

A tear trailed down her face until she tasted salt. "You've given me so much. Safety, stability, and you've comforted me so as I've dealt with rebuilding my business."

"Do you love me?"

He was a beautiful man. Handsome. Kind. She hated the sadness in his eyes and dropped her gaze to where he had placed the ring before she'd ever had a chance to give an answer to his proposal. With a trembling hand, she slipped it off of her finger and held it out to him.

His eyes were clouded and she'd forever regret that.

"I'm sorry." A sob hitched her voice. "But no. Not love."

Now that she was back in her room, Sophia shut off her cell phone and called the front desk to ask that calls to her room be blocked. Then she burrowed more deeply beneath her comforter, until something landed with a plunk on the floor. She sighed and peered over the side of the bed.

Jackson's iPad. Or, rather, *her* iPad.

She winced and carefully retrieved it, checking the screen for damage. With a flop, she settled against her pillow and opened it up. Priscilla had come all this way for mermaid sightings. Well, and to see Meg. Of course.

Sophia shook her head. If only life could always be so light-hearted. She exhaled and made a quick search for Christian's interview, the one Liddy had told her about. It came right up. The photo was captioned "CJ Capra." With his beard rugged and fully grown out, he looked like he had lived in the wilds for many months instead of weeks.

INTERVIEWER: Tell me about the heroine of your book?

CJ: She's brave.

Interviewer: How would you describe her?

CJ: Eyes like wild willow; supple, radiant skin; and hair of raw umber, windswept, like smoke.

Interviewer: Wow!

CJ: And a tail.

Interviewer: (laughter) Sounds like you've actually seen her ... this mermaid.

CJ: Nightly ... in my dreams.

Interviewer: Hmm. So, you're having a hard time moving on without her.

CJ: Most difficult thing I've ever done.

Interviewer: Other than writing a book about a mermaid, that is.

CJ: Oh, no. I did that on *porpoise*.

SHE LAID THERE on that bed and read the interview from beginning to end, then re-read it, alternately laughing and flicking away wayward tears. Christian had a way of pulling diverse emotions from her. She saw that the night she'd been so depressed and he'd cheered her up with those awful reviews he had received.

Sophia set the iPad aside, laughing at the memory. Even in her darkest moments, he could make her laugh.

"Oh, Chris," she whispered into the night. She'd been angry at Christian for ducking out of the hotel without telling her where he'd gone, but after a while, she simply missed him. Their friendship. Wondered how he was and if he would ever surface in her midst. If only she'd had a chance to say goodbye before he'd gone.

She sat up. If only she'd had a chance to say goodbye ...

Sophia threw back the covers and padded across the room. She began to dig through her bags, searching for a piece of paper that had been crumpled and flattened more times than she could count. When she'd found it, she scanned the words again. So many painful, often degrading expressions in one, grammatically incorrect sheet of paper.

Your dresses are ugly—especially that red one.
Makes your hips look large.
Will never sell.

Tears began to form, these larger than the ones she'd shed after hurting Wade. She knew her stepfather had no good excuse. He was truly repentant when he'd found out she read the lengthy diatribe, the letter that Gia had shoved in her face. Still, despite his apology, their relationship never quite recovered from that.

The realization sobered her. How many times had unkind words filled her own thoughts or her mouth in private? How much worse for them to be made public and therefore remain unforgiven?

Tears flooded her eyes now, racing down her cheeks like rain on a sheet of glass. Her hand shook as she stared at the water-streaked note, taking in her stepfather's final line:

You might as well stay here.

"Oh, Daddy," she whispered. Christian was right. Her stepfather had wanted her to stay there, with him, in Italy. The letter was written to make her stay, but it had pushed her away faster. The idea of staying behind had never even crossed her mind.

Nor had it ever crossed her mind that her birth father was out there, somewhere still. And that she had a brother. If she had learned nothing else in all these years, it was that life was unpredictable. So were people. Her half-sister proved that. Sometimes, nothing made sense.

Like why in the world she would hold onto her stepfather's note for this many years and allow it to damage her confidence as it had. She took one more glance at the letter, seeing it differently now. "I forgive you, daddy," she said. And then she ripped the note into tiny pieces and deposited it into the trash.

❧

IT WAS TIME TO GO. Christian had taken off—how many times before? A dozen? Two? Always the same. A carry-on, a personal item, and everything else would be shipped. Not that he owned much else. He'd kept his items in storage too long, paying that ever-growing bill each month, unsure of what was actually in that unit. For all he knew, a family of rats had taken over and were feasting on morsels served on his mother's china.

But he'd made a change in his travel plans this time. This time, Christian had not shipped a thing. Instead, he loaded up the car, anxious to get on the road. Rather than jostling through airport security, he'd be taking the highways from California to Nevada to Utah to Idaho until he found wide open space in Montana.

He got behind the wheel, loaded up the GPS on his phone, released a long-held breath, and headed out. He hadn't traveled by car in years. As he drove, his mother's voice popped into his head. What was it she used to say? Some kind of traveling mercies?

Jesus, Mary, and Joseph, be with us on our way.

He laughed aloud at the prayer his mother had always said, not in a mocking way, but because he hadn't realized, until now, that he'd stored the words somewhere in his brain all these years. His laughter died away and he wished he could call her now.

As he drove, the world moved past him at a high rate of speed. Or was it he who moved past it? Christian reminded himself to breathe. Life was good. His book was doing well. He'd built a strong team despite the odds. He'd overcome his own dumb mistakes to come out on top.

It was enough, wasn't it?

He was approaching the inn. Could not avoid it. Well, not easily. Sea Glass Inn was south of where he had been staying these past few months. If he kept his eyes on the road, he knew he could avoid a glimpse altogether. But a flicker of a memory called out to him and he glanced at the inn one last time. Though he'd lived there for months, the place really hadn't felt like home the last time he'd stepped inside those doors.

Had it?

He swallowed back that memory, one that had started out with possibilities but had ended in lost hope. His heart began to race, so much that he could feel his pulse beating in his throat. In a split second of decision, he thrust his blinker on and changed lanes. One more walk on the path that wound its way around the sea, he told himself. Just one more walk.

SOPHIA HAD AWOKEN EARLY, sleep elusive. One glance at her phone told her what she could have guessed: They all knew.

What happened?

Are you okay?

Do you want some gelato delivered to your room? (That last text was from Priscilla.)

She held her head in her hands, knowing she would need to face them all soon.

And yet ...

And yet, surprisingly, she knew she could. She had done

what was right. The decision was painful. In the end, though, Wade had wanted something from her she wasn't ready to give.

The sound of the sea swept through the open window. She shivered, but reveled in a roar that, though still somewhat new to her hearing, had become welcome. Expected. Despite the early hour, Sophia got out of bed, brushed her teeth, combed her hair with her fingers, and got dressed. She pulled on a soft sweater and leggings, and headed out for a walk.

~

THE SEA WAS as it always was. Ferocious. Beckoning. Distant. Approachable.

He meandered along, surprised by the coolness of the morning. How many times had he strolled this path or sat in the shade wearing nothing but shorts and a worn tee? He stopped at his usual bench, unable to fathom staying for long in this temperature.

That's when he spotted the chapel, warm lighting emanating from within. He slipped inside the small, bright building, and found her there. He froze. She seemed to freeze as well. They stood across from each other, staring.

She opened her lips, as if to speak, her eyes imploring. Yet she said nothing.

He took a step toward her, and she toward him.

Sophia tilted her head, her voice probing, "Chris?"

The voice that had been branded in his mind, that sang out in his dreams. *Man, she was beautiful.* "It's me."

"I ... thought that was you." She paused, her eyes sweeping over him. He couldn't tell if she was shocked or angry, or a little of both. "You shaved."

"I did."

She didn't say anything for a few seconds, and then, "You look good."

"Hmm."

Something shifted in her countenance then. He thought he saw a flit of anger quickly replaced by a small smile. "Don't 'hmm' me."

A broad smile broke out across his face and he hung his head.

"Why did you ... shave, I mean?"

"I was tired of hiding."

She only nodded. "I read your interview."

He sobered and searched her face for affirmation. He didn't just want that from her right now, he needed it.

"It reminded me, somehow, of our time together." She paused, her voice quieting. "I have something important to tell you."

Something like ... let's run away together?

Nervous laughter left her. "Though if I knew I'd see you here I would have at least showered and put on makeup."

And mess with perfection?

When he didn't say anything, she gave her head a little shake, her voice trembling. "Everything you said about my stepfather was right. I'd hung onto his letter far too long." She shrugged. "It's gone now. I've let it go completely."

"Sophia," he said. "I'm so glad."

"I just wanted you to know"

He nodded. He knew a decision like that must have taken some introspection and he longed to know more. But she was likely here to plan her nuptials and he had interrupted her. No doubt she would be getting married soon—if he were in Wade's shoes he wouldn't want to wait either.

He took a step back. "It was good to see you, Sophia. I am on my way out of California now."

Those eyes of hers held him, bright like emeralds. She began to nod, then stopped. Flashed her eyes at him. "Don't go."

He stepped toward her again, reaching for her like an old friend.

She shook her head, her eyes pooling now. "Chris."

He pulled her close, their faces inches apart. She traversed his face with her gaze and allowed the gentle touch of her finger to travel down the length of his scar.

"Does it remind you of that night?" she whispered. Her gentle breathing rose and fell, and those eyes of hers searched his depths. "In the bar?"

He swallowed. "Sometimes scars remind us of things we'd rather forget." He reached for her hand, the one caressing his face, and held it against his skin, breathing her in. "But they can also remind us of how far we have come."

Her eyes closed. "Sometimes they really do."

He released her from his embrace and stepped back. "I'll never forget you, Sophia. I know you are engaged, and I ..." He exhaled, forcing himself to do the right thing. "I wish you all the happiness that you deserve."

"I'm not engaged."

He hadn't known what else to expect from this unexpected meeting, but hearing that Sophia was not engaged? Not in the running. At all.

He quirked a smile at her. "Really."

"Really." She smiled wide at him now, then quickly sobered. She tilted her head, watching him. "What are you going to do about that?"

He did not hesitate. All at once Christian scooped Sophia into his arms, hugging her so tightly her feet lifted from the ground. He flashed her a wicked grin. "How's this for starters?"

Her smile reappeared. "Perfect."

When he finally set her back down, his mouth found hers,

and he kissed her like a man once lost at sea ... who had finally come home.

DEAR READER

If you've read all three Sea Glass Inn novels, thank you so much for keeping me writing! And if this is your first—welcome!—I hope it won't be your last.

Sea Glass Inn really is a magical place. You may have already guessed this, but I used to work in the hotel industry. I was an operator, front desk clerk, sales manager, and later, an event planner. Guess you could say travel is in my heart—and now in my books!

I sincerely hope you were whisked away by Sophia's story. Here's a fun behind-the-scenes tidbit: my daughter, Angie, a fashion designer herself, provided the sketches for the cover model's sketchpad. I'm a grateful momma!

Speaking of gratefulness, I'm thankful to my husband, Dan, for his sacrificial support and love; as well as to my parents and children for always loving and supporting me, Dan and Elaine Navarro, and Matt, Angie, and Emma. Also a thank you to my editor, Denise Harmer, for connecting with me all those years ago, and to my sister-in-law, Rita, for answering fashion business questions for me.

For those who haven't read the end of *Windswept* yet—I see some of you flipping to the back to read this, haha!—I won't spoil it except to say that book 4 picks up where book 3, this one, left off. (Though this novel does NOT end on a cliffhanger!!)

Book 4 of the Sea Glass Inn novel series (title coming soon) will be appearing sometime in summer 2019. Will you watch for it? I hope so.

Oh and one more thing: If you enjoyed *Windswept,* would you help me spread the word by leaving a review or two? I would be SO grateful!

Thank you for reading,

Julie

ALSO BY JULIE CAROBINI

Sea Glass Inn Novels

Walking on Sea Glass

Runaway Tide

Windswept

Otter Bay Novels

Sweet Waters

A Shore Thing

Fade to Blue

The Chocolate Series

Chocolate Beach

Truffles by the Sea

Mocha Sunrise

Cottage Grove Mysteries

The Christmas Thief

All Was Calm

The Christmas Heist

ABOUT THE AUTHOR

JULIE CAROBINI writes inspirational beach romances and cozy mysteries ... with a twist. She is known for spunky heroines, charming heroes, quirky friends, and the secrets they keep. Her bestselling titles include Walking on Sea Glass, the Otter Bay Novels, The Christmas Thief, and more. Julie has received awards for writing and editing from The National League of American Pen Women and ACFW, and she is a double finalist for the ACFW Carol Award. She lives near the beach in California with her husband, Dan, and loves traveling and hanging out with her three 20-something kids. Grab a free eBook here: www.juliecarobini.com/free-book

f facebook.com/AuthorJulieCarobini

🐦 twitter.com/juliecarobini

📷 instagram.com/beachyjewel

Made in United States
Orlando, FL
31 October 2023

38452115R00161